ALSO BY SOPAN DEB

Missed Translations: Meeting the Immigrant Parents Who Raised Me

Keya Das's Second Act

a novel

Sopan Deb

SIMON & SCHUSTER PAPERBACKS

New York   London   Toronto   Sydney   New Delhi

Simon & Schuster Paperbacks
An Imprint of Simon & Schuster, Inc.
1230 Avenue of the Americas
New York, NY 10020

First Simon & Schuster trade paperback edition July 2023

SIMON & SCHUSTER PAPERBACKS and colophon are registered trademarks of Simon & Schuster, Inc.

For information about special discounts for bulk purchases, please contact Simon & Schuster Special Sales at 1-866-506-1949 or business@simonandschuster.com.

The Simon & Schuster Speakers Bureau can bring authors to your live event. For more information or to book an event, contact the Simon & Schuster Speakers Bureau at 1-866-248-3049 or visit our website at www.simonspeakers.com.

Interior design by Carly Loman

Manufactured in the United States of America

10 9 8 7 6 5 4 3 2 1

Library of Congress Cataloging-in-Publication Data
Names: Deb, Sopan, author.
Title: Keya Das's second act : a novel / by Sopan Deb.
Description: First Simon & Schuster hardcover edition. | New York : Simon & Schuster, 2022.
Identifiers: LCCN 2021034823 (print) | LCCN 2021034824 (ebook) | ISBN 9781982185473 (hardcover) | ISBN 9781982185480 (paperback) | ISBN 9781982185497 (ebook)
Subjects: LCSH: Bengali Americans—New Jersey—Fiction. | Estranged families—Fiction. | LCGFT: Domestic fiction.
Classification: LCC PS3604.E2326 K49 2022 (print) | LCC PS3604.E2326 (ebook) | DDC 813/.6—dc23
LC record available at https://lccn.loc.gov/2021034823
LC ebook record available at https://lccn.loc.gov/2021034824

ISBN 978-1-9821-8547-3
ISBN 978-1-9821-8548-0 (pbk)
ISBN 978-1-9821-8549-7 (ebook)

To Wesley, my best friend and partner in all things,
and Koko, who is likely eating these pages as you read them.

You can't cross the sea merely by standing and staring at the water.

—RABINDRANATH TAGORE

Keya Das's
Second Act

Part 1

Part 1

ONE

The wooden box was simple, elegant even. Shantanu Das almost missed it in the unfinished attic, but it was wrapped in a twinkling silver paper, peeking out from behind a stack of other boxes he had already spent the entire day going through, as if it were the lone flower in a garden of cobwebs. Perhaps it was fate, though Shantanu didn't believe in fate. And come to think of it, he didn't believe in much of anything anymore.

Shantanu crawled towards the corner, his knees and back aching with every instance of hitting the grid-like joists below, which were punctuated by pink tufts used for insulation. He silently cursed himself again for not installing a floor and more lights than the lone flickering bulb above. There were dozens of cardboard boxes up here that Shantanu hadn't touched in years until this evening, which he shoved aside like a rescue worker clearing the opening to a collapsed cave. For some reason, there were two folding chairs leaning against a wall, ready to seat guests who would never come.

When he finally reached the box, its top came off easily. Inside, there were dozens of folded-up pieces of paper. Some were folded neatly, while others were crumpled and uneven. Shantanu, sweating in the attic's thick air, ran his hands through them as if they were pieces of sand. At the bottom of the box, there was an unfolded packet of papers held together by a binder clip. Shantanu placed the box on the floor and began to take the folded papers out one by one. On each of them there was a heart drawn with pen. Within the hearts were various messages. Shantanu started reading the handwritten cover messages out loud, despite there being no audience.

" 'Writing a *Great Gatsby* paper the morning of,' " Shantanu muttered. He picked up another one, his confusion rising. " 'Keeping a secret.' "

This went on for a few more. "'Mrs. Bakke's necklace' . . . 'Stealing your penne.'"

Are these mine to see? he wondered hesitantly—but then he realized: *Everyone else has left this house behind. No one will see these if I don't.* And besides: Shantanu was curious. He was an anthropologist. This is what he did—excavated stories by way of clues. Carefully, he proceeded.

Hi you,

We have a sub today for AP History. You know what that means: A MOVIE!! I hope you're having a good morning. I'm so relieved we talked about prom the other day. What straight guys will we have to pretend to want to go with? Mark? John? What fucking awful choices. One day, we won't have to fake it. I'm excited for ice cream later. Okay, I think we have to do some reading or some shit. I'll write you later. I love you so, so, so much.

Pamela

The paper was suddenly scalding; his breath quickened. He felt a slight pain in his stomach and sat backwards, reaching for one of the two mysterious folding chairs. With sweaty palms, he scooped the papers back into the box.

It took a minute, but Shantanu gathered himself. He reached for his pocket with his spare hand, fished out his cell phone. He went to the contact most dear, yet currently most torturous to him. The picture attached to the contact was of a smiling toddler. Now it served as a taunt. There were many messages to her that went unanswered. But Shantanu wanted to try again. He tried in vain to convey calm urgency. Or unobtrusive wonderment.

Can you come home? Please. I need to show you something.

◇

The void in Shantanu's life blasted him in the face the moment he opened his eyes every morning. It was darker in the light than when he closed his eyelids. There was his queen-sized bed, covered by a rarely washed green down comforter and an even less-washed white fitted sheet. A wooden nightstand—a housewarming gift from a neighbor—empty next to the bed, except for an iPhone and a worn-down leather wallet bursting at the seams with credit cards, some of them past due. The walls bare, save for one small painting of a brick building in the French Quarter of New Orleans, its crooked frame swallowed by the surrounding off-white plaster. It was a gift he had excitedly brought home for his family years before from a work trip. Now it was a relic from a life that was no longer his.

His routine was the same. Shantanu would blink his brown eyes a few times and then use his arm to propel his aching fifty-two-year-old body upwards. He would then rub his eyes and take stock of the bags deepening beneath them with each new sunrise. He'd inspect the backs of his hands for signs of wrinkles. He'd squint to pierce through the little strands of hair. The wrinkles stood out more than ever, like overgrown roots to a tree. Then he would absentmindedly run a hand across the seemingly permanent stubble on his face and his ever-expanding paunch. This was his way of confirming he was still alive.

Is this the day? Is this the day it is too late? Shantanu would whisper to himself, though there was no one else in the home to hear him.

This particular morning—a gray, October one—Shantanu stood up and limped across the brown Saxony carpet to one of the two windows in the bedroom, this one overlooking his front lawn. He had a clear view of his cozy housing development nestled in Howell, the New Jersey suburb he knew as home. All the two-story houses looked exactly the same except for their exterior colors. Shantanu remembered the real estate agent—a young, eager, and energetic man named Brendan with blond, curly hair—referring to this place as a "heaven for starter houses." That was more than two decades ago. *Now I wonder if this will be more of a house for the end.*

It wasn't just the houses that looked the same. It was also the people, save for the Dases, and the lawns, which on this block of Hillcrest Drive were perfectly manicured, lush with green grass. None of the blades extended more than six inches from the ground. There was no visible dirt. Except for his home at 2 Hillcrest Drive, where the barely greenish grass was patched sporadically with dirt and patches of weeds cohabitating.

The day the movers carried the boxes from the van into the house, Shantanu stood on the lawn with his arms outstretched, a delighted and pregnant Chaitali looking on while Mitali, then two, clung to her hand, surveying her new playground.

"Do you see this, Chaitali?" Shantanu exclaimed. "I'll make sure this lawn is the greenest in this whole place." His mustache, unkempt and uneven like the lawn, spread with his lips.

Chaitali giggled, an innocent admission of her belief in him. They both had made it. A house with a lawn in a middle-class suburb? A beautiful daughter? With another on the way? Sure, the drab brown carpet in the living room needed replacing—but this was what their Bengali parents had come to the United States in search of: this American dream. The chance to have a lawn.

And yet the grass never grew, no matter what Shantanu tried. One of his first purchases was a seed spreader, bought even before the sorely needed sofas for the living room. He spent multiple weekends strolling up and down the lawn planting grass seed, blissfully listening to the Rolling Stones' album *Sticky Fingers* on a Walkman and gazing with longing at the rest of the block. He would take the hose and water the grass every morning. He had a small mountain full of mulch dumped on the driveway, much to the confusion of the neighbors: Geoff and Betsy Bocchino to the right, Patrick and Carla Brennan across, and Linda Rossi diagonally. Once the weeds started popping up, Shantanu would spend too much time spraying weed killer. But it was like whack-a-mole. The weeds seemed amused by Shantanu, and kept arriving in droves to get a better glimpse. It took years for him to realize that the reason the grass was not growing was that all the other houses on Hillcrest Drive had elaborate sprinkler systems, and, occasionally, professional landscapers to fertilize the lawns. Shantanu was never going to pay for that. So this was the grass (and weeds) that this young family would live with. The Dases would have to make do with a different kind of American dream.

Today, the grass was the same, but his life was different. He sat in the kitchen, back in his usual routine, swirling a bowl of Froot Loops and distractedly scrolling through the morning's headlines on the *New York Times* app. He ignored the slight smell of mold that filled the air. There was some dirt on the cotton bath rug by the stove. *Why did Chaitali put a bath rug by the stove?* he groused. The sink was not as empty as the rest of the house. There were three—about to be four—days' worth of bowls with hints of congealing skim milk on the side, and other assorted plates where crumbs had set up a kingdom.

Neighboring the sink was an elevated wooden counter. Past a collection of spices—red pepper flakes, garam masala, cardamom pods—there was a toaster that produced only hardened sorrow for Shantanu instead of crispy bread. It was silver with signs of wear and tear, and mostly taken over by spiders, where they'd claimed an area ripe to build webs. *At least something in the house has found fertile ground,* Shantanu thought upon seeing them.

There was a pin-up Disney calendar, a gift from Mitali to Shantanu and Chaitali, hanging above the toaster. The thumbtacks holding it up looked like they would give at any moment. Shantanu did not need to consult Mickey Mouse to know what day it was, though the outdated calendar wouldn't have helped anyway. This weekend was Durga Puja, which meant hours of *ragas* to take in and too many *shingaras* to stuff down his throat. It was on this day five years ago that he was taking a slightly burnt bagel out of the toaster when Keya, his younger daughter, then eighteen, bounded into the kitchen sporting a black denim jacket and matching black jeans.

Keya dropped her car keys next to the stove and eyed him for several seconds before softly saying, "Baba, where's Ma? I want to talk to both of you." There was a pause. "Can I have some toast?"

"Ma's upstairs organizing saris for the *annaprashan* next weekend," Shantanu said, chuckling while stirring his green tea. That Saturday was going to be yet another trip hours away to visit Bengali family friends. Swati Mashi's kid was cute, but he'd rather go to the Bocchinos' barbecue instead. "Sure, *sona*, I'll make you some toast."

When he finally turned to look at Keya, she looked visibly stressed. He frowned. Shantanu had never been good at serious talks with his daughters.

Shantanu wished he had been prepared at the time to recognize the distress in Keya's face. That he had known to hug her then. In the years since, he had not been able to let that regret go. Really, he'd never been good at letting go of things, at moving on. But Shantanu knew it was time to move on from this house, from this place, that was both his and not his anymore. Today he would start with the room littered with the most memories, stashed away out of sight and out of mind. Shantanu would spend his day in the attic. But first, the Froot Loops.

◇

Mitali knew the question was coming. It always did. It was a reasonable one, but this time she didn't want to answer it, as she ran her hand around a stemless wineglass, a quarter full with merlot. She admired her manicure from earlier that day: little pink lilacs arranged perfectly on a cream background. Multiple couples, some more cuddly than others, sat nearby. A bearded white man wearing a chic coat ideal for an October evening in New York sat by himself reading Tolstoy. Mitali estimated him to be in his thirties. *Performative*, she thought.

There was what appeared to be a fake silk tree in one corner. English ivy and snake plants, their leaves as long as arms, lined the front window. *Baba would love this*, she thought, recalling her childhood lawn, or lack thereof, on Hillcrest Drive. But then she remembered her anger.

"So what do you want to talk about?" the young man in front of her, Neesh, asked. He spoke quickly, drumming his blistered hands and stubby fingernails on the table.

This wasn't *the* question, but it still caught her off guard.

"Do you usually start first dates off this way?" Mitali asked. Neesh was clearly not the coolest of conversationalists, but at least he wasn't shorter than what he'd listed on his Hinge profile. She could tell he spent at least some time in the gym and didn't mind his outfit showing this off. She wondered whether her own clothes, business casual black slacks and a matching jacket over a blue blouse, were perhaps a bit conservative. *I should've at least worn heels. But for a wine bar? On the Upper East Side?* And she had just come from work—something she probably did too much of—but at least she had the good sense to wear her contacts instead of those hideous, bulky glasses.

"I used to bring note cards, believe it or not," he responded. He took a deep sigh. "I should relax."

"Note cards?" Mitali couldn't suppress a laugh.

"Yeah, note cards, with questions written on them. I used to go to the bathroom during dates and read them just in case I ran out of things to talk about," Neesh said. He allowed himself a chuckle. And a bit of that relaxation. "Now I just ask the other person. You're my note card."

Mitali found this oddly charming.

"Okay. Let's start with what you do," she said. "You said a desk job?"

"I'm an analyst at this boutique hedge fund called Amplitude," Neesh said.

Mitali raised her eyebrows.

"Amplitude?" Mitali asked. *What a terrible name.*

"I lied. I'm not that. I'm an instrument technician at this rehearsal studio in Midtown called Electric Smash," Neesh said. "I just thought 'hedge fund' sounded more impressive. But I fix all the instruments—pianos, guitars, drums—so that people can come jam. You?"

"So you're a music producer?" Mitali asked.

"No, I work the front desk. I just set the instruments up. Plug them in. That kind of thing. I play the drums."

What an odd guy. But Mitali couldn't help feeling relief. A musician. At least that was different from the turnstile of bankers, marketers, and personal trainers she had gone out with in the last three months. The thought of having to feign interest in boutique hedge funds was not something she was keen on. It was why she always picked a wine bar close to her apartment. She was not the sort of person to go too far out of her way.

"I'm a web producer for a marketing agency. I create content for their website," Mitali said, a line she had rehearsed for every date. Every time, the person opposite the table had the same uncomprehending, glassy look: *Content creation. Web producing.* Meaningless buzzwords. Neesh was no different.

"Cool," he murmured, and took a sip from his highball glass, the mint leaves from the mojito taking up more space than the liquid.

"Is it?" Mitali asked, more directly than she meant to. *Ordering a mojito on a first date is a flashy move.*

"Sorry?"

"Is it cool?" Mitali pressed.

Neesh's shoulders tightened. He looked confused, maybe wondering if he'd said something wrong. He began biting his nails—*a habit?*—but quickly stopped himself. His self-manicure would have to wait.

"Is it . . . not?" Neesh volleyed back.

She let the question float between them a bit, deciding she wanted to play with her date some more. She'd reached a point of apathy with dating—trying hard and trying not at all seemed to yield the same result anyway. Neesh had moved from biting his nonexistent nails to fidgeting with the zipper on his leather jacket. She was tempted to like him, but that was a dangerous temptation for someone like her. She might not be worthy of liking someone. And really, at this point, she wasn't even sure if she liked herself.

"It can be. It depends on the client," Mitali said. "When the creative teams come up with marketing campaigns, I come up with interesting ways to present them on our website. In high school, I used to love coming up with television commercial ideas for companies. I would cast celebrities and everything. So I made a career out of it. It's less interesting than I thought it would be. Clearly, this is not something you care about."

"That's presumptuous of you," Neesh shot back.

Both of them let that hang in the air. Mitali shuffled in her chair.

"I'm not good at this," Mitali said. "I'm sorry. I haven't really done *this* much."

Mitali had her shields up. She had recently downloaded the normal dating apps—Hinge and Bumble—but hadn't told her friends, the few she kept in touch with, about it. She didn't want the interrogations or to admit to others that she was making an effort to move forward. She declined to match far more often than she chose to match.

With Neesh, his profile picture was uninteresting: him looking pensively out at some lake. She meant to swipe left, but being a novice online dater, she'd accidentally swiped right. They were matched. Of course, she didn't have to answer his message. But his opening gambit ("Hi! Is this worth a shot? You seem like a Pisces, which means you're probably closed off!") was too strange and tempting to pass up. "Only to assholes," she had responded, and thus began a back-and-forth which had led to this moment. Unbeknownst to Neesh, Mitali was feeling her own sense of vulnerability. But it was because she knew the question was coming.

"No, you are good at this," Neesh said. "I lied about working at a hedge fund."

Mitali felt guilty at his earnestness. He was being polite, engaging, and vulnerable.

"How long have you been in New York?" Neesh tried to hit the reset button.

Mitali received a reprieve. This was safe small talk.

"I went to Rowan and moved to the city right after. So four years, give or take," Mitali said. "Your last name, Desai. Are you Gujarati?"

"Yup. I grew up outside Chicago. Naperville. Went to school at the University of Iowa to study film. Disappointed my parents by trying to pursue a career as a drummer in New York after college. And now I'm thirty-three and fixing instruments so other people can play them."

Neesh looked cheery as he said that, which Mitali didn't know how to take. She sipped the last bit of wine, to which Neesh immediately motioned to a nearby waitress for another glass. But then he caught himself.

"Sorry, I should've asked. Did you want another one? I'm buying. Least I can do for being late. You could tell me more about web production?" His face looked equal parts pleading and apologetic.

Mitali took stock of the sight in front of her: trim, earnest, a full head of hair held up with just a bit of mousse, and bushy eyebrows. His oral fixation—the nail biting and chewing—was an object of fascination for Mitali, especially because of his sharp jaw. Neesh's face was like two faces plastered together, like it was constructed to hide an altogether different person inside.

Neesh's phone buzzed loudly in his pocket. He reached for it and saw a text that made him scowl. He quickly recovered and contorted his face back to a forced grin, but not before mouthing a curse that Mitali noticed.

"You okay?" Mitali asked.

"Absolutely," Neesh said in an almost too-exultant tone. He began to chew on a mint leaf. "Let me tell you a joke: What kind of shoe did Beethoven wear? A flat. I'm sorry, but that's the best I can think of at the moment. I'm not really that funny."

Mitali, in spite of herself, chuckled over this dumb crack even as she wondered about the text Neesh just received. She would stay for another drink. Mitali was committed now.

"You know what? Sure. Yes. Another merlot, please," Mitali said. Neesh's eyes widened, as if he couldn't believe his good fortune.

"That never happens," Neesh said as he waved again at the waitress. He turned his body back to Mitali, who played with her straightened black hair, bangs and all, which fell to right above her shoulders.

"I can't drink too much tonight. I'm going home tomorrow for Durga Puja," Mitali said swiftly, to give herself an out.

"Where did you grow up?" Neesh asked.

Mitali closed her eyes a bit too long.

"New Jersey."

"Edison?"

"No, not Edison. Howell. About an hour south."

Mitali steeled herself. It was coming.

"Nice. Any siblings? I'm an only child," Neesh said.

The question was a gut punch, even though Neesh had no idea of the albatross around her neck. And on every previous date, Mitali stopped at the edge of answering honestly. Usually, she would either say, "Yes, I have a sister. She is in New Jersey," or, "No, I'm an only child." She never wanted to discuss this ever—with anyone. Just thinking about the truth stung.

But maybe it was the wine, or this disarmingly goofy man in front of her. Maybe it was that he wasn't fake. She liked that.

"I had a sister. She died almost five years ago," she said, as matter-of-factly as she could. It was, after all, a matter of fact. "It was partially my fault. I think about it every day." This was, too.

Neesh's head tilted upward and then turned to look out the window at the pedestrians strolling by. The streetlight turned green, and cars began moving. The clatter of glasses never seemed louder to Mitali as they did then. Neesh had no expression. Just as the waitress arrived with Mitali's second glass of wine, Neesh jerked his head back to Mitali and said, "Tell me more about web producing."

Now it was Mitali's phone that buzzed loudly on the table. She swiftly glanced at it.

Can you come home? Please. I need to show you something.

Mitali rolled her eyes and gripped the side of the phone so the notification would disappear. Her irritation about her father often reared its head at sporadic moments.

"Are *you* okay?" Neesh said.

"Absolutely."

They had that second drink. He did not press Mitali about Keya. He was not taken aback when she said that she had never had a long-term boyfriend. He made some more terrible jokes, including one she didn't get about how "Bun Day More" would be in his Broadway musical about hot dogs. She had never seen *Les Misérables*.

"I'm a big musical theater guy," Neesh said, after explaining the joke. "I love Broadway. I used to, anyway."

"You don't strike me as the type," Mitali said.

"Why?"

"You can sit still in a quiet theater for hours?"

"Who said I sat still?" Neesh replied.

There had been a girl he was seeing for a couple months, but it didn't work out, and Neesh did not elaborate. Something about their work schedules not matching up since he went to the studio on nights and weekends and her being, as he put it, "a possible fascist." He bit his nails some more. He liked podcasts and recommended *The Moth*, which was a storytelling show. Neesh said he felt "transported" whenever he listened to it. He acted—at least Mitali thought it was an act—interested in InDesign, the software she used at work. He had this high-pitched laugh that sometimes disrupted those around them. If there was something that seemed unusual for Mitali, it was that Neesh did not want to talk about himself. He did not elaborate on his friends, other than to say he didn't have many, like her. He shied away from discussing his family. He mostly wanted to hear from her, which Mitali found to be a pleasant change of pace from Paul the Finance Guy or Russell the Trainer, both of whom loved hearing themselves talk.

More than anything, Neesh wanted Mitali to like him—that much was clear from his nervous energy. She felt warm. For a few hours on a weeknight, the day before Mitali was to go worship the goddess Durga, she herself felt worshiped.

He paid the tab and walked her home. She had to walk faster to keep up with his long strides. Mitali was surprised by her nerves, too. As they arrived at her apartment building, another question she did not want to answer at the moment loomed. *Should I come upstairs to see your place?* It had been so long since she had felt desired, let alone had sex. It was like she carried the guilt of Keya's death with her everywhere. *Why should I enjoy myself when Keya cannot?* But Neesh didn't ask to come up. Instead, he surprised Mitali once again. Arriving at her stoop, he extended his hand for a shake.

"I don't know what to say in these moments, but thank you for coming out," Neesh said.

A handshake? Thank you for coming out? Not even a hug? She chuckled in disbelief, unsure if she had just been relegated to friendship, and shook his hand. At twenty-five years old, she had never had a date quite like this. *Who is this guy?* His disinterest caught Mitali off guard and simultaneously intrigued her.

"Am I going to see you again?" Mitali finally asked.

"Only if you want to see me again," Neesh countered, his thumb stroking the back of Mitali's hand. Mitali noticed something white sticking out of Neesh's wallet. He followed her gaze down, his eyes widening.

"Those are the note cards," he said sheepishly.

Mitali burst into laughter, genuine laughter. And then she gave him a hug, burying her head in his chest and closing her eyes. She felt his heart thrumming, the safety of its drumlike beat. She leapt up the stairs and didn't look back.

◊

Shantanu grimaced as he drove with one hand on the steering wheel and the other holding his cell phone. He placed his phone on the passenger seat. Mitali had ignored his evening text, which wasn't unusual, but it still cut him nonetheless. *I do this every two weeks. Can't she answer me just once?* He wondered what she could be doing this late at night. *It's actually not that late. What if she's doing nothing? Perish the thought.* Shantanu turned off Route 9, the highway connecting several suburbs in Monmouth County. In Mitali's world, there were Starbucks on every corner. For Shantanu, there was Route 9, where an Applebee's, Best Buy, Wendy's, and Target seemed to reappear every quarter mile. As his hands gripped the steering wheel, Shantanu noticed an aching in one of his wrists the tighter he squeezed. *I suppose this is the price of getting old: pain that you do not recognize, along with the pain that you do.*

The sun had tucked away for the night as Shantanu found an empty parking spot in a complex of condominiums called Maplewood. He turned off the headlights and the engine of his 2008 Honda Accord, and its purr came to a halt. The purr sounded more like a cough every day, but Shantanu adored the car's durability, even as its sage-green paint was chipped.

Shantanu limped down a sidewalk that snaked around some other brick buildings, before arriving at a door with a wreath hanging in front. He knocked twice. No answer. *Is this the day?* Shantanu turned the doorknob and found it was unlocked. *She needs to stop with this.*

He poked his head in and smelled curries, much to his relief.

"Ma?" Shantanu called out while patting on the dark wooden panels that made up the walls in the condo. From the kitchen, he heard a firm, high-pitched yell.

"*Babu*?! In here!" Kalpana said, and Shantanu heard the clatter of a spatula dropping in the sink.

Instead of waiting for him to come to the kitchen, Kalpana moved surprisingly swiftly to the living room to embrace Shantanu, helped by the thick spectacles that took up much of her face and the clutching of her lush *salwar kameez*.

"*Bechara! Ekhene asho! Keycho? Keetchu katcho na!*" Kalpana said, both of her frail hands reaching up to touch his face.

"I'm eating just fine, thank you, Ma," Shantanu said, blushing slightly. He handed her the lilacs he purchased on the way, and then kneeled down on one knee. He bent and touched both of her feet with his hand, and then his own forehead and chest before rising.

"A *pranam? Kano?*" Kalpana was surprised by the gesture. She was three inches shorter than him and proceeded to wrap her arms around his waist.

"Because it's been a month since I have been over for dinner," Shantanu said. "And I know it's Durga Puja this weekend, and I feel that I should be a good Bengali."

"This reminds me. Come here," Kalpana directed. She reached up with both of her hands and brought Shantanu's head closer to hers and murmured, "*Durga, Durga,*" with her eyes tightly shut. Shantanu never quite understood this prayer, but for as long as he could remember, his mother would say it every time he arrived or left the house. He regretted not saying it enough. Maybe Keya would still be around.

"Why are you walking like that?" Kalpana wore a perpetual look of concern.

"I was coming out of the shower and rolled my ankle. It's nothing," Shantanu said.

Kalpana, satisfied with the explanation, beckoned him into the dining room.

"*Esho, esho.* I've made your favorites: *Shorshe maach. Chingri maach. Mangsho. Aloo posto.* The *posto* is because you need some vegetables, and I know all you eat are those frozen pizzas at home," Kalpana said as she marched to the kitchen, which was considerably smaller and cleaner than Shantanu's.

Shantanu took a seat at one of the six chairs of the dining room table, which was covered by a tablecloth and then a separate plastic sheet. Kalpana came out carrying steaming-hot CorningWare dishes of curry: The mustard fish he so adored. Shrimp with cauliflower. A chicken curry with hot peppers. Sliced potato prepared with poppy seeds.

"*Bhosho*, Ma. Those pizzas are good," Shantanu said.

"You need to eat better, *babu*," Kalpana said as she placed metal serving spoons in the dishes. "I am seventy-seven. I won't be around too much longer to make this for you."

"Don't say that." Shantanu turned his eyes upwards as he rolled up the sleeves on his plaid button-down shirt and prepared to mix the rice and curries with his hands. Kalpana set a small dish of raw onion slices and green chilli peppers next to Shantanu's plate.

"You're right. I am seventy-five according to my Indian government records," Kalpana chortled. "Perhaps, *babu*, I am still just a baby. But I really don't have much time left!"

Kalpana's brightness brought a slight and rare smile to Shantanu's face. She had suggested that he move to Maplewood, something that seemed attractive in the moment. But someday, perhaps soon, Kalpana would be gone. *Maplewood is a suburban tomb*, Shantanu thought, before chiding himself for thinking in such grim terms.

Shantanu was hungry, which he realized as he spooned the balls of rice into his mouth with his hands, only interrupting to gulp water from the plastic cup Kalpana had set out or to nibble on a piece of onion.

"Do you want *luchi*? I can make *luchi!*" Kalpana insisted. Shantanu declined. He had all the carbs he needed right in front of him.

"Dr. Das, how is work going?" she asked, raising her eyebrows and sarcastically stroking her chin.

Shantanu considered the question, unsure of whether he should say what was next.

"This semester is going fine," Shantanu said, casually adding, "I might leave in a year. I've put in enough time. Rutgers likely wants new blood."

Kalpana nodded and said nothing, though her slight frown said much more. After the meal, Shantanu helped clean up, over Kalpana's objections. He hand-washed the dishes and spooned copious amounts of leftovers into Tupperware to take home later. Kalpana refused to use her dishwasher. She didn't trust it, which was a source of great amusement for Shantanu. Every couple of minutes he would feign putting a plate in the dishwasher to tease his mother, who would strenuously object.

Shantanu suggested they watch a movie together.

"I was hoping you would say that," Kalpana said with a smile, which exposed her missing tooth. She walked to one of her two bedrooms and returned with a VHS tape labeled *Goopy Gyne Bagha Byne*. Kalpana did not have a DVD player, let alone any streaming networks. She had her VCR and the movies she and Shantanu's father, Amitava, had accumulated over many decades. Shantanu, upon seeing her choice, snickered.

"How many times have you seen this now?" Shantanu asked.

"Too many and yet not enough," Kalpana retorted.

The Bengali-language fantasy, a black-and-white classic from the 1960s by Satyajit Ray, tracked two quirky, bumbling, untalented musicians who were granted the power to create whatever clothes and food they wanted at a moment's notice, travel anywhere, and the ability to hold an audience spellbound with their musical talents.

"Imagine that? If you could make clothes whenever you want?" Shantanu said.

"You would still wear that same shirt with stripes every day," Kalpana retorted without taking her eyes off the screen.

Right as the duo arrived in the kingdom of Shundi, Kalpana suddenly grabbed the remote control and shut the television off.

"What's that for?" Shantanu protested.

Kalpana sighed.

"I don't want to pretend anymore, *babu*. I am worried about you." Kalpana moved closer to Shantanu on the couch and put a hand on his shoulder.

"I'm fine," he responded tersely, wishing that she would turn the television back on.

"Has it really been five years?" Kalpana said.

"Almost." Shantanu steeled himself.

She turned away from Shantanu, beginning to tear up.

"Something for you to remember: It hasn't just been five years for you. It's also been five years for me. And Mitali. And Chaitali."

Shantanu didn't know what to say. So he did not respond. He was finding this to be the case in many of his conversations.

"Did you call my granddaughter?" Kalpana said.

"I texted, but she hasn't responded," Shantanu answered, embarrassed.

"Don't be angry at her," Kalpana soothed. "Did she tell you she is coming to take me to the puja this weekend?"

Shantanu was reticent. She hadn't told him, but this was not unexpected. The pujas were not for him. Not anymore. Mother and son sat in silence. All that could be heard was the sound of a dehumidifier plugged in next to the sofa.

"Something I love about your kids: they've always called me *shomadidi*. That's not a real term. They're supposed to call me *dida*. But they loved me so much that they made up my own title," Kalpana said, her tears becoming more visible. She took off her glasses. "Your baba loved Keya too. I wish he lived to see who Keya became."

Shantanu gave a distasteful look.

"Don't you dare fault your baba," Kalpana snapped.

Shantanu stayed silent. He didn't want to argue.

"He grew up in a different time. He did not know how his words would be taken. You are looking to blame someone else, when—" Kalpana stopped herself. She used the *dupatta* hanging off her *salwar kameez* to wipe her eyes.

"Go ahead. Say it. *Bholo*," Shantanu said softly. "You're right. *Choop khore thako na.*"

"*Babu*, I don't mean it. I just miss her," Kalpana said. "I did not expect her to go before I did."

With that, Kalpana straightened up on the love seat, a possession that was a source of deep sorrow; a reminder of what used to be. She had allowed the family to buy her and Amitava the new furniture for Christmas one year. Keya had eyed the navy-blue color at the store and jumped on it as an eight-year-old to mark it as the one for *shomadidi*. Amitava only enjoyed the sofa for two years before dying of a stroke.

The more Kalpana straightened up, the further Shantanu slumped on the couch.

"I'm going to stay alive as long as I can for you," Kalpana said, looking intently at Shantanu. "But, *babu*, you need to *be* alive."

"Ma, can you not talk as if every second of your life is on borrowed time?" Shantanu said, his eyes fixated on the still television screen.

"*Bechara*, we are all just buying time," Kalpana said. "Some of us just have more money to play with than others."

TWO

The next morning, Shantanu was on the third floor of a commercial building off College Avenue in New Brunswick—about a fifty-five-minute drive from Howell—crammed into a tiny waiting room, thumbing through a two-year-old issue of *National Geographic*. He was the only one in the room, and hoped it would remain that way. He didn't want to run into any of his students.

Shantanu was deep into the magazine's cover story—"Healing Power of Faith"—and almost forgot why he was there to begin with. On the inside flap, the subheadline read, "You're not just what you eat or do, or think. You are what you believe." He didn't notice Dr. Lynch standing in the doorway, coughing loudly to get his attention. Shantanu jerked out of his print-inspired trance and saw a figure more than six feet tall, sporting a gray seersucker suit and a full head of a perfectly executed blond comb-over.

"Would you like to come in?" Dr. Lynch said in a smooth, kind tenor.

Shantanu scrambled to put the magazine down and grab his briefcase while Dr. Lynch held the door open for him, wearing a grin that matched the energy of the seersucker suit. Shantanu limped through the doorway and found two brown task chairs with arched backs sitting opposite each other, adjacent to a cluttered wooden desk—not too unlike his own office. There was also a couch. Shantanu glanced uneasily at Dr. Lynch, who gave him a look that said, *Wherever you want*. He chose the chair closest to the door.

"What can I do for you?" Dr. Lynch said warmly, holding a notebook, surrounded by multiple degrees hanging on the wall behind him. On it, there were pictures hugging the diploma with Dr. Lynch and people Shantanu assumed were the doctor's family.

"This is my brother and me at a Police show in the eighties." Dr. Lynch pointed to one of the frames. "That was a fun one. I'd tell you more about it, but I don't believe doctor-patient confidentiality goes both ways." He pointed to another frame, one of a young Dr. Lynch on the beach: "I took some time off and lived in Australia for six months in my twenties. It's where I met my wife."

There was a poster of Grant Hill in a Duke University jersey. A dream catcher hanging off the ceiling in one corner. *A gift from a patient, perhaps?* A framed note on lined paper that simply said, I AM MY OWN BIGGEST OBSTACLE. *He looks younger. In his forties, maybe.*

"Do you prefer Dr. Das or Shantanu? Am I pronouncing that correctly?" Dr. Lynch said.

"Shantanu is fine, thanks. And you?"

"Harry is great," Dr. Lynch said. He rolled up his left sleeve to show the copious amounts of hair on his forearm. "My kids think my name is a result of all the hair. You know. 'Hairy.'"

As an anthropologist, Shantanu had spent decades being an expert in how humans behaved, yet how bizarre it was to be in a room across from someone in a different field to understand himself. He had felt less nervous all those years ago when he was defending his thesis—an exploration of how migratory patterns were linked to public health in urban areas.

"How does this work? What do I say?" Shantanu asked, feeling ridiculous. "Indians aren't typically known for going to seek therapy," he reminded Dr. Lynch, as much as himself.

If Dr. Lynch had thoughts, he remained guarded. He just smiled.

"So what do you want to talk about?" Shantanu said.

Dr. Lynch's gaze was unwavering. He hunched forward in his chair, put both elbows on his knees, and rested his face on his hands. Unnerved by Dr. Lynch's stare, Shantanu studied Dr. Lynch's face just as intently. *Does he have no wrinkles?*

"You came here for a reason, Shantanu," Dr. Lynch said. "You said on the phone you thought you needed some help. So let me help you. It's my job. Tell me about yourself."

Shantanu ran through a short version of his life story, aware that he was wasting valuable time in his allotted forty-five minutes: He had been a professor at Rutgers for almost twenty-five years. He did his undergraduate and PhD at Rutgers, too. He had been in New Jersey his whole life: his parents, who were in an arranged marriage, settled in Hillsborough—about an hour north of Howell—after immigrating from Kolkata. Initially, Shantanu's grandfather on his father's side objected to their marriage, because of how dark Kalpana's skin was. But beyond the colorism, Shantanu's grandfather had always been choosy, and he was always finding something wrong with prospective wives, so he relented, at Amitava's insistence, so he didn't have to deal with the shame of having an unmarried son for too much longer. For his part, Amitava was just tired of waiting. That didn't stop Amitava's parents from openly grumbling about whether Kalpana was worthy of their son and derisively referring to her as someone who belonged to the lowest caste in society.

"I have a daughter who lives in New York. She's been alive for as long as I've been a professor. She's vibrant, but we don't speak often," Shantanu said. "I had another one. And lately—"

Dr. Lynch interrupted.

"I'm sorry, did you say 'had'?" he said.

"Had. Yes. I lost my younger daughter five years ago, which is why, I suppose—"

"What did you mean before? When you said, 'Indians aren't typically known for going to seek therapy'?"

"We're not. My parents thought therapists were for"—Shantanu mimed quotes— "*crazy people.*"

There was a nod of understanding from Dr. Lynch. Shantanu paused.

"Maybe I should come back next week. I've given you plenty to chew on," he said.

"But you showed up empty-handed," Dr. Lynch said instantly and with a straight face.

"I'm sorry?" Shantanu said.

Dr. Lynch repeated himself and then Shantanu understood the joke.

"Shantanu, please. You've come this far. I interrupted you when I shouldn't have. I'm sorry. In my defense, I never said I was a good therapist," Dr. Lynch said.

◇

Shantanu wished that night was a blur, like so many other nights in his life. But no matter how much time passed, he could still recall the details seamlessly. He stood by the toaster when Keya walked into the kitchen. Minutes later, she had gathered the entire family in the living room. Shantanu could vividly remember how radiant Chaitali looked, her hair in a bun and wearing a Rowan University T-shirt. This was the last night they were still in love. Mitali, then a junior in college, was home for a surprise visit. Well, she called it a surprise visit. It was more of a laundry and free food drive-by.

Shantanu sipped his green tea, while Mitali and Chaitali crowded next to him on the green, fluffy living room sofa. Keya pulled up a nearby chair that was typically reserved for guests. Shantanu had no idea what this talk was for. Most of his conversations with Keya for their entire life centered on academics. He figured Keya wanted to tell them what colleges she was going to apply to.

"Ma. Baba. Didi. I have to tell you all something." Keya sat there, biting her toast, unable to look at her family. She preferred her toast almost burnt, with large dollops of butter on it.

"You need to see the saris I'm going through upstairs," Chaitali said. "I'm making you try some on."

Chaitali was tender. *She always was*.

"Please listen."

"I know you smoke pot," Chaitali said. Mitali burst out laughing. They always teamed up. They were even wearing the same pink pajama pants that night.

"What?" Shantanu was horrified. "What is this?"

Chaitali chided him.

"Shanti, who cares? She's eighteen. It's not the end of the world," Chaitali said, chuckling along with Mitali. "If you did some gange, it would make your office hours more fun."

"This is not funny! How long have you been doing drugs, Keya?" Shantanu said sternly. "All your extracurriculars. National Honor Society. Student Council. It will mean nothing if you're in jail."

Keya rolled her eyes.

"I don't smoke pot, you idiots," Keya said.

There was something different in her features, a desperation. She was clutching the toast just a bit too hard. Her knees were bent, her arms hugged around them.

"Is it cocaine?" Mitali cut in.

Shantanu gave her a dirty look. Chaitali didn't love that line either.

"Quiet, Mitali," Chaitali scolded.

Keya took a deep breath. "You know my friend Pamela?"

All three were taken aback by the question.

"Are you asking us if we know Pamela?" Mitali said.

"Your friend who comes over *all* the time?" Chaitali chimed in.

Even Shantanu, who was not overly involved in Keya's social life, knew Pamela. Keya paused, searching.

"*Sona*, what's wrong?" Chaitali said more delicately, as Keya began to tear up. Mitali straightened in her seat.

"I don't know how to tell you all this. I'm just going to say it—" Keya stopped and wrung her hands before quickly separating them. Then held her palms out and stared at them, as if she didn't recognize her own limbs. "I like her. And she likes me. And I'd like to take her to Durga Puja this weekend."

"Well of course you like her. She's your friend," Shantanu said.

Keya furrowed her eyebrows.

"She wants to go to Durga Puja? Of course she's welcome!" Chaitali said. "It's nice of her to want to come."

"Yes, but I want her to come as my date," Keya said.

"That's very funny," Chaitali said. "She can be all of our dates! The car will be crammed, but the more the merrier."

"Are you listening to me?" Keya said.

"I think so?" Chaitali said.

"Ma," Mitali said. Only she understood.

"No, not as friends," Keya said. "As my *date*. I like *girls*. Like you and Baba like each other."

Shantanu and Chaitali were nonplussed as the living room grew painfully quiet. They exchanged mystified glances. And when it came to his daughters, Shantanu often turned to Chaitali to act as a translator. When her face showed bewilderment, he felt like he received permission for his mind to become a minefield of incomprehension. Even more than wanting to be told what to say, Shantanu wanted to be told what to think. And on this rare occasion, Chaitali's glance at Shantanu told him that she was looking for the same from him.

"Is anyone going to say something?" Keya asked. It was more of a plea.

"How long have you known?" Mitali said first. Shantanu knew his daughters were close—or thought they were, at least, from conversations he overheard between them. Mitali would call once a week to help Keya with her college applications. *Surely, they would have discussed crushes? Apparently not.*

"How have you never told me before? Why am I finding out at the same time as Ma and Baba?" Mitali accused, more than asking. The look on Keya's face wasn't one of shock, Shantanu would realize later, but terror.

"Only Pamela knew. She swore me to secrecy. And besides," Keya said indignantly, "it's none of your business."

"Well, you could've made it my business." Mitali recoiled, and before she could stop herself, she blurted out, "And so what? This is all supposed to fall to *me* now?"

"What's that supposed to mean?" Keya shot back.

"Getting married. Giving *them* grandchildren," Mitali said, a finger pointing at their parents. Keya looked wounded. Mitali looked ready to dive into a rant but held her tongue as Chaitali groaned from the couch. She was mystified no longer. It was finally dawning what, exactly, Keya was trying to tell them.

"On second thought, we don't know Pamela that well," Chaitali said. "I don't think it would be appropriate to bring her to the puja." She pursed her lips. Her face hardened. Shantanu rarely saw her like this.

"You just called her my 'friend that comes over all the time,'" Keya said, seemingly unnerved. "Of course you know her."

"How do we explain this to all the Bengalis? What will they think? All of them will think this is highly improper."

"*Them*," Keya said.

Shantanu, however, drifted away somewhere else. Finally, coherence began to form. He thought back to Amitava, his father, who would routinely refer to same-sex relationships as "unnatural." He remembered him saying so in front of Mitali and Keya, and not having the courage to contradict him in front of them. He had no courage in this moment either. He let himself feel the shame his father would have put on him.

"*Sona*, you are eighteen. You are going through a phase," Shantanu said, placing his teacup on the glass table. "My friend, Dr. Sanjay Mehta, is a clinical psychologist. He is very famous and popular at Princeton. I think he can help you manage this phase and exit it."

He sensed this was the wrong thing to say almost immediately, but he was reacting instinctively. Shantanu was an academic by trade, a doctorate. He was used to rigorous analyses and challenging his students to have foolproof arguments. Yet when the moment came for him to consult logic, he failed. It would haunt him.

"I don't understand. Ma, you're a librarian. You don't think you've ever checked out a book to a gay person? Baba, don't you have gay students at Rutgers?" Keya said. Her face no longer registered fear. She looked appalled.

"Of course I do, but—" Shantanu said.

"But they're not *your* daughter. So not your problem."

"Keya!" Chaitali raised her voice. "Don't yell at your baba."

"Enough! *Choop khoro!*" Shantanu bellowed. "We will not hear any more of this. You are a great many things, Keya. You aren't this."

"*This* is who I am. And you are fucked up."

"Keya!" Chaitali gasped.

"You don't talk to me like that. You aren't a disgrace. You are not like the white kids," Shantanu said sternly. Mitali was frozen, realizing the situation had unraveled. "We didn't raise you here so you could be like *them*."

I did, though, Shantanu later thought. *I raised my daughters to be exactly like them.* Keya could not bear to look at any of the three of them. Finally, she let out a cackle.

"But I *am* a disgrace," she said, grabbing her car keys and purse. "I thought you guys would understand." With that, she bolted out the door. No one stopped her. Only Mitali watched her through the front window as Keya turned her car out of the development.

Chaitali turned to Mitali.

"Were there signs of this?"

"I don't know," Mitali said. "It's not something I thought much about."

Chaitali turned to Shantanu, who seemed like he was in a trance.

"*Suncho*, what should we do?"

"There's nothing to do. She is fine," he said, the uncertainty dripping off every word. "This is a phase."

Shantanu caught himself thinking about the times he would come home from school as a teenager and tell Amitava about being bullied. Amitava barely glanced at him as he too would call this a phase. *And he was right*, Shantanu thought. *Eventually everyone leaves high school and grows up.*

He didn't have anything else to add. All he could hear was his father's voice seared into his thoughts, saying the word "unnatural" over and over again.

◇

"Please continue," Dr. Lynch said gently.

It didn't take a psychologist to see Shantanu's hesitance to tell him the next part of the story. Shantanu looked up at the ceiling. He hoped it would fall on him.

"We didn't speak again for two months. And then she was gone."

"Was it—" Dr. Lynch didn't want to finish this question, Shantanu could tell. *He must be a parent*.

"Ah, she passed," Dr. Lynch finished with a statement instead of a question.

"I don't want to discuss this anymore," Shantanu said, trying to compose himself. "I don't know why I'm here."

"I get it," Dr. Lynch said. "Why *are* you here?"

"I don't know. I was drinking too much."

"Why is this your fault?" Dr. Lynch asked.

"I'm sorry?" Shantanu said. He would not look Dr. Lynch in the eye. He kept his head turned away.

"I said: Why is this *your* fault?" Dr. Lynch repeated.

"We didn't try to make things right with her. *I* didn't," Shantanu said, his eyes suddenly welling.

"Do you think this is what Keya would have wanted for you? Do you think that she died thinking you didn't love her?" Dr. Lynch said.

"Yes, I do," Shantanu said without skipping a beat.

"Are you eating well? Are you still drinking?" Dr. Lynch asked. Shantanu could not read his tone, but he said that he ate as much as he needed to and that he had stopped drinking.

"We're almost out of time," Dr. Lynch said, eyeing the clock on top of the door. "But we have plenty to talk about. I'd love for you to come back, Shantanu. We need to explore your relationship with your two daughters and your wife."

"Ex-wife."

"Ex-wife. Yes. Will you come back?"

Shantanu didn't answer.

"Can you help me?" Dr. Lynch asked.

Once again, Shantanu found Dr. Lynch to be different from what he expected.

"With what? Aren't you supposed to help me?"

Dr. Lynch leaned back against his chair and looked towards the ceiling.

"Dr. Das, before you leave today, I would like you to consider something. Death is what you say it is. I firmly believe that."

"What does that mean?" Shantanu said as he rose from the chair and reached for his briefcase.

"Death can be permanent. It is, in most ways," Dr. Lynch said. "But there are ways for people to live that don't involve being alive. And there are ways to be dead while still being able to breathe."

Shantanu put on his black zip-up windbreaker. Dr. Lynch stood as well.

"It's up to you—no, us—to find the former and rid you of the latter," Dr. Lynch said. "You're not ready today. That's fine. But help me do that. This is a journey, and I'd like for us to go on it together. You should know that you're not just dealing with grief. There's also significant trauma."

Dr. Lynch extended his hand. His look into Shantanu's eyes was so piercing that Shantanu had to stare back. He nodded and rose to leave. On the way out, he grabbed that *National Geographic* issue he had been reading.

◇

"I like your new *gari*, Mitali," Kalpana said, sitting in the back seat of the 2016 Honda Civic. "I rarely get in cars. *Bhoi pai!*"

Mitali jerked her head to the left as she guided the car on an entrance ramp and onto the Garden State Parkway.

"It's not a new car, *Shomadidi*," Mitali said, over the sound of *The Moth* podcast that filled the space. "It's a rental. And there's nothing to be scared of. I don't understand why you don't sit in the front seat."

As soon as she said that, Mitali regretted it. *Of course there is something to be scared of.* She inched farther away from the guardrail. Kalpana shuddered as she watched the trees and highway signs fly by. Her white hair fluttered in the wind from the slightly rolled-down window.

"It is safer back here," Kalpana said. "That's why when you were young, you were not allowed to sit in the front. And I don't sit in the front because the front is for parents. *Thomar Ma-Baba.*"

Mitali chuckled at the arbitrary lines in the sand. *The front seat is for my parents?*

"Did you call your ma?" Kalpana asked.

"No."

"Did you call your baba?"

"No."

"*Eeesh. Amra kee korbo?*" Kalpana said.

"There is nothing for us to do," Mitali answered, easing her foot off the gas pedal, making sure to keep the car going at the speed limit and no more. She glanced at Kalpana's troubled face in the rearview mirror. "I'm sorry, *Shomadidi.* I will call them tomorrow when I am back in the city from puja."

"*Eeesh.* I wish they would come. All your *mashis* and *kakus* would love to see them," Kalpana said wistfully. "Thank you for taking me. I know this will be your first one since—"

"I wanted to see you," Mitali said. She changed lanes.

"So, are you dating? Is there a boy?" Kalpana asked.

"*Shomadidi,*" Mitali said, her anxiety suddenly rising. She wondered whether she should tell her grandmother about her date.

"Or a girl!" Kalpana said. "Sorry, *beta.*"

Kalpana's question hung in the air—Mitali still hadn't heard from Neesh since the hug. Maybe the initial impulse—the handshake—is what was relevant. Maybe she put him on the spot, and he was being nice. And Mitali found it unnerving just how much she was hoping to receive an entreaty of some sort from him. *This feels unnatural.*

Kalpana suddenly cried out.

"Mitali! *Asthe! Asthe!*" she said, as she clutched her seat belt. The speedometer suddenly read ninety miles an hour.

"I'm sorry, *Shomadidi,*" Mitali said. It just occurred to her that she had never discussed a love interest with a family member. Look how it had gone the last time her family tried that. "No," she said. "I haven't met anyone."

◇

As Mitali pulled into the driveway of her childhood home, she felt a familiar sense of dread. This place was cursed to her, and the state of the lawn served as a reminder. Mitali could see a lone light on in the dining room from the outside of the house. Other homes in the development had put up Halloween decorations and set out pumpkins. There were none at 2 Hillcrest Drive, though.

Should she knock? It was her home too, she supposed, but the door was unlocked. She didn't see any signs of life—the walls were bare, and her father was nowhere to be found. She crept upstairs and went to her bedroom. Everything was the same. The medals. Her favorite comforter. The pillows stacked exactly how she liked them. There were some CDs fanned out on the dresser. *I forgot how much I liked listening to Good Charlotte.* A drawing Keya made of her. She found her high school yearbooks in the closet, along with a binder of stamps from the one summer she decided to be a collector. Mitali turned to her bed, crouched underneath and pulled out a paddle that was still stashed there. This was from one time when she went kayaking with a high school friend, and she was so good at it that she insisted on keeping it. At some point, she didn't always hate living here.

Keya's room looked untouched from the doorway. She couldn't bring herself to enter but could see Keya's drawings sprawled out on her desk, and the lyrics she painted on the wall. As she leaned in, she heard shuffling downstairs.

"Baba?" she called out. "Are you there?"

She walked to the stairwell. At the bottom, Shantanu stood there, staring up at her. He looked like he had seen a ghost. He dropped the box he was holding.

"Mitali!" Shantanu gasped, a mixture of shock and elation.

"What are you doing down there?" she said.

"What are *you* doing up there?"

"I just dropped *Shomadidi* off after the puja and I thought I would stop by," Mitali said. "I'm sorry. I forgot to text you back."

"It's okay. Did you eat? We can order something," Shantanu said, speaking excitedly. "It's so late! Will you stay the night?"

Mitali considered the opportunity to sleep in her old bed, something she hadn't done in, what, years? She was tired. She had spent an entire day hugging and giving *pranams* to dozens of sympathetic *mashis* and *kakus* she hadn't seen in years, not since Keya's funeral. No one brought up Shantanu. Or Chaitali. Or Keya, for that matter. Surely they all gossiped when Mitali wasn't nearby, about her parents' divorce, about her dead sister. But no one would be rude enough to do it to her face. She was like a ghost to them, much to her relief and her amusement.

There had been an imposing ten-armed, life-sized wax Durga figure in the high school cafeteria, which Mitali stood next to, along with Kalpana, with her arms clasped in front of the goddess. Hundreds of other Bengalis stood nearby. Everyone's hands were clasped around flowers handed out by the *mashis*, and the pandit led chants for the group to repeat.

Durga was on a *Singhasan*, the platform upon which gods are placed, depicted as vanquishing Mahishasura, a demon king. Mitali didn't pray often, but the sounds of the *dhak* being rhythmically pounded nearby, and the *mashis* blowing conch shells or using their tongues to make melodic noises made her nostalgic.

A *mashi* strolled by and sprinkled peace water—*shanti jol*—on the devotees, after the group chanted invocations. Mitali had prayed selflessly— that Chaitali and Shantanu would find peace. She had prayed, selfishly, that Neesh would text her. Mitali remembered that as children, she and Keya would always laugh at getting wet, and at night after the ceremony ended, they would chase each other and toss their own *shanti jol* on each other, much to the chagrin of Shantanu and Chaitali. "It's for peace!" Keya would assure them.

For one day, Mitali was transported back to her childhood. But that trip down memory lane, as she stood outside Keya's room, was enough for one day.

"No, I need to get back. I ate the shitty *khichuri* they always have. Glorified *daal*. I came because I saw your text. What's with the box?"

Shantanu looked at the box that he had just dropped on the floor. He bent down, fiddled with its top, and picked it back up.

"I was in the garage," he said. "I'm cleaning up because I'm thinking about selling the house."

Mitali didn't have much sorrow about this, although she did like how untouched her room seemed.

"You're selling?"

"It's time," Shantanu said matter-of-factly. "What do I need with four bedrooms?"

Mitali walked down the stairs. "So did you want me to go through my room?"

"No, I found some stuff in the attic the other day I wanted to show you. Come."

Mitali and Shantanu walked to the dining room, where several open cardboard boxes, a metal carton, and a wooden box were laying on top of a table.

"Look at this one," Shantanu said, pointing at one that was tagged AL-BUMS and ripping the masking tape off the top. Inside, there were several envelopes filled with developed photos. "I found these in the attic."

Mitali took her coat off and draped it on a chair. In her entire life, she had gone into the attic only twice.

"Your mother must have never gotten around to putting these in actual albums," Shantanu said.

Mitali began flipping through them, occasionally flicking off dust that had accumulated. There was one of Mitali and Keya as babies. Another two at their *annaprashans*, both of which were held at the same Rutgers banquet hall. *Keya did much better with eating the* payesh *than me*. Mitali wearing a batting helmet and a softball uniform with HORNETS lettering on it, and Chaitali with one arm around her and giving a thumbs-up to the camera.

"That must have been when you were around twelve," Shantanu said, looking over Mitali's shoulder. "Softball was how I made you a Yankees fan."

"Was I any good?"

"You sat down in the outfield when games were going on, so take that for what it's worth," Shantanu said. Mitali laughed, flipping through more of the pictures.

A photo of all four of them at someone's wedding.

"Whose was this?" Mitali asked. "Maybe Shalini and Sourav?"

Mitali felt a pang when she came across a resplendent picture of Keya in a red silk sari with gold embroidery. She looked to be around ten. This was from her Bharatanatyam dance days. *This must be from one of the pujas that year.*

"Oh my gosh," Mitali said. She held the photograph up for her father to see. "I remember this one. She stumbled a bit during the *naach* and was upset the whole car ride home."

Mitali and Shantanu spent the next hour perusing the contents of the boxes on the table. There were two of old clothes. One was only of saris, likely belonging to Chaitali. The metal carton was full of old sneakers and sandals, as well as a deflated basketball.

"I didn't think I was that bad a shooter," Mitali said.

"Do you remember when NASA found one of your jump shots on the moon?" Shantanu teased. There were hints of smiles they used to share.

"Baba, did you really bring me here to look through old boxes?"

"There's something else," Shantanu said.

He slid the wooden box, still twinkling, in front of Mitali. She took in the series of folded pieces of paper and the packet. Mitali gave Shantanu a quizzical look.

"Unfold them," Shantanu said.

Mitali took out one of the squares, on which was written "Last Five Years" in purple pen surrounded by a heart, and unfolded it.

Hiiii!

We have an English test today, so I don't have much time to write a note. But I just wanted to give you something to open before

*lunch. Dad is being a dick again about college, and my mom just
stands there and watches it. I'll tell you more later. But it's more
of the same. Okay, the teacher is handing out papers.*

Love, Pamela

"This was in the attic?" Mitali said. Shantanu nodded. She reached into
the box and fished out two more notes to read them. Her pulse quickened
and she dropped the paper.

"These are love notes," she said breathlessly. "All of these. How did
they get to the attic?"

Shantanu gestured that he didn't know.

"Did she *hide* these up there?" Mitali said.

"That's what I was thinking," Shantanu said. "It's possible."

Mitali closed her eyes.

"How many of these did you read?" Mitali asked.

"Just one."

He immediately reached for more notes to open and winced from the
pain in his knees as he did so. Mitali stopped him.

"Baba, maybe we should stop," she said. "They are hers."

"She's *dead*," Shantanu said fiercely. He took a breath and looked towards the attic. "She died."

"I know that, Baba," Mitali said. "Please. Let's not do this right now."

"Death is what we *say* it is," Shantanu said.

Mitali reached for the wooden box and ran her hand over it. Keya
would have spent hours picking out this paper, Mitali thought. It was
bright and screamed of optimism, much like Keya. Suddenly, Keya felt
very alive. Mitali noticed tears forming in Shantanu's eyes and couldn't
help her own. That was when she noticed the packet of unfolded papers
held together by a binder clip sitting underneath the notes. She pulled
them out, as if they were wreckage being pulled from the ocean.

There was a title page with the words *The Elm Tree*. Mitali began
leafing through the unexpectedly heavy packet. It was about eighty pages,

formatted inconsistently. Some page corners were bent, others were fully wrinkled. There were handwritten notes scribbled in the margins throughout. One, on page eight, read in purple marker, "Should we cut?" with a bracket around a scene. The first page had a character list, giving the biographies for six people. One page that Mitali came across had a giant, circular stain on it. Presumably, someone had left a glass with liquid on it for too long. Another one was hard and crusty and littered with ink blotches; the victim of a full-on spill, it appeared. But even still, it took a minute or two for Mitali to comprehend what this was. Each page had lines of dialogue on it.

"This is a play, Baba," Mitali said.

"A play. I didn't even look at those papers. I figured they were a school project or something."

Shantanu tried to peek at what Mitali was holding. Both of them wanted to devour every word that was hiding in the box.

"She's *not* dead." Shantanu's voice trembled. "She's right here. My *sona* is right here."

As Mitali handed the packet to her father, her phone buzzed and her eyes widened at the text. It was from Neesh, a photograph from the front desk of the studio, captioned *Slow night*. As Mitali's eyes went from the box on the table to Shantanu intently reading *The Elm Tree* to the text message, she clasped her hands around her phone as if it were one of the flowers from the puja hours before.

She closed her eyes and mouthed to herself, *Durga, Durga*.

◇

The days became longer for the Dases after Keya stormed out that night, until they became an eternity. Occasionally, Shantanu, Mitali, and Chaitali would catch themselves staring at the driveway, hoping to see Keya's car pull up. But Keya never showed her face in the daytime, her bouncy curls nowhere in sight. She came and went from the house, almost entirely right after dawn or at night, without speaking to anyone in the family. If only Keya had still relied on Shantanu for rides.

Pamela didn't come over after that night. Mitali went back to college a couple days later. Shantanu and Chaitali ended up going to Durga Puja alone, parrying questions from friends about how Keya was doing by saying she had a stomach bug. Chaitali would leave food out for Keya that went uneaten.

They never once discussed that night's conversation. Chaitali no longer surprised Keya with visits at the nearby Target, where Keya worked part-time on weekends. The Dases tried to pretend Keya's coming-out conversation did not happen, except for the fact that Keya was no longer having *any* conversations with her family members. Texts went unanswered. On the rare occasions Keya crossed paths with her parents in a hallway, she would stare determinedly straight ahead. If they weren't going to see her, she was not going to see them. That went for Mitali, too. Shantanu and Chaitali preserved the facade of a united family outwardly, whether in conversations with friends, co-workers, or, bizarrely, each other. As far as they were concerned, the path of least resistance—pushing the memory of that talk with Keya deep into the crevices of the earth where it could never be heard from again—was the safest choice to make.

Maybe they could force normalcy with sheer will. The only time they brought up Keya was when Shantanu mused about whether Keya was keeping up with financial aid applications. Chaitali pursed her lips and didn't answer. She had more trouble than Shantanu at pretending. But they still refused to acknowledge that Keya was gay, until Mitali was home for Thanksgiving break. When Mitali arrived, the home was cold and joyless.

"Ma. Baba. We handled that very poorly," Mitali said abruptly at the kitchen table, Keya nowhere to be found. "Do we know where Keya is?"

"Pam— Work, maybe?" Shantanu said.

Mitali's guilt over not being immediately accepting had been overwhelming in the preceding weeks. She had not been able to focus in class. She had been trying to use weekend parties—and the free alcohol that came with them—to distract herself. It wasn't working. The silence weighed on all of them, but Mitali, as the older sister, felt a particular burden.

"Handled *what* poorly?" Chaitali said, but she knew. She had just gotten up from the table to make hot chocolates, the family drink of choice, while standing on the cotton bath rug she had inexplicably put in the kitchen. Shantanu, meanwhile, scanned real estate listings. He didn't have the money or interest in buying another property, but he might as well dream and see whether prices were dropping.

"Keya," Mitali said. "She hasn't spoken to me in a month."

Chaitali and Shantanu exchanged glances. Suddenly, Chaitali put a hand on her head and burst into tears. Mitali realized this was perhaps the first time anyone had even spoken her sister's name aloud in weeks.

"You're right, Mitali. We didn't handle that well." Chaitali looked as if a boulder had been removed from her back. "I was just so shocked. I didn't know what to say," Chaitali said. "Shanti?"

Shantanu put the listings down.

"I've done some research," he said, a bit lighter now that the tension had popped. "I need some time to learn more about it. But I think therapy for her is the best answer."

"*Therapy?!*" Mitali said with an uncharacteristic impetuousness. "You don't need more time. Neither do you, Ma. She doesn't need therapy."

"Perhaps this is not a phase. But the last month has been unbearable. We cannot live like this," Chaitali said.

"Mitali, you don't understand," Shantanu said. "This isn't how I grew up. Baba was different."

Chaitali placed steaming-hot cups at the table. The trio sat around the kitchen table sipping their drinks, planning out a second conversation, while *unnatural* rang in Shantanu's head.

"But we need to make sure that she knows we love her, first and foremost," Chaitali said.

"I'm googling the right things to say," Mitali offered.

"Maybe it will help if we tell her that of course it's okay for her to bring Pamela to Durga Puja next year," Chaitali said.

"And that she's *gay*, Ma. And that she's gay. It's okay that she's gay," Mitali repeated sternly.

"Right, of course. This is all just so sudden," Chaitali said. "What will the other Bengalis say about us?"

"Who cares?" Mitali nearly shouted.

"Right, who cares," Chaitali replied, though a bit reluctantly. "Right, right."

She spilled some of her hot chocolate. Her hands were shaking. "She is my daughter. How did I not know this? *Suncho*? Say something."

"And we have to apologize," Mitali added. Shantanu was quiet, deliberating. His eyes were focused on the bread crumbs by the toaster as he tapped his fingers together. He kept thinking of Keya saying *I don't understand*.

"The upside to that conversation is that she doesn't smoke pot," Shantanu said with a reassuring smile. "Everything else is immaterial. Mitali, call your sister. Actually, no, text her since she's not answering our calls. I heard her leave this morning. Have her come back. We will tell her everything is okay."

"I'm calling her," Mitali said, grabbing her phone and furiously swiping the passcode. She held the phone to her ear as Shantanu and Chaitali watched nervously. After three rings, the Dases could hear Keya's voice mail. The call was screened. Mitali set the phone down and put a hand on her head, just like her mother moments before. Chaitali hung her head.

"Let's give her some time," Shantanu said. "We may not have a big mansion," he added, as he picked up his real estate listings again, "but we surely have time."

THREE

At fifty years old, Chaitali had never planned on being a newlywed again. Who could? Certainly, the thought of marrying someone else before either of her daughters married was unnerving. She was sure her parents, who had died before Mitali was born, would never have approved. *Divorcing a respected anthropology professor? What shame to our family!* Yet there she was at a town hall obtaining a marriage license to Jahar Ghosh, a partner at a corporate law firm and a widower ten years her senior. There was no ceremony, owing in part to the shame they both felt in remarrying. Chaitali didn't even tell her sister in California until afterwards. And even if they did throw a party, Chaitali wondered, would Mitali have come? She carried this guilt, complicated by the fact that she was happier than she had been in a long time. Not happy, exactly, but happier. After they signed their marriage license, Jahar had put his hand on hers and said, "There is no shame in love, Chaitali." But there was undoubtedly shame. Mitali hadn't forgiven her for leaving Shantanu. Nor did Kalpana. Wherever Keya was, Chaitali was sure she was angry at her too.

It was Jahar's jovial presence that caught Chaitali's eye at a family friend's house—Shalini's—shortly after the divorce papers were signed. The dinner party was filled with his dramatic stories of contentious negotiations with opposing lawyers, supplemented with jealousy-inducing bits about adventures in his New York City life: weekend hikes, Lincoln Center ballets, and lots of restaurants. He'd talk of frequenting French bistros where the occasional diplomat, author, and actor could be spotted at separate tables at once. But as Chaitali struck up a conversation with him by herself that night, she found a man who was deeply lonely. Just like she was. It turned out they both could bond over grief: Jahar's wife, Supriya, had died two decades prior. They clicked. They both knew pain.

Unlike Shantanu, Chaitali opened her eyes every morning to a cacophony of color. Clothes of various shades tossed around on the floor, which she had meant to pick up the night before. The flowery wallpaper in the primary bedroom punctuated by several picture frames featuring smiling children. One was of Keya. There were three of Mitali. The burgundy-red Berber carpet, upon which Chaitali spotted the same stubborn stain from a spill months ago that she had been unable to remove. Maybe it came from the half-empty wineglass on the nightstand she always liked to use. There was no stillness in this house, it seemed.

The smell of bacon wafted upstairs, as did the sound of a television turned to CNN, which was blaring the mundane outrage of an anchor discussing another Trump tweet. Chaitali tilted to see the time on the digital clock: 7:45 a.m. On cue, she heard the roar of a school bus's engine as it drove through the Candlelight development. The lawn was perfectly trimmed and green, as she could see outside the window closest to the bed, one of three windows in the primary bedroom. The grass was aided by the sprinkler system that she and Shantanu had not sprung for in a previous life. No weeds were welcome here.

"Chaitali, can you come down here? You have a guest," Jahar's voice boomed, as it always did. But this time, he sounded unsure of himself. She realized he had turned off CNN. Chaitali wasn't a fan of unannounced guests—of course, her thoughts wandered to that night five years ago when Officer Giggenbach solemnly arrived at their doorstep. *Who would come by the house this early in the morning?*

"I'll be right down!" she yelled back.

Chaitali rushed to the en suite bathroom and splashed her face with cool water. She did not notice her wrinkles. What she saw was a new life. A new beginning. And unmistakable guilt.

She didn't bother changing out of her pink bathrobe as she strolled down the stairs. She was not supposed to be at the library until noon anyway. On the eighth step of the winding stairway, Chaitali wished she had changed out of her bathrobe.

Shantanu was standing in the doorway, next to Jahar. He was holding a shimmering box. Her ex-husband was perfectly shaven, wearing a plaid shirt—*what else?*—that was tucked into tan khakis over an increasing belly. *He's gained weight*, Chaitali thought, before chiding herself. Even if Shantanu had cleaned himself up since she'd last seen him, he still looked disheveled next to the tall lankiness of Jahar in his crisp white undershirt and a more-salt-than-pepper beard as perfectly manicured as their lawn. Even so, Chaitali's breath caught in her throat as Shantanu came into view.

"I'm sorry to barge in like this," Shantanu said. "May I talk to you in private?"

This had never happened before, and Chaitali did not know what to do. Shantanu and Chaitali had not been in the same room since Mitali's college graduation, a strained affair in which neither party wanted to take part. Jahar had a tortured look on his face, but he said nothing, only looked to Chaitali for guidance. And yet, Chaitali couldn't help but feel her fondness for Shantanu rise within her.

"Of course," Chaitali said with an air of formality. "Can I make you some chai?"

Shantanu took his black dress loafers off and left them by the door. Chaitali pointed him towards the adjacent family room, filled with reclining chairs and a wooden desk with merger agreements on them. Jahar, not knowing what else to do, politely exiled himself upstairs, while Chaitali made the tea and brought cups out.

"How are you?" Chaitali said, partially wondering if this was a dream.

"I'm hanging in there, thank you for asking," Shantanu said politely, and with a formal stiffness. He nodded towards the stairs. "He didn't have to go upstairs."

"I heard Mitali went to puja with your mother," Chaitali said, to change the subject. "Shalini told me she looked lovely."

Shantanu was still focused on the stairs.

"The last time I saw Jahar, he was just a *kaku* to the kids at Durga Puja," Shantanu said with a smirk. "Now he's their baba." *We might as well get the passive-aggressiveness out of the way*, Chaitali thought.

"Did you come here to fight about this? Now?" Chaitali began to feel irritated and felt her attraction for him melting away. He slowly sipped his chai.

"No, not at all," Shantanu said, and she could hear in his voice a note of regret, of longing. He reached for the box he had placed next to the chair and handed it to Chaitali. "I should have called."

"So what do you want to talk about?"

"Look what I found in the attic last week."

Chaitali took the box and held it in her lap, simply gaping at it. She was as still as a statue.

"Aren't you going to open it?" Shantanu asked, perplexed.

Chaitali maintained her posture. Her striking brown eyes fixated on the artifact. How did he come to find the box?

"Chai?" Shantanu pressed again.

"Of course, I'll get you some more," Chaitali said robotically, her eyes still on the box.

"I meant you." Shantanu's brow furrowed. "Chaitali."

Chaitali stood up and put the box down on a low table between them. As she did, the reclining chair jerked back and forth. Chaitali met Shantanu's blank gaze and found herself in a familiar position: she couldn't communicate her shock or her pain at seeing the box and, frankly, at seeing him.

"You found this already," Shantanu said, now realizing.

She nodded yes.

"Shanti," Chaitali said plaintively, using her old nickname for him.

The memory of discovering the box washed over her. She remembered the bruises on her knees when they hit the wooden joists as she rushed to put the papers back in the box and shove it back in the corner.

"I found it in the attic when I moved some of Keya's clothes up there," Chaitali said. "After the funeral."

"How come you never told me?" Shantanu said, reaching for his hot mug.

"I didn't want to upset you," Chaitali said. "And we had stopped talking. I was mad all the time."

"You were *mad*?" As Shantanu spoke, a grandfather clock bounded to life. "You were mad. You were so mad that you didn't think this was something your family would want to see."

"You don't get to lecture me, Shanti," Chaitali said through gritted teeth. "You were not sober enough in those days to listen to me. I was so alone!"

Shantanu glanced at the grandfather clock and the bookshelf directly next to it, where Chaitali could see he was eyeing its contents. One of the books on the shelf was a copy of *Jane Eyre*. All the books there belonged to her. Chaitali couldn't say this aloud to Shantanu, because it would give him too much satisfaction. But she imagined what he was thinking. And it made her slightly insecure. Shantanu was probably internally mocking Jahar, that he didn't give a shit about *Jane Eyre* or other books, unlike Shantanu. And he'd be right. *But there is a life outside of literature.*

In a way, it was a book that brought Shantanu and Chaitali together in the first place. When Shantanu first laid eyes on Chaitali at a coffee shop in New Brunswick while he was a doctoral candidate, she had a book in her hand. He was immediately drawn to her but didn't have the courage to approach her. He also didn't want to interrupt Chaitali while she was reading, she would find out later that night, something she found appealing. As well as his filled-out, bit-too-slick side-part on his head.

"So you packed your bags. And really, how alone were you?" Shantanu remarked. Chaitali looked stricken. They were both reminded of their last years of marriage.

"I *never* had an affair," Chaitali said, looking Shantanu directly in the eyes. He put the mug on the table and exhaled deeply. Shantanu let his body sag on the chair. He signalled that it was time for a détente. Chaitali thought back to the coffee shop and the fortuitousness of running into Shantanu at a party that night. They laughed over wine and crackers. The two stood in a corner, away from everyone else, and talked about their parents' inability to stop discussing the cultural impact of Rabindranath Tagore and the virtues of communism. They talked about pujas—Chaitali's in Houston, Shantanu's in Hillsborough. Chaitali was visiting a friend and was looking for apartments in New York City after recently graduating with a teaching degree she had no interest in using. They held hands while discussing the Rolling Stones.

"I'm sorry, Chai. I know you didn't. You are, as always, right." Shantanu looked wounded at having to admit that. He looked at Chaitali's hands. Chaitali recognized the look. He wished he could hold them. Chaitali drew her hands towards herself and straightened her back.

"Did you ever read any of the notes?" Shantanu said.

Chaitali tried to let her frustration seep into the living room like carbon dioxide.

"A couple, but I stopped," Chaitali said. "*She* hid that box up there because *she* didn't want it to be found."

"Mitali suggested the same thing," Shantanu said. "Is that really why you stopped?"

"Yes, but there was another reason." She sighed. "Keya is dead. No amount of reading these letters is going to bring her back to life again."

Shantanu nodded in understanding.

"Shanti, there are some days where I have trouble remembering what she was like," Chaitali said. "Do you ever find yourself feeling that way?"

"Not yet, no. And I will not let you forget your daughter."

"Every now and then, I wish you would," Chaitali said, looking down at the rug.

"You don't mean that."

A hush came over the room, except for the ticking of the clock.

"I don't mean that," Chaitali finally said. She wished he would leave, and perhaps whatever was left tethered between them made him rise, taking the box from the table.

Chaitali felt like she was stuck on a treadmill from the past.

"I hope you find some peace, Shanti," Chaitali said.

At the front door, Shantanu struggled to put his shoes on, and she felt almost sorry for him. She recognized the ways their bodies were failing them more these days. But it was no longer her place to feel those failures with him.

"What is peace but just another precursor to war?"

Chaitali gave the faintest hint of a smile. "I see you've been watching the History Channel again."

Shantanu smiled back and turned towards the driveway.

"Have we lost Mitali?" Chaitali asked.

"Pieces of her, possibly."

"Did you know that we weren't the first ones Keya told about being gay?" Chaitali said.

"I assume she told her friends. Pamela, of course," Shantanu said, stiffening in the cold breeze from the open door.

"No, Shanti," Chaitali said. "I meant the first in *our* family."

◇

APRIL 2013

"*Suncho!* You were late and look at where we had to sit!" Chaitali chided Shantanu as they climbed into seats near the back of the auditorium at Howell High School. Mitali waved at some former classmates and teachers a couple rows away before sitting next to her parents. She had not been back at her alma mater since the alumni football game the year before. As a college sophomore, one was still thought of as a conquering hero when one returned to school.

"Traffic, Chai. You know how Route 18 can get. Ma, are you comfortable?" Shantanu said. "Here, take the aisle."

Kalpana, wiry frame and all, easily strolled by while holding her turquoise sari, and sat in her seat. All of them were holding folded packets of paper, the cover reading HOWELL HIGH SCHOOL'S FINE AND PERFORMING ARTS CENTER PRESENTS *42ND STREET*. The auditorium was packed, as it usually was for the spring musical. Shantanu could not help but notice the sea of white in the seats, some of them giving Kalpana's sari an extra glance.

"Do you see her name?" Chaitali said, turning the pages of the program. On the fourth page, she found a cast list. Her fingers ran down the list until she came to a section titled "Ensemble." There was the name in 12-point Times New Roman: Keya Das.

"I really have no idea why she decided to do the musical," Mitali said as she scanned the room for more familiar faces. "Can she even sing?"

"It'll be good for her college résumé," Shantanu said. "Chai, do you remember when we saw that Broadway show when we first met?"

"It wasn't a Broadway show. It was *Stomp*."

Chaitali was still looking at the playbill and saw another name she recognized, this one under a heading titled "Production." Pamela Moore was a set designer for the show.

"How nice," Chaitali murmured to no one in particular.

The show was a spectacle, as many Howell High School musicals were, with lots of tap dancing, show tunes, and elaborate 1930s costumes. There was a professional pit band. Shantanu found it unsettling to see Keya alternating between an oversized bright pink blouse and a beige jumpsuit. Her hair was more curled than he had ever seen. But otherwise, she was smiling. In every scene she wore a grin that was as wide as it could be. Shantanu was grateful that it wasn't Keya in a scene early in the show which involved a kiss between Dorothy and Billy. Otherwise, he was enjoying himself.

"Is she this old? Weren't she and Mitali just up to my knees? Wasn't I just teaching her how to read?" Shantanu whispered to Chaitali during a scene change. She was so engrossed in the show that she did not hear him.

Every time the ensemble appeared onstage, Chaitali would have to keep herself from leaping out of the chair. During one of the showstopping numbers—"We're in the Money"—Keya was performing choreography that involved her doing the Charleston. She looked a bit off-balance, but that was only noticeable if audience members were staring only at her, as all the Dases were. But the Dases didn't notice anyway.

Kalpana had to shield the lilacs she brought from Chaitali's restless legs. Chaitali's lip curled during "Sunny Side to Every Situation." Keya had a line to sing all by herself: "With no bonds and no stocks/In your little safe deposit box/You can never be affected by inflation." Even though

Keya's voice wasn't as confident as some of her more seasoned castmates, she sounded heavenly to four particular audience members who sat third row from the back.

Did you know that she could do that? Mitali mouthed to her mother, who, again, was too focused on the show to notice.

During the final bows, which involved the entire cast performing goodbye choreography, the audience relentlessly applauded. The Dases were on their feet. Even Kalpana, who could not be on her feet for long, would not stay seated.

In the lobby outside the auditorium, family members and friends crammed together to await the cast.

"Is there a bathroom?" Kalpana asked. "I should go now. Before I get run over by this herd."

Mitali pointed down the hallway that was partially blocked off.

"Do you want me to take you?"

"No, *beta*, I can go."

Kalpana trudged around the barrier and headed down the hallway. She could hear screams of laughter and cheering around the corner. There were discarded costumes on the ground. She came to the first door and peeked her head in. It wasn't a bathroom, but rather a classroom. Kalpana kept walking, audibly frustrated that the bathroom was so far away. The next door was closed. Kalpana pushed the door open softly. Another classroom. Kalpana sighed. She was about to close the door and go on her way when she heard a noise: lips smacking. Kalpana's eyes traced the noise to the corner of the room, behind set pieces and an upright piano.

It took a few moments for Kalpana to comprehend the sight of Keya locked in a full romantic embrace with a classmate Kalpana was familiar with but whose name she didn't know. Yet there they were: Keya and a girl, passionately kissing. The kissing stopped. Keya grabbed the girl's face and said, "Did you *see* all those people clapping?" The girl looked horrified, as her eyes met Kalpana's in the doorway. Keya's head turned as well.

"*Shomadidi!*" Keya, still wearing her makeup and costume from the show, yelped. "I can explain!"

Kalpana backed out of the room, and the heavy door slammed shut on its own. She walked as fast as she could down the hallway, back to the rest of the family.

Ten minutes later, the lobby was filled with cast members greeting audience members. Mitali received a text from Keya: *Go home! I'll see you guys there!* Chaitali saw the text and would have none of it. *Ma wants you to come say hi right now*, Mitali replied. Kalpana hadn't said a word since returning.

"Ma, are you okay? You look pale. I know it's late. We'll get you home," Shantanu said. Kalpana remained quiet. Finally, Keya appeared, looking sick. Chaitali ran to her and enveloped her in a bear hug.

"That was *so* good!" Chaitali said, almost throwing the bouquet of lilacs at her. Shantanu and Mitali followed close behind with their own hugs.

"Do that dance again, the one from that tap-dancing song," Mitali teased. But Keya did not look like she was in the mood to dance. In fact, she looked fearful, her eyes wide and trained on Kalpana.

"*Sona*, are you okay? You seem tired like your *shomadidi*. But you're eight hundred years younger!" Shantanu said.

"I'm fine," Keya squeaked out.

Chaitali spotted Pamela, who was wearing all black and her hair in a ponytail, down the hallway. If Chaitali was any closer, she might have spotted some of the makeup from Keya's face smeared on Pamela's T-shirt.

"Pamela! Come here!" Chaitali said. Pamela clearly heard her, but she ran the other way down the hallway. The Dases, except for Kalpana and Keya, didn't notice the strange interaction.

"Go to your cast party," Shantanu said. "Don't stay out past one a.m. We will be up waiting for you. Call us when you get there and when you leave."

"Baba, let her live," Mitali said. Keya was still in a state of shock from before. Kalpana seemed to be in a distant place. "Although I would like to note that I wasn't allowed to go to parties when I was in high school."

"Keya?" Chaitali said, stroking her younger daughter's face. "Maybe you should come home. You look flushed."

Keya looked Chaitali in the eyes.

"No, I'm all right. Thank you for coming," she said in a hushed voice.

She abruptly headed back down the hallway and yelled, "Thank you for coming," again over her shoulder.

◇

A week later, Kalpana was sitting on the couch that Keya picked out for her. Keya's head was in her lap as she stroked her hair. The remnants of tears stained her face.

"*Shomadidi, thumi amar upore*— What's the word?"

"*Rheghe*," Kalpana answered.

"Yes, *rheghe*. Are you *rheghe* at me?"

"No, I am not angry at you, *sona*," Kalpana said. "I don't quite understand it. But I am quite old. Everyone your age is like a . . . what's the word? Those things. From up there."

Kalpana pointed to the sky with her free hand.

"An alien?"

"Yes, that. You are all that to me."

"I'm not that different," Keya said. "I just love Pamela."

"You don't know what love is, *bechara*."

"Do you?"

Kalpana was taken aback. *Perhaps my granddaughter isn't as young and foolish in the way I was.*

"Your *dadu* and I were not married out of love. We were married because our parents thought they knew best," Kalpana said.

"Were you ever in love?" Keya pressed.

"*Bechara*, it is not something I ever think about," Kalpana said. "We did not need to be in all this 'love' that girls your age talk about. I miss your grandfather sometimes. He is the only person I have ever been with. Is that love?"

"It's tolerance," Keya said.

"Exactly! *Teek teek!* It is tolerance!" Kalpana said. "I tolerated him for many decades. That is true love!"

The two shared a cackle.

"He came to this country before I did," Kalpana continued wistfully. "He used to write me handwritten letters about how much food there was here. And how big everything was."

"Letters?" Keya perked up.

"Yes, *sona*, letters. That's how we used to communicate in ancient times. One time, he wrote about a slice of pizza the size of his head," Kalpana said. "I enjoyed writing back and forth. And looking at every envelope, hoping that my husband wrote to me from America. I don't know if that was love. But it was not nothing. Eventually, we raised a son together. He became a doctor of a sort. He has a wife who shows respect to me. And two daughters. What more could we have asked for?" Kalpana said.

"Do you think *Dadu* would have approved of me? If I taught him about it?" Keya asked.

Kalpana looked away and transported herself into her memories.

"He came from a different time," Kalpana said. "I don't know."

But she did know: Amitava had been rigid.

"So did you," Keya said.

"Your *dadu* was a fossil," Kalpana said. "He was strong-willed. I have tried to be an ocean that changes with the tides. His family used to mock me behind my back because of my skin color. An *untouchable*, they used to say. I know what it's like to be judged by something you do not control."

"You are full of tolerance," Keya said, as she turned her body on the sofa and gripped her grandmother. "Thank you for not telling Ma and Baba."

◇

"Ma knew? Before we did?" Shantanu said. His ears were ringing.

Chaitali reached an arm out and held Shantanu's elbow.

"How do *you* know about this?" Shantanu demanded.

"Ma told me after Keya was gone," Chaitali said. "She didn't tell you because she didn't want to hurt you. She didn't think you could handle it. Mothers don't go out of their way to hurt their children."

Chaitali paused and then shook her head in sadness.

"In most cases," she added.

"Why does everyone treat me like I'm an ancient ruin that will fall apart at the slightest touch?" Shantanu said.

"Because you *were* exactly that. We all were. We are no longer together because we didn't realize it. You understand, right? Surely, by now, you must."

Shantanu didn't answer at first.

"But Ma told you," he finally offered.

"She did," Chaitali said. "But not willingly. I always sensed she knew more than she was letting on. I pressed her."

"She should have told me."

"Maybe," Chaitali considered. "But it wouldn't have brought Keya back."

FOUR

Mitali pressed the buzzer of a drab building, an overgrown concrete slab which seemed to have sprouted from the sidewalk where it didn't belong. She was wearing a sleeveless dark green dress, black heels, and a white cardigan, which was not enough to keep her from shuddering against the cool fall wind rustling her hair. She had put a lot of work into this outfit, spending hours to get ready, although much of that effort was aimed at creating an air of effortlessness.

"It's me!" Mitali shouted into the speaker.

When she heard the front door unlock, Mitali threw the heavy double door open in relief and stepped inside, where she was immediately met by a stairwell. With no elevator in sight, Mitali prepared herself for an expedition up the stairs. Neesh had repeatedly warned her that he lived on the sixth floor, and that it would be fine, even encouraged, to skip his invitation to Brooklyn. By the third floor, her legs were unhappy with her. By the fifth, Mitali was out of breath. On the sixth floor, she saw Neesh waiting in the doorway. He was wearing a slightly wrinkled orange V-neck sweater on top of faded, poorly fitting jeans.

"Crown Heights is a lot farther from the Upper East Side than I thought," Mitali wheezed. She thrust a bottle of red wine into his chest. "But still less than the distance of your apartment from the ground."

And Neesh was holding a bouquet of roses.

"These are for you." Neesh took the wine and put the bouquet in Mitali's hands.

"You got me roses," Mitali said, a confused look on her face.

"Yes, from the bodega down the street," Neesh said.

"Thank you, but we're at your apartment. Where should I put them?" Mitali said, as Neesh ushered her inside.

"Ah, I didn't think of that," Neesh realized.

"No worries! This is nice and can brighten, I guess, here. Do you have a vase?" Mitali said.

"I didn't think of that either," Neesh said. "I figured you would have one. Ah, but we are at my apartment. Never mind. How about a cup?"

"Sure. Why are they so cold?"

"The flowers?"

"Yeah."

"I put the flowers in the fridge to keep them fresh."

"Flowers in the fridge." Mitali shook her head with a laugh.

Neesh walked to the kitchen and reached for a tall plastic cup to fill with water, which gave Mitali a chance to take in Neesh's apartment. It was somehow both small and sparsely filled. The space wasn't comfortable or warm. There was an electric drum kit in the corner. A fish tank in another one. Two lava lamps of different colors. A large television in the living room and one shoddy couch, which had cushions with visible rips. On the wall hung one solitary frame of a Playbill from the Broadway musical *Rock of Ages*. Mitali could see a broom—its bristles caked with dust and dirt—sticking out of a closet near the pasty blue front door.

Mitali took a seat on the couch.

"It's too bad you have to work tomorrow night." Mitali raised her voice so Neesh could hear.

"I couldn't find someone to cover my shift," Neesh said, stepping out of the kitchen, holding a cup with the roses to place on the coffee table in front of the couch. He stacked some books—a Bruce Springsteen autobiography being one of them—next to the cup to keep the flowers from toppling over.

Neesh and Mitali had been seeing each other weekly for about a month, but this was her first time at his apartment. He had stayed at Mitali's once but had barely made an effort to invite her over, which she found surprising. When Mitali mentioned this later, Neesh used his roommate, whom Neesh revealed as an aspiring forty-two-year-old actor named Hector, as the reason, suggesting that Hector spent all his time in the living room and would not give them any privacy.

"Where is your roommate?" Mitali asked.

"He's either at his boyfriend's or he's at work," Neesh replied. "He works nights as a security guard."

"I thought you said he was always home."

"Oh, when he's not working."

It was now that Mitali wondered if Neesh had resisted inviting her over because of his apartment, which managed to have just enough space to seem barren. Mitali felt self-conscious about the way she had been presenting herself to Neesh. *Do I come off as someone who needs to be with someone rich?*

Tonight was notable for another reason: it was Thanksgiving. After graduating college, Mitali had typically spent Thanksgivings holed up alone in her studio, despite Kalpana's pitches to come home. Her grandmother's promises of keeping up the tradition of Thanksgiving *luchi* at her condominium weren't enough after her parents got divorced. Shantanu would joke every Thanksgiving that since it was purportedly celebrating pilgrims and Indians, the day was actually supposed to be a tribute to Bengalis. It didn't make sense, as Mitali and Keya would loudly point out to Chaitali's delight, but it allowed Shantanu to go into his yearly lecture about the faults of colonization. Holidays without Keya were quiet and desolate, except for when Shantanu and Chaitali would snipe at each other.

Mitali was surprised to find out after their third date that Neesh wasn't going home for Thanksgiving either: a night at an improv show at Upright Citizens Brigade, during which Mitali had to physically place her hand on his knee to keep it from bouncing in restlessness. This briefly brought up a painful memory: seeing Keya in *42nd Street*, and her mother's knee bobbing up and down in her seat, but Mitali quickly buried it.

The show was Neesh's idea, but Mitali found herself fascinated by the stage. Who knew a human acting as a deer in a doomed romance could be so funny? *Is this what Keya felt?*

They held hands for the rest of the show. Neesh's knee stayed still. As Neesh walked Mitali to the subway afterwards, he had told her that he didn't typically fly back to Naperville during the holidays. His parents owned an antique store in Chicago they were busy with, he said, and didn't really celebrate the holidays. Mitali's intuition told her that there was more to that story, but it was only their third date. And where did her irrational suspicion end and genuine instinct begin?

"If you are going to be in the city for Thanksgiving," Neesh had said to Mitali before she took the stairs to the subway platform that night, "come trek to Brooklyn. We can have Thanksgiving pad Thai. Or not. I don't know."

It wasn't a ringing invite, but Mitali said she would think about it, before awkwardly inviting Neesh to her apartment.

"Do you, uh, not want to go home?"

"Oh, do you want to get another drink?"

"Uh, yes, we can. But I was also thinking we can go somewhere else."

"Food? Another show? It's kind of late."

"No. Never mind."

Dating in college was so much simpler for Mitali. The stakes were lower. There were parties and accompanying flings. A cursory exchange of glances. A courtesy exchange of names and biographical information. Some dancing. Back to the dorm room. See you never again, unless absolutely necessary. Rinse, wash, and repeat. In high school, Mitali had a crush on the student council president, Zach Levinson, but he was dating her friend, a cheerleader named Rachel Osborne, which Mitali only found out when she worked up the courage to ask him to go to junior prom. It was a humiliating experience. She ended up taking a well-meaning classmate who sang in the school's a cappella group, Justin Dalessio. She declined his kiss at the end of the night.

"What I meant to say is that you could come back to my apartment, if you feel like it."

"Oh." Neesh looked like he was caught off guard. "Do you want me to?"

"Do you want to?"

"If you want me to."

"If you want to!"

"I can't tell if you want me to."

"Well, it's up to you."

"It's up to you, too."

The conversation wasn't efficient, but Neesh did end up back at Mitali's place and stayed the night. As he was fast asleep next to her, Mitali decided that Thanksgiving would be a no-go. She would spend it in her apartment, like every year. Mitali had serious misgivings about celebrating a holiday with someone she had only recently met. For her, Thanksgiving, or any other holiday where families gathered, was a day reserved for solitude. And besides, Neesh's invitation seemed half-hearted to begin with.

But then a phone buzzed on the nightstand next to the bed. Mitali reached for it and realized it was Neesh's phone. She looked over at him. Even in the dark, she could see he was on his side and his back was turned to her. Whether it was curiosity, mistrust, impulse, or all three, Mitali picked up the phone and read the text Neesh was sent. It was from an unknown number.

Don't contact you again? You think this is that easy?

Mitali placed the phone quietly back on the nightstand and stared at the ceiling. An ex-girlfriend? A telemarketer who couldn't take a hint? Someone else he was seeing? A wrong number? Mitali realized she actually knew very little about Neesh. Where he came from. Why he didn't have many friends. Why he hadn't pushed her to come over.

She changed her mind. She would go to Brooklyn for Thanksgiving and investigate for herself. *Investigate*, Mitali thought. *What is wrong with me?* In the morning, she told Neesh she would come, and that she was looking forward to it. She meant it, too. But she also wanted to investigate.

At Neesh's apartment, Mitali and Neesh scarfed down Thai food on the shoddy couch, as *A Charlie Brown Thanksgiving* played on the television. They had to crane their necks slightly to see around the flowers in the plastic cup.

"Do you wish you were with your family?" Mitali asked, taking a bite out of a piece of crab rangoon.

"Nah."

She could certainly understand not wanting to get into the mess of family—look at her own, she reminded herself—but wasn't that what people in pursuit of one another did? Shared things about themselves, even the messy, ugly bits?

"Nah? That's all?" Mitali said.

"There's not much to say," Neesh replied, his eyes trained on the TV. "I spent my weekends going to flea markets, yard sales, and auctions with my dad. Looking for great deals on old things. Sometimes, we'd overpay."

He began gnawing on his plastic fork.

"Were you close?"

"What is close?"

"Did you talk about stuff growing up?"

"We talked about antiques."

"You don't have any antiques in here."

"You haven't seen my broom."

"Did they like your friends?"

"I've always had associates. Not friends."

That's a strange thing to say, Mitali thought, but before she could examine whether this was a red flag, Neesh sighed and gave in, perhaps sensing her annoyance bubbling.

"My father got his real estate license after coming here from India," Neesh said, as if reciting a line he had heard many times. "Fourteen dollars in his pocket, the whole thing. He used to work as a banker after graduating school in India. But getting a regular nine-to-five was difficult for new immigrants."

A landlord Neesh's father knew had a few small properties which Neesh's father purchased. All throughout Neesh's childhood, his father kept collecting. There was no trinket too small or lamp too big for the storage space that he rented. Eventually, between the rental income on the properties and savings he had accumulated as a real estate agent, Neesh's father opened his own shop.

"Jigar Desai. A self-made man who loves *things*," Neesh said mournfully, letting his resentment slip. "Old things, specifically. He loves things more than his wife. Or any human, really. All those trips out of the country. *Things*."

Neesh finished his glass of wine with an aggressive gulp.

"He used to walk into the house and say, 'I grew up having nothing. And soon, I'll fill my warehouse with the world. What will you do?'"

"You've done plenty, Neesh. I'm sure your father knows that."

Mitali felt this was the right thing to say, but it occurred to her that she didn't know if it was true. What had Neesh accomplished? He didn't seem keen on telling her. Mitali moved closer on the couch, not an easy feat given the thinness of the cushions.

"Sometimes too much," Neesh said.

Mitali spooned the remaining pad Thai onto her plastic plate.

"I haven't seen my parents in eight years. They don't want to see me," Neesh said. "And I don't want to see them. Thanksgiving or otherwise. My last name is the antique."

After dinner, they headed outside for a walk. The sidewalks were empty, as many New Yorkers were out of town. Mitali wore Neesh's University of Iowa sweatshirt, since it had only become chillier. Neesh had on his leather jacket, the one he wore on their first date. *He looks handsome*, Mitali thought. *If you're only going to wear one coat, might as well look good in it.*

Both of them had their hands shoved inside their pockets.

"I'm sorry," Neesh said.

"What?"

"I'm sorry."

"For what?"

"All this talk about me. I didn't ask about you. One of my note cards says 'Ask about her.' But I left them at home."

"You don't need note cards, Neesh."

"You really don't know me. So why aren't you with your family on Thanksgiving?"

"I stopped going after my sister died. What was the point? And then my parents got divorced. And instead of choosing between the two for the day, I chose neither. So much easier."

As they kept walking, Mitali counted the squares of concrete on the sidewalk in her head, to help fill the silence.

"Five years," Mitali said. "I feel like I just called her yesterday. But it actually has been five years."

Neesh's silence felt like a quilt around Mitali's shoulders. His listening, rather than offering advice or sympathy, put her at ease.

"You know, I went home the other day and my dad showed me this box he found in the attic," Mitali said. "It had a bunch of love notes to my sister and this play she wrote."

"A play," he said, perking up. "What about?"

"I didn't read much of it. I left it with my dad. Something to do with coming out."

"She was gay?"

Mitali nodded. Neesh didn't press, but he began to play with his zipper when they arrived at a stoplight.

"We never talked about it," Mitali said. "I wonder if I would have told her about you if she was still around."

"Why wouldn't you have?"

Mitali stopped. She had never had a serious partner before, and so had never considered the question. And though it had only been a handful of weeks, Neesh was the closest thing. There was something about him—his willingness to listen, the leather jacket, his opening up about his father earlier—that made it easier for Mitali to talk about her late sister.

"She was always so intimidating. Always successful. Great grades. Pretty. The *mashis* and *kakus* always seemed to gravitate more towards her. I was always jealous, deep down," Mitali said. "Trying to keep up with her—to be as good as her—made me feel vulnerable. I didn't want to be vulnerable around her. Or about her. Vulnerability isn't something our family did."

A brief breeze kicked up, sending leaves flying down the sidewalk.

"Do you want to know the truth? When she came out to us, I didn't take it well."

Neesh continued to walk.

"Don't you want to know why?" Mitali said.

"If you want to tell me."

"We were a happy family. Picture perfect in many ways. And I thought she pierced it. I was afraid at that moment. I blamed that beautiful soul for disrupting us, when in reality it was me. And my parents."

"We all fuck up," Neesh said.

"Have you ever fucked up like *that*?"

Mitali saw a fleeting moment of fear in Neesh's eyes. She thought of the text message she'd seen the other night.

"Have you?" she pressed again.

"We *all* fuck up."

Mitali didn't like how closed off Neesh seemed, nor did she like feeling suspicious. *What is he not telling me?* She couldn't shake the sense of foreboding that emanated from him; that he was hiding something. But there was a certain warmth, too. This made her more attracted to him in a way, as if he were her equation to solve. In time, Mitali thought, she would. But it was early still, and maybe he was just doing what many men were unwilling to do: listen. *Stop overthinking it.*

"Tell me more about the play," Neesh said, as if on cue.

"The one in the box? Honestly, I don't remember. It's with my dad. Something about an elm tree. Why?"

As they crossed the street, Neesh looked absorbed in thought.

"What?" Mitali repeated.

"I'd love to read it," Neesh said.

She should read it too, she realized. She was so focused on the folded notes that she didn't think to see what was in the play. But in hindsight, reading the play was probably less of a violation of privacy.

"I guess I can get it from my dad. We were never much of a theater family."

"I actually love reading plays," Neesh said, surprising Mitali. "I was a drummer in the pit band for *Rock of Ages* when it was on Broadway. I know theater. Before that, I was a stagehand for an Off-Broadway show." *This drummer in the leather jacket uniform was a theater dork?*

"Wait, so you *were* a professional drummer?" Mitali's mouth was agape. "For how long?" She caught another brief flash, this one a look of regret on Neesh's face.

"Four months."

"So you didn't just pursue this as a career, as if it was something to be chased. You caught it."

"It didn't work out."

"How come?"

"It just didn't."

"You're not going to tell me why?"

Neesh stopped walking.

"It's not worth going into. I was a drummer. I'm not one any longer. I work at a front desk."

She sighed.

"Okay," she said, easing off. Month one, after all.

As Mitali walked a few more paces, she heard the pounding of footsteps. Abruptly, and without warning, Neesh ran up the front steps of the nearest apartment building and yelled loudly, "Stop acting so small. *You* are the universe in ecstatic motion!" His arms were wide, and his face was turned towards the sky.

Is he possessed? Was there something in the pad Thai? She turned to the rest of the street in embarrassment, but to her relief, they were alone.

"Neesh, what are you doing?!" Mitali whispered loudly.

"One of my favorite quotes from Rumi," Neesh answered, still holding the pose. "Or maybe it's someone else. Who cares?"

He finally put his arms back by his sides and walked towards a bemused Mitali.

"What *was* that?" Mitali asked.

"How am I supposed to know?"

Mitali didn't know either. One minute, he was closed off and putting flowers in the fridge. The next, he was a professional drummer screaming Rumi quotes outside in the cold. The surprises made her smile, which was another surprise. And then she asked herself a question that she found petrifying: *Is this what falling feels like?*

◇

MARCH 2003

"This store has our name on it," Jigar said to Neesh. "Do you know what that means?"

Neesh groaned behind the glass counter of Desai Antiques, which was nestled in the Lakeview area of Chicago. He immediately regretted it when a slap from Jigar sent him careening backwards. Even as he was knocked off-balance, Neesh took care to avoid the ceramic bowls that lined a shelf behind the counter.

"Careful you don't break anything," Jigar growled, as Neesh rubbed his face. "You disrespect me with your attitude. You disrespect the Desai name on the front of this store. You disrespect yourself with drugs."

"Is there anything else? Or can I go now?" Neesh said, his face stinging. He was used to his father's explosions at this point. Sometimes his mother Bhavika had taken the brunt of it. But as he got older, Neesh had become more audacious, stepping between his mother and father when the situation called for it. Next year, he would be in Iowa, ready to watch films for homework and pursue his dream of becoming a sound engineer. He would be in college, far away from his domineering father. But still, he was tempted to grab Jigar by the ugly sweater vest he was wearing and thrash him. A recent growth spurt meant Neesh was almost taller than Jigar for the first time in his life. Jigar was clean-shaven, with a visible potbelly. He had no hair on his head and didn't exercise at all. Most of his time was spent here, at the store.

"You hate me," Jigar said. "But one day you'll be like me. A man. I built this place. And you will respect me for it. Rather than wasting your time with the stupid drumming."

Kill me now, Neesh thought to himself. *I never want to be like you.* Jigar was not finished.

"What will you do with your drumming?" Jigar hissed. He absentmindedly busied himself by grabbing a cloth and polishing some of the watches in the case in front of him.

"Where will it lead? Respectable income? Reliable income? Any transferable skills? I should ask the school district for a refund on my property taxes. They didn't teach you anything."

At the flip of a switch, Jigar's anger turned into a pleasantry, as a middle-aged man wearing a Cubs cap, sunglasses, and a black sweatshirt walked into the store, the first customer of the day. He was stocky and had an unkempt goatee. Neesh couldn't help but notice how the customer held his arms jutted out like a wannabe bodybuilder. He looked familiar, Neesh thought, but he couldn't place him. Jigar shoved a broom into Neesh's hands.

"Sweep around the counter and then you can go," Jigar whispered.

"How can I help you, young sir?" Jigar turned on the charm.

"I'm just browsing, thank you," the man said with a heavy voice. He turned to a glass case in the back corner where several porcelain figurines lined the case. "Can you unlock the case so I can get a look at these?"

"Of course. Neesh, help the man."

Neesh placed his broomstick against the cash register and grabbed a key chain bigger than his hand that was hanging off a nail. He trudged to where the man was standing. As he got closer, Neesh noticed the man's head swiveling, observing the rest of the store. His sunglasses were still on.

"I see you looking around." The jolliness with customers never stopped with Jigar. "I don't blame you. We have so many things here I hope you'll consider buying."

Neesh unlocked a glass panel and slid the door to the right. As he reached for some of the figures, he heard a click and felt steel against his head.

"Don't fucking move, towelhead," the man growled intensely. "Back up slowly and put your hands where I can see them."

Neesh did as he was told, though all he could hear was the hammering of his heart. Jigar looked stricken. Another man walked in, somehow even huskier than the first, but dressed the same: baseball cap and a sweatshirt. Both men nodded at each other, and the second man locked the door so their heist would be uninterrupted.

"Get a bag," the first man directed Jigar. "Fill it up with cash from the register and as many things from here as you can."

Jigar was frozen.

"Do you think I'm fucking joking? Do it!" the man yelled. His accomplice stood by the door, arm on the handle, ready to flee at a moment's notice.

"This is my life's work," Jigar said, folding his arms. "I won't do anything for you."

"I will blow this motherfucker's head off!" the man yelled. Neesh felt the man's nails digging into his neck, causing him to grimace. Jigar made eye contact with Neesh. "Or I'll drag him away and you won't see him ever again, terrorist."

"*Bapuji*, please," Neesh pleaded. "Do what they say."

Jigar weighed his options. He looked away from Neesh and at the collectibles in the store.

"You may do what you wish with him," Jigar said serenely, as Neesh looked on with horror. Jigar's eyes were glassy and his face expressionless. "You will not take anything in here."

"Are you fucking crazy?" the man with the gun said. He tried to say something else but was interrupted by Neesh somehow socking him in the face with the oversized key chain. The assailant was momentarily stunned, and the gun dropped. Neesh came at him again with a ceramic bowl that was within arm's reach and broke it over the would-be burglar's head. The man let out a yell, while his partner now looked petrified. He quickly unlocked the front door and sprinted through it, apparently more fearful than his posture let on. The man who was still in the store was able to crawl to his gun—a small revolver—but Neesh leapt on him, hitting him over the head with another figurine within arm's reach, causing the burglar's baseball cap to fall off. The burglar covered his head with his arms, flipped on his back, and kicked Neesh away. Neesh fell backwards into a table. More dishes shattered on the ground. Jigar, rooted to his spot, put one hand on his head.

The man grabbed his baseball cap and gun, which were both still nearby. He scrambled to his feet and stumbled towards the entrance. With his back turned to Neesh, the man pointed the gun backwards and fired. The bullet sailed into the back wall of the store, well above Neesh and Jigar, and, somehow, not into any of the silver teapots meticulously arranged on the shelves attached to it. The man didn't turn around to see if he had hit anything; he just kept running.

Neesh, his eyes wild, climbed to his feet, panting. Jigar, on the other hand, still had not moved. As Neesh used his T-shirt to wipe sweat from his face, Jigar went behind the register and picked up the broom. Neesh hoped for some sort of concern from his father. But he knew hope in Jigar was a fruitless exercise.

"Clean up the mess you made," Jigar snarled, before heading to the back room.

FIVE

Shantanu remembered the mustache. It was the first thing that stood out when he opened the door that December evening in 2013, to find Officer Jim Giggenbach standing at the door of 2 Hillcrest Drive, looking solemn. So perfectly shaped, without a speck of gray in it and not a strand out of place. It didn't complement his buzz cut. Shantanu did not recognize him right away, but realized he had seen this mustache before.

"I'm sorry to bother you, Mr. Das," Giggenbach said, standing unusually straight, with both hands on his waist. "We've met before at the high school. Is Mrs. Das home?"

Thanksgiving had come and gone. Keya had not come with the family to Kalpana's, like every other year. She simply texted Mitali, *I have work*, and left that morning. Those days, Keya already existed as a ghost, coming and going, with her family catching glimpses through windows or around corners. Shantanu found it odd that Kalpana did not object more to Keya's absence, but chalked it up to Kalpana's preference to avoid arguments. Now, it was two weeks before Christmas, and the Dases wondered if they had waited too long to have a discussion with Keya. Mitali wanted to sit Keya down immediately. Chaitali and Shantanu didn't want to impose anything on Keya. And Shantanu, meanwhile, was doing more research, trying to get comfortable with the thought of a gay daughter.

"She's upstairs," Shantanu said. "Is there something I can do for you?"

"Do you mind if I come in?" Giggenbach asked cautiously.

Keya must have been caught doing something—sleeping in her car, or maybe she was smoking pot after all. It was then that Mitali emerged on the stairs, carrying a bag of laundry.

"Jim! O.J.! What are you doing here?" Mitali said.

"Hey, kid," Giggenbach said, a deep baritone ringing through the doorway, his head now in a slight bow. "Back from school, huh?"

"I haven't been speeding, I swear," Mitali laughed. He weakly smiled back.

Shantanu let him in. By now, Shantanu could sense something was wrong. Mitali went to go get Chaitali, and they gathered on the couch, the same fluffy green one from which they had all last spoken to Keya.

"There's been an accident," Giggenbach said.

Shantanu could barely hear a single word for the rest of the conversation. There were snippets he caught: A slippery curve. An icy road. Veering into a guardrail. An accident, they were sure. Nothing the EMTs could do.

"We're guessing she saw a deer and swerved too quickly," Giggenbach said. "I'm so sorry."

There was no forgetting the anguished cries that escaped his wife and daughter. He watched them collapse into each other's arms, he himself unable to move. *Unnatural. Unnatural. Unnatural.* Those words, ringing like a prophecy, a warning, melting into an icy hatred—for his father, and for himself.

While the day of Keya's death remained vivid for Shantanu, the aftermath was not. It made the *Asbury Park Press*, a local paper. One of Keya's friends was quoted in the article, describing her as a "free spirit." The police called the crash an accident in a press release—the sudden turn possibly a result of deer scampering across the road, as the officer had said. This didn't quell rumors, nor Shantanu's own doubts.

The memorial service, at Thompson's Funeral Home in neighboring Freehold the next week, was a blur. Shantanu could still hear, if not see, the conch shells being played by some of the family friends from the Bengali community. It was Keya's *mashis* who played the conch shells, while their husbands—Keya's *kakus*—stood uncomfortably nearby, unsure of whether to approach Shantanu or not. Jahar was there too, one of the few then-unmarried *kakus*. They had all heard these conch shells at the Durga Puja months prior, more jubilant then. Now, their haunting wails filled a funeral home. Shantanu wore a white dhoti, Mitali and Chaitali wore white saris. Many of Keya's classmates and teachers from Howell High School came dressed in black, not knowing any better. Most of them looked unfamiliar to Shantanu, except for those he had seen onstage for *42nd Street*. As Shantanu shook hands with the attendees, he thought to himself, *How little I knew about her.*

Something else didn't escape Shantanu's notice: Pamela never showed up.

Those who knew Keya from school set up a roadside memorial near the curve where Keya's car hit the guardrail. The principal, Mrs. Jones, stopped by, with the air of a visiting monarch. It was Shantanu's job to coordinate the *niramish* food for the attendees, since elaborate meat-based curries were out of the question. Kalpana insisted on cooking, and that Shantanu take her to the roadside memorial to drop off some lilacs. Chaitali and Mitali refused to go.

The Dases were present that day, but only physically. Kalpana wept in a corner. Keya's most recent yearbook picture—encased in an elegant frame—sat next to the closed casket, which was adorned with flowers before being sent to the crematorium.

After the funeral, nothing was the same. Shantanu took the rest of the year off from Rutgers, while Chaitali, not wanting to be at home with Shantanu, asked for more responsibilities at the library. Mitali, even as her parents urged her to take time off from school, stopped making surprise visits home. Kalpana was the glue who tried to hold the family together. She insisted on weekly dinners, followed by a Bengali movie. Chaitali would not sit on the sofa that Keya picked out. Kalpana would call every night. It didn't work. In the five stages of grief, Shantanu stayed in anger for the longest, before moving on to bargaining, and then depression. Acceptance had yet to come.

It did not help that Shantanu developed a taste for whiskey shortly after. They all inwardly blamed each other for Keya's death. Shantanu and Chaitali blamed Mitali for not being aware of what Keya wanted to tell them. Chaitali and Mitali blamed Shantanu for being too much like

Amitava. Shantanu and Mitali blamed Chaitali for saying it wouldn't be "appropriate" to bring Pamela to the puja. But more than anything, they each blamed themselves.

In their own ways, they had made Keya feel unseen.

◇

"What was Keya like?" Dr. Lynch asked. Shantanu found himself focused on the therapist's *Star Wars* sweatshirt, a significant change from the previous appointment's seersucker suit.

"She was funny. Smart. Fearless. Got good grades. She was in the high school musical. I remember that when we took her to the beach, we had to constantly tell her not to swim out too far. I used to joke to my friends that she'd point out at the horizon and say, 'I want to go *there*.' My other daughter was more into sports, but Keya was more of a creative type."

"Did you ever talk about dating?"

"No. We didn't talk about that kind of stuff."

"What did you do together? Just the two of you?"

Shantanu locked and unlocked his fingers, not unlike what Keya did when she told the family her secret.

"Not enough. It was a lot of picking her up and dropping her off. Friends. Work. School. Occasionally we'd all go to the movies. Or relatives' houses. I always thought that we'd bond more as she got older. We ran out of time."

"Do you think she loved you?"

Shantanu thought of Keya hanging around his knees on the dreary front lawn, begging him to pick her up.

"Yes."

"Then why didn't you say you loved her the night she told you she was gay?"

The amusement disappeared. Shantanu tensed.

"I should have."

"Rejection is often a much more powerful emotion than acceptance," Dr. Lynch said. "What does a dog do when it catches its tail? It doesn't know what to do. That's acceptance. That's something we all strive for. And only a small handful of us have it."

For a few moments, the only sound in the room was the heater in Dr. Lynch's office and the voices of students mingling on the street below. Giggenbach's face appeared in Shantanu's mind. And then Amitava's.

There was that night, when Shantanu was a teenager, and Amitava found out an unmarried co-worker at Bell Labs, where Amitava was an engineer, had come out of the closet. At dinner, he called it *jhoghonno*.

"Why is it terrible?" a young Shantanu had asked.

"Because it is unnatural," his father answered, with that booming voice of his. He had a slight hunch as he walked, but he still remained an imposing presence. "You are never to live that kind of a decadent lifestyle. Brahma meant for men to be with women when he created the universe."

There were comments like that all the time. When Shantanu asked Amitava if he could go to the 1980 Elton John concert in Central Park, Amitava said no, because he didn't want Shantanu emulating John's behavior, since he had come out as bisexual. When Don't Ask, Don't Tell passed in 1993, Amitava wondered out loud, "What is happening to this country?" Chaitali rolled her eyes. Amitava even avoided hugging men, opting for firm handshakes or shoulder slaps. If there was ever a news story involving gay rights, Amitava would shake his head, cluck his tongue, and change the channel, sometimes in front of Mitali and Keya, who were too young to understand and push back. Kalpana never corrected her husband. Shantanu knew she believed it wasn't her place.

"My father was very controlling," Shantanu told Dr. Lynch. "He was insistent I go to Rutgers, so I could be close to home. He didn't want me to become an anthropologist. I actually initially went here to become an engineer, to make him happy, and switched my major without telling him. He didn't take that well."

"Lots of secrets. Did he love you?" Dr. Lynch said.

"In his own way," Shantanu said. "He was proud of having a son with a doctorate. He only got his master's. My father would always say, 'You have more work to do.' That's how he lived. There was always more work to do."

"But why did his approval of Keya matter that night?"

"I couldn't get my father's face out of my mind," Shantanu said. "He was there. Hovering. Like a hot-air balloon. He died thirteen years ago, and somehow I still worry about disappointing him."

"Go on."

"I thought about grandchildren, and maybe not being able to have any. I froze. I thought it was maybe a phase."

Unnatural. Unnatural. Unnatural.

Shantanu forced the voice out of his head.

"These are all excuses. Not good ones," Shantanu said. "Poor Keya. I had more work to do. I always thought I was open-minded. And then when something different came to my doorstep—"

"You closed the door," Dr. Lynch said.

Shantanu buried his face in his hands and then ran those hands through his hair, what was left of it.

"The morning of Keya's death, were you okay with her sexual orientation at that point?" Dr. Lynch asked.

Another sigh from Shantanu.

"Be honest," Dr. Lynch added. "The answer you want to give and the truth are two different things."

"I'm not sure," Shantanu said. "I wanted my daughter back. I was still hoping counseling might be able to fix it, I think. I thought I could take my time to figure things out. And maybe convince her otherwise."

"Was she the one who needed fixing?"

The question cut Shantanu. Dr. Lynch tapped a pen on his head as he considered where to take the conversation next.

"Why do you think Keya died?" Dr. Lynch asked.

"What do you mean?" Shantanu said. "I told you. The police said it was a car accident. She probably was on her way to Pamela's or something. Or this park near our house, Echo Lake."

" 'The *police* said,' " Dr. Lynch said, putting an emphasis on *police*. "Do you not believe that it was an accident?"

Again, Shantanu tensed.

"I don't know."

"I guess what I'm asking is—"

"I know what you're asking," Shantanu said tersely.

"I'm asking, Shantanu, if you don't believe the police. Do you think she drove the car into a guardrail on purpose?"

"It wouldn't be the first time a police investigation turned up incorrect results."

"You're being an anthropologist," Dr. Lynch said. "Looking for hard evidence and data. But this isn't an academic exercise. Dig for me."

Shantanu squinted his eyes and tried to sneak a glance at Dr. Lynch's diplomas without him noticing. He couldn't make out the lettering, and Shantanu wasn't that good at being sneaky.

"Duke University for my doctorate," Dr. Lynch said. "But I agree with you. That doesn't mean I know what I'm doing."

Shantanu looked apologetic but chose to move on.

"She was angry at the end."

"How do you know she was angry?"

"It was obvious."

"What made it obvious?"

"She didn't talk to us."

"She could have been hurt by your reaction. That's a different emotion. Or she could have been giving you space. You seem convinced that she was angry."

At the moment, it was Shantanu who was angry, although he was unclear why. For a second, he imagined himself throwing the chair he was sitting on through the window.

"What difference does it make?"

"It makes all the difference," Dr. Lynch said. "You're punishing yourself for a suicide that likely wasn't one. You are giving yourself only the permission to suffer instead of to grieve."

"You're saying I didn't do anything wrong?"

"I'm saying that's the wrong question. You're an academic. Focus on the facts that we know: that car could have crashed any night. It could have crashed before she came out. After. You have no proof that your last conversation with her was the cause of her death, and focusing on that will only hurt you more."

"Maybe I want to hurt."

"Ah."

Dr. Lynch put his notepad down on the floor next to his chair and moved his chair a bit closer to his patient.

"Visibility is an interesting term," Dr. Lynch said. "I used to do a fair amount of couples therapy. And half the challenge is navigating the power dynamic between couples. The other half is visibility, making two people see each other."

"What's your point?"

"So much of this is your fear of having made Keya feel invisible," Dr. Lynch said. "You are being invisible to yourself right now. And, likely, to your daughter. And when you started drinking, you made your wife feel invisible."

"Ex-wife."

"Yes."

Shantanu reached for his bottled water and took a gulp. He thought back to all his visits to the road where Keya crashed. Even though the site had been cleared and the guardrail replaced, Shantanu kept going back to where Keya last saw life. The only evidence that remained was the roadside memorial. He had done hundreds of land surveys, often for the government. Could there really have been a deer? Could the car simply have swerved like that? But he was no crime scene investigator.

"I went to the crash site, you know," Shantanu said. "Three, maybe four times, in that first year."

"Why?"

"I was trying to figure out why it happened."

"What did you find?"

"Nothing."

"You were trying to figure out if it really was an accident."

Shantanu didn't reply.

"I'm here to tell you, my anthropological friend, that answer was never going to be at the crash site. No matter how badly you want it to have been."

◇

I really should become a vegan, Shantanu thought to himself that evening as he rolled a cart through Stop & Shop, the closest grocery store to his house. *It would be much healthier.* He still walked with a noticeable limp as he navigated around shoppers, but at the moment, it was his left knee that ached. These trips to the grocery store—always on Fridays—never lasted long. It was busier than usual, likely due to Christmas next week. He got himself new boxes of Froot Loops, packets of ramen, onions to slice for the ramen, skim milk, some boneless chicken thighs, bananas, and white bread. His favorite part of the grocery trips was going to the frozen food aisle. One of the benefits of divorce, he found, was being able to pick various processed pre-made dinners without Chaitali getting on him about eating healthier. And yet, Chaitali's voice was louder than his internal one about his diet.

As he stood in front of the freezer, hand on his chin, he heard a woman's sunny voice behind him.

"Shan-TAN-oo?"

A middle-aged blond woman appeared, wearing a silver necklace with a cross dangling at the end, looking like she was either on her way to a board meeting, or church—or a church board meeting.

"Shan-TAN-oo! It's been too long!"

He couldn't place her, not at first.

"Oh, I'm Janine. You know, Pamela's mother."

Now it dawned on Shantanu.

"That's right."

Janine rolled her cart to the side and embraced an awkward Shantanu, while giving him a kiss on the cheek.

"How have you been, Shan-TAN-oo? I just came from the mayor's office." Something about her voice got on Shantanu's nerves. Its timbre was bright and thin. She sounded like she was constantly hosting a television show. And he didn't ask where she had just come from.

"I'm fine, thank you," Shantanu said stiffly. "Uh, how's . . . Roger, right?"

"That's it, Roger," Janine said. "He's doing great. Business at the furniture store got iffy for a while, but it's on an upswing right now." As she said "upswing," she swung her hands upwards. "I'm just going to address the elephant in the frozen food aisle. I've been meaning to reach out for years. I was so sorry to hear about your daughter. She and my Pammy were so close."

"Thank you," Shantanu said quietly.

"I prayed for you when I heard the news," Janine said, her voice turning restrained. "I enjoyed your daughter. She was an absolute sweetheart. You probably don't remember, but she came into our store with you guys and picked out a sofa for her grandmother. She was a tyke back then. She didn't know Pamela yet."

Of course, Shantanu remembered. That *was* the Moores' store. But still, Shantanu found this exchange disorienting. *Shouldn't Janine be angry at me? Judging me? Surely Pamela told her everything.* He stood there and wished he could go back to picking out frozen foods. Janine was not one to let an uncomfortable silence persist.

"I'm sure you don't want to talk about this," Janine said. *I don't*, Shantanu thought. "But Pamela was never the same after what happened."

"Really?"

It was less a question and more a statement. *Here it comes*, Shantanu thought. *The punishment. The "How could you be like that towards your daughter? Look what you did to mine."*

"She rarely came out of her room," Janine said. "She stopped singing in the house. She stopped talking about auditioning for acting school. She refused to go to college, even though she had straight As up through senior year. You remember, she wouldn't even go to the funeral. In fact, she stopped going to church with us, period, Lord forgive her."

Janine, for the first time, looked burdened.

"Now she's a server at this restaurant down Route 9. The Ivy House. Do you know it?"

"Yes, I've been a couple times. We took the family there after my older daughter's high school graduation. This stuff takes time."

The answer you want to give and the truth are two different things.

Janine nodded.

"One thing I wish she'd do is meet someone. I know the grieving process takes a while. But five years? And to completely change her future? But that's God's will," Janine said, now thumbing her cross necklace.

Five years is nothing at all to grieve someone you love. Shantanu's self-loathing bubbled to the surface, almost as much as his loathing for Janine. *This is the punishment. This is Janine saying she knows what happened. This is her not-so-subtly criticizing me for taking companionship away from her daughter. She's just trying to pierce me.*

"Huh," Shantanu grunted. "You know, I'm not feeling so well. I should go."

"You must come to the house sometime," Janine said with a look of what appeared to be sympathy. "We'd love to have you and your lovely wife over."

He smiled vaguely by way of answering, and instead of grabbing more frozen fish sticks, he wheeled the cart towards the front of the store. *That was deeply unpleasant*, Shantanu thought to himself as he watched his items get checked out in the express lane. He considered making another drive to the crash site. Shantanu hadn't been in years. *There must be something there.*

◇

"Thank you for coming to lunch," Jahar said, spooning crisp potatoes onto Mitali's plate, while Chaitali was hunched over a simmering pot of butter chicken at the stove, standing on a purple bath rug made of cotton. Mitali nodded and tried to transform her face into a smile but could not quite get there. Getting even a slight response was enough for the towering Jahar. He turned his head. "Leave that, Chaitali. I'll bring it to the table."

"I know you typically love your grandmother's holiday *luchi*," Chaitali said, relinquishing pot holders to Jahar. "She gave me this recipe for the *batta* chicken years ago. I've never tried it before, though."

Mitali no longer knew how to act around her mother. This was the first time she had seen her since Chaitali had officially entered her new life a year ago, with a new husband.

"So do I still call you Jahar Kaku?" Mitali asked. She could still figure out which buttons to push. Chaitali's face hardened, but Jahar played it off with a laugh. He was in the Christmas spirit, as was evidenced by the brightly lit tree in the living room, and the stocking above the kitchen doorway. None of these compared to the sweater he was wearing, with a horrific-looking Santa Claus smiling across his chest. Chaitali opted for a red-and-green-striped sweatshirt.

"You call me whatever you want," Jahar said. "I'm not your baba. I'm someone else's, though."

"You have a son, right? I don't remember him coming to the pujas."

Chaitali turned the heat up on the thermostat and sat down at the table.

"Would you like some wine, Mitali?" Chaitali asked.

"I have to drive," she said. Mitali noticed her mother recoil slightly upon hearing this, an involuntary reflex.

"I do have a son," Jahar said. "He's a bit older than you. He didn't come to the pujas, no."

"And why is that?" Mitali said.

"It was complicated."

Mitali was about to ask more, but she caught a look from Chaitali that said, *Don't press on this.*

Once all three of them were seated, Jahar bowed his head and muttered a prayer. Mitali caught Chaitali's eye, her mother shrugged, and soon they were all spooning rice, potatoes, and chicken into their mouths.

"How's work going?" Chaitali asked.

"Fine," Mitali answered.

"Are you still liking your apartment?"

"It's fine."

"Do you think you'll stay in marketing?"

"It's fine."

As the plates emptied, the clatter of utensils made up the majority of the noise from this Christmas lunch. Chaitali stopped trying to make conversation.

"We went ice skating in Bryant Park the other day," Jahar said, trying to punctuate the utensils with a voice.

"Ice skating," Mitali said curtly. She dropped her fork on the table in contempt.

"Yes. I had never gone before."

"Well, I'm sure Ma was quite familiar with how it works."

"Mitali," Chaitali warned.

"It's okay," Jahar cut in.

"Is it? We used to go every year," Mitali said angrily. "Baba used to take us."

"Yes, and now I go with Jahar Kaku. Is that so bad? Why must my happiness be such a sore spot?"

"You should call him *suncho*. He's your husband."

"Watch your tongue, Mitali."

"I'm glad you're doing great, Ma. In this beautiful, big house. With a replacement baba. With a nice lawn. A nice car. Some of the rest of us have to live real life."

"Excuse me, Mitali," Jahar said. His voice did not have any hint of malice. "It's Christmas. I must insist you have some spirit."

Something about Jahar's thundering voice and the innocence with which he said that broke through the tension in the room. Chaitali pursed her lips and began clearing the table.

"Every Christmas, I like to smoke a cigar. It's an indulgence in my old age I allow myself. Would you like to join me on the back porch?" Jahar asked Mitali.

Mitali looked uneasy. She barely knew Jahar. She had met him a handful of times, at family friends' houses and occasional pujas. They had never had a conversation.

"I have an extra one for you," Jahar said.

"Jahar!" Chaitali yelped from the kitchen. Her mother's disapproval was enough for Mitali to follow Jahar to the porch, where the cold of winter surrounded them. Jahar took two cigars out of his pocket and lit them. He handed one to Mitali, who, upon taking a drag, immediately felt the burning in her chest, causing her to double over coughing.

"That'll warm your insides, won't it?" Jahar chuckled.

"I've never had one of these before," Mitali admitted.

She took some deep breaths and tried again. This time, the drag was not as overpowering.

"Thank you for coming today," Jahar said stoically. "I know your mother misses you."

Mitali stared at the cigar, and then at the backyard. It was bare, except for a shed in the back corner.

"We've only been here a year, but the work on the house is coming along quite nicely," Jahar said. "Your mother wanted to keep the job at the library. And she wanted to make it easy on you to visit both of your parents. Did she tell you that?"

"No."

Mitali remembered two vivid conversations with Chaitali: the first was during senior year of college, when both of her parents called to inform her about the divorce. Chaitali did most of the talking, saying they both still loved her but that this was best for all of them.

"You mean best for you," Mitali had said, slightly inebriated in her dorm room, sipping vodka mixed with orange juice on her extra-long twin bed. "Baba, do you have something to say?"

Shantanu did not. Mitali hung up.

Then there was the call about one year ago, when Chaitali, in stilted, concise terms, quietly told Mitali that she and Jahar had been seeing each other and that they had gotten married. And that they were moving in together. Mitali hung up then, too.

"Your mother misses you," Jahar said. "And after twenty years of being alone, I've finally found meaning in something that doesn't have to do with mergers and acquisitions."

He took a drag, and the smoke billowed out from his nostrils. "Please try to open your heart to us," Jahar offered.

The dryness in Mitali's mouth made her uncomfortable, but she didn't want to show it. When they headed inside to exchange Christmas presents, Chaitali was already waiting next to the tree. Mitali reached under the tree and fished out a box with Chaitali's name on it. It was wrapped in newspaper.

"I'm sorry, Ma," Mitali said. "I didn't have wrapping paper."

"That's okay," Chaitali said, as she gently took the paper off the box and opened it. Her eyes widened at the small clay pot with a sunflower etched on it.

"I know you like gardening and sunflowers. I took a ceramics class," Mitali said with a hint of pride. "Somehow, it didn't break on the way down here."

"You made this?"

Chaitali seemed genuinely touched and reached for a hug. Mitali gave a solitary pat on the back, while her shoulders seemed to stiffen.

"And this is for you, from the both of us," Chaitali said.

Mitali opened the box, which was properly wrapped. Mitali reached inside and felt the spine of a book's dust jacket. She took it out: Rabindranath Tagore's *Chokher Bali*.

"It's a first edition. We somehow found it at a rare bookshop in the city," Chaitali said. "You know I also love old books."

"It's considered one of Tagore's formative works and one of the first modern novels of India," Jahar said.

"Thank you, Ma. Jahar Kaku."

"Do you know what it's about?" Chaitali asked. Mitali said no.

"It's about how the main characters handle love. Both forbidden and otherwise."

Subtle, Mitali thought. Still feeling the burning in her throat from the cigar, she went to the kitchen to get a glass of water and laughed to herself about the bath mat by the stove. New house, same habits. Minutes later, she returned to the living room and told them that it was time for her to get going: Shantanu and Kalpana were her next visit. On the way out of the house, Mitali gave Jahar a *pranam* instead of a goodbye: the act of touching his feet out of respect. Jahar protested, as many Bengali elders often did.

"Stop! Stop!" Jahar said. "Come back when you can."

Chaitali walked Mitali to her car and watched as she turned the key in the ignition. Mitali lowered the driver's-side window and her mother leaned in. Mitali felt a touch she hadn't in years: her mother running her hands through her hair. She closed her eyes and felt them watering suddenly.

"I remember doing this whenever you hurt your elbow playing softball," Chaitali said. "Thank you for coming today. Are you okay? Please tell me you're eating something other than toast." Chaitali hesitated, but she finished her thought. "This last year has been hard without you."

"Your life doesn't seem hard," Mitali said.

"It's not empty, no," Chaitali answered. "But I will not apologize for that."

Chaitali leaned in to kiss Mitali on the head.

"This doesn't seem fair," Mitali said. "To Baba. To me."

"My baba used to say, 'Life isn't a compass that points north,'" Chaitali said. "There was no going back after Keya."

"I'm sorry I was rude to Jahar Kaku," Mitali said. "But I can't help but be mad about all of this. Still. You didn't just leave Baba. You left us."

"I didn't leave you."

Chaitali said this without a hint of frustration or defensiveness.

"He stopped by the other day, your baba," Chaitali said, continuing to run her hands through Mitali's hair. Jahar watched from the doorway. "And he said something funny, that peace is another pathway to war."

"Baba came over? Why? To knock Jahar Kaku's teeth out?"

Chaitali chuckled.

"I heard you found the box in the attic."

Mitali bobbed her head.

"Your baba has been at war with himself ever since Keya," Chaitali said. "But I'm trying to heal. Jahar has helped me do that. That box should be buried along with everything else. So we can all heal. Your baba. Me. You. Us."

"You know what's funny?" Mitali said. "You were so worried about what all your Bengali friends would think of Keya. And here you are now. Divorced and remarried to someone in the community. You aren't so worried about your public image now, are you?"

Chaitali turned towards the house, where Jahar was now peering out the window.

"Someday you'll understand all of this."

"And if I don't?"

"Then I'll have lost a second daughter."

SIX

Neesh was hunched over the bar counter at his favorite local haunt, the Grassy Knoll, a grungy dive bar about a quarter mile from his apartment in Crown Heights. He had a highlighter in one hand and a Guinness in the other.

The bar, surrounded by a convenience store and an apartment building, was mostly empty during weekday afternoons, giving Neesh the space he needed to pore over a pile of papers with visible folds on them, damp from bottled water that was also in Neesh's backpack. Fortunately, it was a copy—one that Mitali had made of *The Elm Tree* when she returned to the city after Christmas.

Daytime availability was one of the benefits of working nights at the studio. His roommate Hector had introduced him to this place. Sometimes, Hector said, he would stop by and run his audition monologues for the bartender, Julia, which was a confusing sight for pedestrians who happened to be strolling by.

Julia, with white hair always in a ponytail, liked to weave into any conversation she was having that she was sixty-two. Neesh didn't know her last name, just that she was sixty-two and loved Dean Martin, hence the pictures of the Rat Pack all over the place. The owners never came by, Julia said, because they trusted her to run the place.

"If ya can't trust a sixty-two-year-old to get a buncha hoodlums drunk, whaddya even doin' out here?" Julia once said to Neesh with her signature raspy voice. Julia became a bartender late in life because she was bored living alone at home, and people provided better company than the dozens of cats she fostered at any given moment. She also liked to talk about growing up in Nashville and her weekends spent watching her soon-to-be-husband's band. She came to New York with him to pursue a record deal. Two divorces later, Julia was across from Neesh, serving him beers, often on the house, because she liked that he was a hard-luck musician too.

Following the cover sheet, there was a list of six characters: Preethi and Kate, both eighteen years old, and their parents. Neesh turned the page.

[CURTAINS UP: PREETHI and KATE are sitting under an elm tree.]

PREETHI

I feel insignificant.

KATE

You are insignificant.

PREETHI

But I actually *feel* it right now. It's right there in front of me—like I'm standing in front of one of those Charlie Brown Macy's Thanksgiving Day Floats. I'm a small, small individual.

[Kate nods and reflects.]

KATE

Does that feel cathartic to you?

PREETHI

That feels hopeful to me.

KATE

Being small?

PREETHI

Being an individual.

[Kate ponders.]

KATE

I need a vacation.

PREETHI

From what? It's not a vacation if it's just life.

"What are ya readin' there, Neesh?" Julia cut in. Neesh looked up to see her holding a broom by the cash register, sweeping bits of sawdust to another pile of sawdust that looked like it could have covered the entire bar's floor.

"It's a play. Something like *Three Tall Women*," Neesh said.

"Never heard of it," Julia said. "Only play I've ever seen is that *Hamlet* one. You ever see that? It sucked!"

Julia cackled, and Neesh continued to read. But first, he grabbed some straws within arm's reach. He peeled one open to chew on.

An opening scene featuring Preethi and Kate, best friends in high school. Preethi talked about being bullied, while Kate comforted her. They both had to go home for dinner. Scenes with each of their parents. Preethi's parents were friendly, but lectured her about grades. Kate's mother and father did the same—a clever bit of echoing. Preethi wanted to take a gap year after high school, but her parents rejected the notion out of hand. On one of the early pages, there were handwritten notes scribbled with a marker. "PREETHI'S MOM" was circled with a note that said, "WHAT SHOULD WE NAME MY PARENTS? DO WE HAVE TO NAME THEM?" Some lines were starred. Others were crossed out. Preethi and Kate often returned to the elm tree.

"This is decent," Neesh said out loud to no one in particular. His restless foot began bobbing up and down.

As the play progressed, Kate and Preethi increasingly addressed the audience. Neesh began making notes.

[PREETHI steps towards audience.]

PREETHI

Significance in the grand scheme of things is irrelevant.
Significance to one person though—that's the stuff gold is made of.

[KATE steps towards audience.]

KATE

I believe in cosmic forces. That planets and stars align exactly as
you need them to.

[KATE and PREETHI walk back to the elm tree.]

PREETHI

I've been coming to this tree for two years with you, and I still
don't know anything about myself.

KATE

Do you blame me for that?

PREETHI

I thank you for that.

Next to that last line, a smiley face scribbled with faded marker. Neesh
took his highlighter and penned, "Could be interesting blocking here."
Some of the writing is sophomoric, Neesh thought. Preethi and Kate
sometimes referenced a teacher named Ms. Kanoople. *But still. Impressive for high schoolers.* Some of it made Neesh laugh with a high-pitched
squeal that filled the empty bar.

[AT THE ELM TREE.]

PREETHI

I thought of an idea this morning.

KATE

I'm pregnant.

PREETHI

WHAT?!

KATE

. . . with anticipation.

PREETHI

Oh my god, don't do that again. Anyways, a comic called "Archie."

KATE

I'm sorry, did you just say that you wanted to create a comic called "Archie"? I think someone beat you to that by, like, forty years.

PREETHI

No, no, no. The comic would be [*PREETHI elongates the syllables*] "Rrrrr-Cheeeee." A samurai superhero.

[*KATE stares.*]

[*PREETHI looks embarrassed as she realizes the ridiculousness of her idea.*]

PREETHI

Well, he's a really calm samurai.

KATE

I think the next time you wake up in the morning with an idea
like that, you should go back to sleep. Hell, I do that even when I
don't have an idea.

At the end of the first act, Preethi and Kate gathered again under the
elm tree. Neesh wrote in, "Simple set." The characters discussed their
days. And then:

PREETHI

I think I have feelings for you.

KATE

Really?

PREETHI

I think so. I know so. The way I feel about you, I don't feel about
anyone else. I think about you all day. I wonder what you're
doing. When you're going to be home so I can call. When I'm
going to be home so you can call. Every text brings me a sense
of relief that you're there. We just spend so much time together.
Please tell me you feel the same.

KATE

Oh.

PREETHI

I take it back. Ignore me. I don't mean it. I'm just drunk.
Although, I've never had a drink. I don't know why I said that.
Sometimes I just say things and I just blurt them out—

KATE

Preethi, stop.

PREETHI

Stop what?

KATE

Talking. Give me a second.

[A BEAT.]

PREETHI

Oh god. This is it. Well, this has been fun! See you around. Or not.

KATE

I feel the same as you do.

Underlines in purple and green markers in that last line.

PREETHI

How long have you felt this way?

KATE

Awhile. You?

PREETHI

Awhile. What do we do?

KATE

I can't tell my parents. I would be shunned at church. My mom would hate me.

PREETHI

I can't tell mine either. But we have to try.

[Act I ends.]

The second act began with Preethi and Kate with their respective parents. The stage directions said they were to be on opposite sides at once. *Again, the echo*, Neesh thought to himself. Both of them lost their nerve. Kate's parents said they'd received a call from Ms. Kanoople about a Saturday detention for skipping a previous detention. Preethi's parents wanted to begin looking at colleges. Eventually, they both told their parents the big secret. Neither conversation went well. Kate's parents gave a lecture about Adam and Eve and Leviticus.

Preethi's parents reacted by discussing the embarrassment this would cause in the Bengali community. They saw Preethi's revelation only through how it would affect their standing with them. Both sets of parents expressed the desire for grandchildren. On both ends of the scene, Preethi and Kate ran off the stage at once. There was a scene in Preethi's room, with her mother. The parents were only labeled PREETHI'S MOTHER/FATHER and KATE'S MOTHER/FATHER. Preethi's mother knocked on the door and told Preethi that she was sorry for what happened. But that she needed to understand how important Bengali culture is. She added, "If my mother knew that America would corrupt her granddaughter like that, she would have stayed in Kolkata."

And then, the play ended. Neesh turned the page and there was nothing more. He flipped the papers on their back and saw only blank pages. Neesh reached into his backpack to see if there were more pages. There were not.

There's something here, Neesh thought. A vision briefly appeared in Neesh's wandering mind: It was nighttime. He was signing Playbills for adoring fans outside of a large theater with Mitali at his side, while wearing a tuxedo. Mitali was staring at him as if she wanted to be nowhere else. She looked impressed; flashbulbs were going off. At the end of the line of people, Neesh spotted his father, who was waiting with a Playbill and a marker. Neesh smileed as he proceeded to ignore him and then walked away, his arm around Mitali.

Neesh snapped out of his daydream and saw the Guinness in front of him. He was reminded how far he was from that vision and how, at any second, Mitali would find someone better. Someone more *normal*. Someone making better use of a degree, who had a relationship with their parents, and could afford the airfare to fly to them. Someone who worked in the daytime and could go on vacations to beaches or to Europe.

And besides, it had been years since Neesh had read a play. He had told Mitali that he loved reading them. This wasn't a lie, per se. In Neesh's previous life, he *did* love reading plays, especially when he had first arrived in New York and became a stagehand. He loved learning about theater and being around it. But after what happened with *Rock of Ages*, it became too painful to sift through scripts.

He furrowed his brow, took out his phone, and dialed Mitali. He was out of practice, but he was sure this play was impressive. *But did it ever get finished?*

"Hey," Mitali answered in a hushed tone. "I'm at work."

"I know. But this play you gave me. Have you read it?"

"I started it."

"Do you have it with you?"

"I have a PDF. Neesh, I'm at work."

Neesh could hear phones ringing through the receiver.

"I know. Pull it up. What does the last page say?"

He could hear Mitali hit some buttons on a keyboard. Neesh imagined her hunched in an office chair as if she were smuggling contraband on her cell phone.

"It ends with something about Bengali culture."

"And you're sure that's the whole thing?"

"Yes, Neesh, why?" Mitali said. "I. Am. At. Work."

"They didn't finish writing it," Neesh said. "Interesting."

"Why is that interesting?"

"Your sister is a really talented writer. I have a bit of a wild idea. Hear me out?"

"What is it?"

Neesh unwrapped another straw and put it in his mouth with his free hand and then began drumming his fingers on the table.

"It needs work, obviously. I don't know how to say this without sounding delusional, so I'm just going to say it."

"Neesh. What?"

"We should stage it," Neesh said.

"Stage it? You mean, like, do her play?"

"Yeah, exactly."

Neesh was interrupted by a loud voice he immediately recognized, which said, "Well, look who it is!" He seized up.

"I've gotta go," Neesh said hastily.

"Do you want to come over tonight?" Mitali said. "Neesh?"

Neesh ignored Mitali and disconnected the call. He couldn't believe his eyes. It seemed like the oxygen had been sucked out of the room.

"What can I getcha?" Julia asked the newcomer, who sat next to Neesh and dropped Neesh's backpack on the ground with the sawdust. Neesh gave Julia a look of *He's not supposed to be here.* But she didn't notice.

"Whatever Neesh here is having."

Julia nodded and went to get a beer glass to wipe off.

"What are you doing here?" Neesh looked horrified. He looked at the door, as if expecting there to be more unwelcome visitors.

"I was walking by and saw you."

"*Here?* Were you following me?"

"Calm down."

"I told you I didn't want to see you again."

"*Calm. Down.*"

Julia returned with napkins and two waters.

"Who's yer friend, Neesh?" Julia said.

"I don't have friends. This is Sandeep."

Julia, the keen bartender that she was, this time recognized that she should not inquire more and walked away to get Sandeep's beer.

"You used to greet me with more affection," Sandeep said. Even sitting, Sandeep was taller than Neesh, and heavyset, with a full head of black hair visible under his winter cap. His hair was curly and stretched down to right above his shoulder. There were some specks of white, more than usual for a thirty-five-year-old. Then again, Sandeep, as Neesh remembered, had led a stressful life.

"Can I get a hug and a kiss?" Sandeep said.

"That's a nice coat," Neesh said wryly. It was just a North Face, but he didn't intend to mince words with Sandeep. "I doubt you could show me a receipt for it."

"Oh, *now* you've gone straight."

Neesh closed his eyes and tried to summon his daydream again. Instead, only his father came to mind. *Soon, I'll fill my warehouse with the world. What will you do?*

"Jared got in touch recently."

"He's out of prison?" Neesh said. "So that's why you texted. You trying to get the band back together?"

"Yeah, bro. He's out. A couple months ago."

Sandeep reached to put an arm around Neesh. Neesh blanched.

"Buddy, I went to visit Jared a couple times," Sandeep said, his breath smelling of cigarettes. Julia emerged from the back room, stealing glances at her only two customers while dropping off Sandeep's Guinness. "He ain't mad anymore. I told him I had a nice package waiting for him. And besides, I run things now."

"Well," Neesh said, not meeting Sandeep's eyes. "Good for you."

"Granted, every day he says something about how *you* only got a misdemeanor and he got a felony."

"He was carrying a gun," Neesh said.

"Which you testified to. It was a tiny revolver. It's not like it was an AK," Sandeep said.

Neesh picked up a napkin to wipe foam from his lips. He was sweating.

"We betrayed him," Sandeep said. "You know that."

"It was your fucking idea. You turned first. Whatever this is, I don't want any part of it." Neesh lowered his voice now, even though they were alone. "You know I lost my job because I met you guys? And I haven't been able to find solid work since. I work an hourly job. I have eight hundred dollars in my checking account. And I'm thirty-three."

"Yeah, that Broadway shit. None of us told you to do coke backstage! We were focused on bigger things, man."

"Stop," Neesh said. "Stop, stop, stop. Your father would fucking kill me if he saw me with you right now. And he really helped me out."

"Fuck my father," Sandeep said. "He doesn't know shit about me."

"You guys okay over there?" Julia called again. She had swept the same spot on the bar floor for several minutes.

"We're good," Sandeep said. With that, he raised his beer glass and took a big gulp. He took out his wallet and left a crumpled twenty-dollar bill on the counter. "I'll get this one. You get the next one. I came up with that shit for Jared because I wanted to keep you out of jail. He was going anyway. I didn't want both of you to go down. You never believed we gave a shit about you."

"There's not going to *be* a next one," Neesh said. "And if you know what's good for you, you'll stay away from Jared. You know all he thinks about is getting his."

"You motherfucker." Sandeep grabbed Neesh by the collar.

Neesh locked eyes with Julia, who shifted her frail hands on the broom like a weapon.

"I don't turn my back on my friends so easily. Jared doesn't want revenge. He's having trouble getting on his feet, is all. We're the reason he went away for so long. You don't want to fucking hang with us anymore, fine. You think you're too good for us now, fine. Fuck it. But we have a debt to Jared. We did that shit for you. And you didn't mind then."

Neesh pushed Sandeep off him and sprang up from the barstool. He walked to an ATM in a back corner near a bathroom. He beckoned for Sandeep to follow him. Neesh took out his ATM card and withdrew five hundred dollars. He bit his lip and a receipt emerged showing what was left in his bank account. There was only a couple hundred left. But nonetheless, he shoved the wad of twenties into Sandeep's hands.

"Give this to Jared. It's almost everything I have. Consider my debt repaid," Neesh said fiercely.

Sandeep, for the moment, looked satisfied.

"*Debt*," he said, a smug grin on his face. "Cash isn't the only kind of debt in our line of work, brother." He went to get his coat and left the bar.

"What *was* that, Neesh? I was ready to beat the shit out of him," Julia said, still with her hands on the broom in an aggressive posture.

"Nothing stays buried," Neesh said bitterly. But the stack of papers on the bar caught his eye and Neesh remembered why he was here to begin with.

He returned to Act II and picked up his highlighter to mark a passage he liked. Preethi and Kate were back at the elm tree.

PREETHI

I feel so alone. Like, I have no one outside of you to talk to about this.

KATE

Me too. But at least you have your sister.

PREETHI

My sister and I never talk about our love lives. I don't even think she's ever dated anyone. I asked her if she had a boyfriend once when we were watching a movie. She said she doesn't date because she has never met anyone willing to go to Medieval Times with her.

SEVEN

B y the song's end, sweat soaked Neesh's shirt. He put one of the drumsticks in his mouth as he readjusted the snare, which had moved several inches off its original position. *This rehearsal room has the worst rug for the drums*, he thought. Neesh didn't stop bouncing on his drum throne or keeping time on the high hat throughout the whole process, a delicate act. Even with the faulty rug, Electric Smash, the Midtown studio, was the closest place to a temple for Neesh, where he could worship at the altar of the drums.

He made eye contact with Sandeep, who was fingering a complex line on the bass, while Jared riffed on the guitar. They were crammed into a small room, with just enough space for a drum set, a bassist, a guitarist, and a keyboardist, although the keyboards sat empty for this session.

"Watch me!" Neesh yelled to the band, like a general leading his troops into battle. He felt at home. "WATCH ME!"

And like a soldier might, Sandeep and Jared obeyed without hesitation. Neesh blasted the cymbals with a fill he liked and then whirled around the whole kit, toms, bass, and all—to signal the song's ending.

Jared, the oldest of the group, smirked as he waved his arms through his guitar strings like Pete Townshend. Neesh rolled on the crash cymbals, before he skillfully nailed a final hit, bringing silence to the room for the first time in nine minutes. For a few moments, the only audible sound in the rehearsal studio was the whir of the fluorescent lights on the ceiling and labored panting from the trio. Neesh took out his earplugs.

"That. Was. Good. Shit," Sandeep declared, collapsing into a chair. "Yo, Neesh, you are a metronome. I've never jammed in 7-8 before."

"Fuck, fuck, fuck," Jared joined in, with his typical high-pitched voice. "FUCK! That was GOOD. I can't even hear right now. My ears are ringing."

Jared was the shortest, skinniest, baldest, and cleanest shaven of the bunch, but what he lacked in stature, he made up for in vitality and authority.

"Neesh, come here, you devilish fuck," Jared said, now taking back his usual position as general. "Do this bump."

He laid out the white powder on a chair and organized it into several lines for each of them. Sandeep bounded over and cut Neesh off.

"Interception!" Sandeep yelled, throwing his head at the chair. Neesh backed off. Sandeep was significantly larger, and Neesh never wanted to test him physically. But Jared had no such hesitation, and grabbed Sandeep by the collar and tried to throw him backwards.

"Chill out," Jared said. "He goes first."

Sandeep was barely moved by Jared's shove, but looked disappointed and stepped back, nonetheless. Neesh got on one knee next to the chair and did his lines. Sandeep followed suit. The effects were immediate for both of them.

"7-8 time! 7-8 time!" Neesh and Sandeep yelled in unison, while Jared did his line.

"Keep it down," Jared scolded as his head jerked up. "Don't get us kicked out of here by that old bat."

Neesh laughed as he sat back at the drum set and began to play a drum roll on the snare drum, ready for more. But Jared stopped him and tossed him a flask. He didn't feel at home many places except here, surveying his kingdom of things he could expertly strike with precise rhythm.

"You coming out tonight?" Jared asked, putting the powder back into his backpack.

"Nah," Neesh said sheepishly. "I got shit to do."

"Bro, what do you have to do?" Sandeep cut in dismissively. "The stage shit? That play ran for like a month and it closed. You got no plans. You haven't worked in months. You don't want to come out because you can't pay for shit."

"Enough," Jared said. Sandeep fell silent.

"Stage*hand*," Neesh said. "That was a good gig. Made film school almost not a waste of time. Too bad it didn't run longer. Thanks for reminding me I'm too junior for these other shows coming out."

"Man, quit that shit and run with us." Sandeep crawled to the chair for another line. "You're one of the best drummers I've ever heard. We can go on tour and all that. Really piss our dads off."

"Nah, man. I just joined Local 802," Neesh said to Sandeep's blank stare. "The Broadway pit musician's union. I've been talking to the dudes behind this new show, *Rock of Ages*. It's Off Broadway but it's going to make the jump. They need a rehearsal drummer. I'm young, but I'm hoping they'll let me sub in and do some spots. Pays well. All that shit. If it goes well, I'll sub in when they do previews and shit."

"A real professional drummer, huh?" Jared said. "Good for you, man. I knew when you answered our flyer you were the real deal. That guy, Gary, setting you up?"

"Gary Whyte, yeah."

"When are we gonna play out?" Sandeep asked.

"When we're ready," Jared said. "We still need to get tighter."

Neesh took a chug from the flask. The burn in his throat from the combination of mostly vodka and some fruit punch made him grimace. He tossed it back to Jared.

"Let's go to a bar," Sandeep said, looking at Jared as if awaiting permission.

"Why not?" Neesh said. "We had a good practice."

"I gotta come down first," Jared said. "Deep, take my card and pay for the room. We'll meet you at that Irish spot on the corner. Have an old-fashioned waiting for me."

"Yes, *sir*."

Sandeep gave a sarcastic salute before he unplugged the XLR cord from the amp and packed his guitar into a soft case that he could sling onto his shoulders. He dutifully took the credit card from Jared and left room C. Neesh got up from the drum set and sat on the floor near Jared, his back on the bass drum. They heard a knock on the door, and Griselda, the co-owner of Electric Smash, appeared in the doorway. She was a tall redhead in her fifties with cigarettes sticking out of her pockets.

"You guys almost done in here?" she asked with a hoarse, gravelly voice.

"Sandeep went to go pay. We're packing up," Jared said. Griselda gave a thumbs-up and closed the door.

"I heard Johnny is sick," Jared said, lowering his voice.

"Her husband? How bad?" Neesh said.

"Bad. Liver stuff. Griselda is pretty much running this place by herself."

"She looked stressed."

Jared reached for his backpack and took out an envelope and handed it to Neesh.

"Before I forget, that's five hundred bucks or so," Jared said. "Should help you with rent for the month."

Neesh felt ashamed as he took the envelope. He put his sweat-soaked T-shirt in his mouth.

"Thanks." Neesh, even with the cocaine soaring through him, felt chastened. "And thanks for giving me the money for the union dues."

"Don't mention it," Jared said.

Neesh put the envelope in his back pocket.

"Don't you ever worry about getting caught?" Neesh had wanted to ask this for months. But in the year of becoming close with Jared and Sandeep, he had never worked up the courage. But Jared had insisted on helping with his rent the last several months. Neesh didn't have a job. He wanted to be on another show's crew, but there were no openings. They were in the height of a recession. And he was not going to call his father for help.

"Getting caught?" Jared was incredulous, before he let loose a cackle. "I've got this check-cashing stuff on lock, man. I'm making more money than you'll ever make as a drummer."

"The scamming shit never bothers you, huh?" Neesh said.

"Why should it?"

"You don't think it's fucked up? The drugs are whatever. Ripping off old people on Craigslist and shit?"

"Man, what is fucked up? You think if you work *really* hard, you're gonna climb some ladder and boom, your life is made? It's not. You gotta make your own ladder."

Jared handed Neesh the flask. Neesh took a drink and handed the flask back.

"Sandeep is in on this shit too, huh?"

"He's useful. I guess I only run with dudes who have daddy issues. Between you and your shit with the antiques and Sandeep's corporate dad who kicked him out, I've got a type."

Jared took another swig.

"Let me tell you something, Nice Neesh. If life was what we were taught as kids, you wouldn't have all that college debt, because your dad would've paid for school. You know he had the cash."

"Yeah."

"And you wouldn't be unemployed for months, because some other show would've hired you."

"It takes a while," Neesh said. "Budgets are tight."

"It always takes longer for people who look like you."

This guy is explaining racism to me? Neesh thought.

"What about people that look like you? All the meritless shit benefits fuckers that go to the beach craving a tan."

"I don't go to the beach, you know that," Jared said. "Let me tell you, though, my dad was such a sucker."

"No he wasn't," Neesh said tamely.

"He was. Worked all his life at that dumb bookstore. For years. And then once the cancer hit, that was it. We sold the place for less than it was worth to try to pay the medical bills. I'll never forget it. And it wasn't enough. I told him: 'Let's do a fundraiser. Let's mark up some books. *Do something.*' He wouldn't bite. That won't be me." Jared spit on the floor.

He added, "The *money* is where the real merit is. That's why I'm not mad at the banks for getting rich off people like my dad. My father didn't die from cancer. He died from a lack of imagination."

◇

Gary Whyte happened to stumble across Neesh at the rehearsal studio in the fall, when he was walking by a room where Neesh, Sandeep, and Jared were playing. He watched the trio through a tiny window on the door in room C and was impressed by Neesh's (cocaine-fueled) energy.

"You've got that Liberty DeVitto–Billy Joel glow," Gary Whyte told Neesh when they crossed paths in the building lobby later.

"Your white hair is fucking wild," Neesh could only manage in response, letting his high show more than he intended. "I want spikes like that too."

"Yours will be like this if you keep drumming like that," Gary Whyte said. "And I figure with a name like Gary Whyte, I better have white hair. You have time for a drink?"

Neesh couldn't believe his luck as he sat next to Gary Whyte on a stool at O'Brien's on the corner. Gary Whyte told him that he was the main drummer for *Rock of Ages*, which was still Off Broadway but preparing to make the leap, and that he had been a professional pit musician for twenty years. He regaled Neesh with stories of touring the world with Gloria Estefan and other traveling Broadway shows.

"I know drummers when I see them," Gary Whyte said. "You, sir, are a drummer. Can you sight-read?"

Gary Whyte slammed Neesh on the back, which slightly alarmed him. "Yes."

"Who taught you?"

"Uh, me."

This was a lie and Neesh had no idea why he said it, other than wanting to seem more impressive. Neesh did learn plenty on his own from purchasing instructional books, but the high school band teacher taught him how to read music.

"Good. Listen, *Rock of Ages* isn't like other musicals. This isn't some *Oklahoma!* or *Kiss Me, Kate* shit. The band is onstage. Which means it's not enough to be a good player. You've gotta have stage presence. More Keith Moon than Ringo. You know what I mean? I'm going to have to wear a costume. But I've had some trouble finding a reliable sub that the musical director likes. Lots of great players. But not a lot of presence. Any interest?"

Can coke cause hallucinations?

"Are—are you serious?" Neesh stammered.

"As serious as herpes."

"What?"

"Yes, I'm serious. You part of the union?"

"No."

A bartender brought over another round of drinks: a Guinness for Neesh and whiskey on the rocks for Gary Whyte.

"Thank you, Darlene," Gary Whyte said, slipping a fifty-dollar bill onto the table, before turning back to Neesh. "Join the union. Local 802. The conductor has to sign off too. He's the guitarist for the house band. But I think he'll like you. We play a lot of classic rock: 'Don't Stop Believin',' 'Hit Me with Your Best Shot,' 'We Built This City.' You can handle being energetic on that stuff, right?"

"I think." Neesh couldn't help but spot several blisters on Gary Whyte's hands. "You should tape those up when you play."

Gary Whyte looked confused, and then eyed Neesh with a look of amusement.

"I need you to not think. I need you to know," Gary Whyte said. "What I'm doing for you right now doesn't happen. It takes years for musicians to get to a Broadway pit. You're still a baby. But I've got a good feeling about you."

"I know."

Neesh's first show came three weeks into the Broadway run. Gary Whyte had a long-scheduled week off. "A twenty-years-late honeymoon with Wife Two," Gary Whyte told him. Neesh had spent weeks auditing the show, learning the onstage mechanics and taking detailed notes. He was to be paid a thousand for the week. He memorized cues, when Gary Whyte would play to the crowd and what fills were used when. Neesh marveled at the packed houses and the audience members that would headbang along with the thuds of Gary Whyte's bass drum hits. He saw the show so many times that his feet would mimic some of the choreography onstage as he sat in the back of the house and watched yet another run-through. He kept tabs on what critics were saying. The *New York Times* theater critic, Nicholas Simmons, called the show "absurdly enjoyable," much to his excitement. Neesh didn't want his meal ticket to close before he got the chance to call himself a professional drummer. And he impressed the show's director in some rushed rehearsals.

A half hour before he went onstage for his debut, Neesh was in a backstage bathroom, trying to adjust his makeup.

"Do I need this?" Neesh said out loud to his reflection. He heard a voice inside his head that told him he did. *If you screw this up, and are more Ringo than Keith, you're going to be back to taking handouts from Jared, figuring out how to pay rent.* Neesh couldn't counter that voice. He made sure the bathroom door was locked and took out the bag of white powder that Jared had given him a while back. *You shouldn't do this. But why not? No, come on. You don't need this. I do.* Neesh set out two lines and snorted them. He tucked the baggie into his coat pocket and headed out. He was ready to play Broadway.

Neesh took his place on the stage. The curtain rose and he heard the audience roar, the first time he had ever experienced anything like this. Neesh had never come close to playing in front of a crowd like this in his high school band that his father so loathed. He wondered what his father would say once he found out that he was playing for a Broadway show.

His first song, "Just Like Paradise/Nothin' But a Good Time," featured a tom-heavy intro combined with an extended guitar solo. Sweat bounced from his face as he struck his set with as much force as he could muster, taking in the drum's booming through the theater. By the time "We're Not Gonna Take It" came around, Neesh was more relaxed, at least as best he could relax. The part came naturally to him. Muscle memory from weeks of auditing kicked in. At one point, he made eye contact with an attractive woman in the front row. He winked. Neesh felt like a rock star, and it wasn't just the cocaine.

At intermission, the music director approached him and shook his hand.

"Good job," Dennis said. "You've got game. Watch your tempo. You're a little hot in a couple numbers, but you're doing great."

Neesh went to the bathroom again to prepare for the second act. When the show came to an end, the audience gave a standing ovation, as was typical for *Rock of Ages*. Neesh was short of breath but wanted to take up residence inside this moment. He had not invited Jared and Sandeep. They weren't the kind of friends he cared to be in the seats. But even if no one he knew was bearing witness, he had made it—he was a professional drummer. When the cast pointed at the house band for a bow, several actors pointed at him, per Broadway tradition, to single out someone making a debut. Neesh played a fill on the toms to acknowledge the crowd and the cast. Then the curtain came down. And Neesh let out a deep breath. It was the greatest night of his twenty-three years living. He went home and slept until two p.m the next day. He was awoken by a phone call from Gary Whyte, who called from Puerto Rico to congratulate him.

"Heard it went great," Gary Whyte said. "More Animal from the Muppets than Ringo."

Subsequent shows that week went just as well. When Gary Whyte came back, he told Neesh that he would be the main alternate on drums, and that he would recommend him for other shows. If all went well, Gary Whyte said, Neesh would become one of the most in-demand subs in the city.

Gary Whyte's word was true. Soon, Neesh was filling in at rehearsals once or twice a week on average for various shows in development or about to open. Neesh was making enough money from occasionally playing for *Rock of Ages* and for practices that he was able to make his rent. But he found himself with minimal savings: much of the extra money he had went towards cocaine. Especially as two lines before *Rock of Ages* performances became three. He no longer had a need for a band, so he stopped reaching out to Jared and Sandeep. And he didn't need them for drugs anymore. One of the cast members was a steady supplier.

For four months he'd been thriving, and still, backstage, Neesh was not used to what he saw in the mirror. He adjusted his wig, which made him look like he had wild, shoulder-length black hair. His ripped jeans felt tight on him, as did the leather, faux-diamond-studded vest. Months ago, the costume designer said this was by choice and that it shouldn't affect his playing.

"Don't rub your eyeliner," she said. "I've told you every night and you still always rub your eyeliner."

"Sorry, Clara," Neesh said in a dressing room reserved just for musicians. Almost habitually, he put one of his hands up near his face before Clara, always anxious before a show, slapped it away.

"You look good," Clara said, admiring her work. This was her twentieth Broadway show, and she was the kind of costume designer who would still be sewing for musicals on her deathbed.

"This is like Halloween," Neesh said. "Well, I don't actually know what Halloween is like. I never dressed up as a kid."

"Trust me. This is better than Halloween," Clara countered. "You get paid in cash and applause instead of Kit Kats."

The show began as it normally did. Neesh blasted the toms during an early number. The movements were becoming more mechanical and practiced. He had the routine down pat. As the show went on, Neesh noticed Dennis looking at him strangely onstage, but quickly covering it up. The audience, not knowing any better, did not notice his face. Neesh didn't make anything of it and kept playing.

At intermission, Neesh headed for the bathroom, but he was stopped in his tracks.

"Did you forget something?" Dennis said.

Neesh turned around.

"No?"

Dennis walked up to Neesh, took him by the arm, and led him to a corner where nobody would notice them.

"These were by your kit. In full view of the whole cast."

Neesh felt a rush of anxiety as he noticed Dennis holding three bags of white powder.

"Do you keep cocaine in your costume pocket during a show? Are you fucking high right now?"

Neesh squirmed. *I forgot to put them back in my coat pocket. Fuck.*

"Finish the show," Dennis said menacingly.

"Do you really think I'm the only person who's high right now?"

"The others know better than to leave it lying around on the set."

He turned around and walked away.

The second act went off without any incident. Dennis often looked at Neesh and smiled, as he normally did during the course of the show, but Neesh could feel the glances were more forced than anything else. The bows came to resounding applause as they usually did, but Neesh did not have the same enjoyment. Dennis walked offstage once the curtain came down and the houselights went up. He didn't say a word to Neesh, who also left, occasionally mumbling a "Good show" to cast members.

And that was it. Neesh did not receive a single call to fill in for *Rock of Ages* again. There were no more calls to play for rehearsals, either. At first, Neesh thought this was a quirk of the schedule, that shows didn't need a substitute for a bit. He called Gary Whyte after a few weeks. Gary Whyte didn't answer. Neesh called again a week later. Nothing. Neesh realized something was wrong when a third call went unanswered a month later.

One evening, the week before Thanksgiving, Neesh was at home nervously eyeing his flip phone between drags of a joint. He stayed at his apartment most nights, just in case he got a call that Gary Whyte was sick and the show needed a fill-in. All those nights, the phone rarely buzzed . . . until tonight. It was a text from Gary Whyte. Neesh sprang up to open his phone to read.

Don't ever contact me again—GW. Neesh sank back into his couch.

That was it. There would be no more costumes. No more bantering with
Clara. He reached for another joint.

◇

"Here's what I got." Neesh handed Jared an envelope at his Williamsburg
studio, which, as far as New York City studios went, was roomy. Jared was
sitting on his king-sized bed, which took up about a third of the room.
On the opposite end of the room from the bed, there was a small, framed
picture on the windowsill of a young boy with a middle-aged man and
woman. They had their arms around him.

Jared opened it and rifled through the cash, mostly consisting of twenties and hundred-dollar bills.

"How much is this?" Jared asked. "Never mind. I got it."

He laid out the bills individually and counted them. Neesh walked
across the hardwood to the windowsill. Outside, he could see the Williamsburg Bridge and the East River. The people looked like ants below,
scurrying about. Neesh picked up the picture frame.

"Are these your—" Before Neesh finished his question, he was cut off.

"Three pairs of tickets? Outside of Madison Square Garden?" Jared
stared piercingly at Neesh. "How long did you stand out there?"

"Hours," Neesh said quietly. "It's the Knicks. Why do you think people
will pay that much money to scalpers for a dog-shit team like this?"

He didn't actually stand out there very long.

Jared looked disappointed, but then shrugged. He counted out half the
money and gave it to Neesh, who walked back to the bed. Neesh scowled
and shoved the money quickly into his pocket.

"Don't look like that," Jared said. "You came back to *us*. Don't forget.
The holidays would've been a lot colder if I didn't pay your heating bills."

Neesh had no answer and turned to leave. His father's words rang in
his head: *Clean up your mess.*

"What did you think of the tickets?" Jared asked when Neesh reached
the door. Out of the corner of his eye, Neesh saw an open closet which had
what looked like dozens of unopened basketball sneakers.

"What do you mean?" Neesh said.

"They looked like the real thing, right?"

"I don't know," Neesh mumbled. "I've never been to a Knicks game."

"It's some of my best work," Jared said, looking at his computer.

Neesh made another motion to leave.

"Don't go back to MSG for a bit in case you're recognized," Jared called out. "And we have to get you a real job, so you have some legitimate income."

Neesh barely heard him as he headed down the hall to the elevator. When it arrived, Neesh was startled by the large figure with an overcoat and a winter cap stepping out. The curly hair was unmistakable.

"The prodigal son!" Sandeep sneered, carrying a backpack. Neesh gave him a dirty look as he tried to brush past him, but Sandeep placed his palm on Neesh's chest. His face softened.

"Yo, my bad," Sandeep said. "I'm just joking. You good? How was MSG?" Neesh let his shoulders sag.

"Cold, huh?" Sandeep interpreted the silence. "I know you hate this."

Again, Neesh was tight-lipped.

"What do you hate most? The scamming? Or living with not being better than us?"

Sandeep's words were biting, and both of them knew it.

"We aren't much to Jared," Neesh said, extending his arm to hold the elevator open.

"We're friends. He's gotten both of us out of tight spots. Me especially."

Neesh didn't have to be reminded of Sandeep's bitterness towards his father, who wouldn't let him move home after dropping out of Rutgers. Of course, Neesh could understand fathers leaving open sores to be picked at, but Sandeep was more vocal about his.

"So this is a loyalty thing," Neesh said. "You let him lead you around and dump on you out of loyalty."

"Loyalty. Desperation. All branches of the same tree, brother," Sandeep said. "We both have a parent who died before it was their time. We get each other."

Sandeep paused.

"He was hurt when you left the band. Once you hit the big time, you stopped talking to us and didn't want to be around us coke-snorting scammers. I wouldn't do that shit to you. Even now."

"He wasn't hurt," Neesh said. "He lost a potential recruit. He had me marked from the start. That's what the rent money and shit was for."

"Keep your voice down. His place is right there," Sandeep whispered. "You don't give him enough credit. It's not Jared that cost you the Broadway gig. You did. He gave you a parachute."

Neesh did not see his current circumstances as a way out. Just the opposite: he felt trapped. He knew Sandeep was right. It was a prison of his own making. And he was increasingly risking a real prison.

"Well, it took him no time to replace me—Jamal, that new drummer? Do you think he considers us friends?" Neesh said.

"Man, Jamal can't even play a 7-8. But I think Jared's a good dude," Sandeep said. "Somewhere in there. But, man, I make too much money off him to care about the question."

EIGHT

This is a colossally stupid idea, Shantanu thought as he gazed up at a brick building on a Saturday afternoon in January. He had never done anything like this, a point that Mitali made as she gave him his Christmas gift weeks before.

"Couldn't you have just given me a new razor or something?" Shantanu told Mitali that Christmas evening at Kalpana's, examining the contents of the envelope he had opened. "A briefcase? Spring semester starts soon."

Mitali laughed. "Baba, this will give you a much-needed jolt."

"So will sticking my finger in an electric socket."

Kalpana reached over and pinched Shantanu's cheek at the dinner table, where a few stray pieces of *luchis* were scattered on a plate, along with other curries.

"Don't say that, *babu*."

"Merry Christmas, Baba. I think this will be therapeutic."

But I'm already seeing a therapist, Shantanu wanted to say. But he opted for a simple thank-you instead.

The sign on the awning read GEORGE STREET PLAYHOUSE. Two mammoth trees surrounded the awning and took up almost the entire building on the New Brunswick sidewalk. They sprouted out of a bed of bushes that also neighbored the theater's entrance. Shantanu considered hurling himself into the bushes rather than walk inside the theater.

"I guarantee you that you are in the right place." A shorter, heavyset man with a brown topknot poked his head through the front door with a smile. "Staring at it won't make it any righter."

Shantanu fumbled in his jacket pocket and took the envelope out.

"I'm here for 'Improv Comedy 101: Learning the Basics,'" Shantanu said, walking up and handing him the piece of paper. Mitali said she had gone to see an improv show recently and that this might be fun for Shantanu to try. Shantanu couldn't help but notice that Mitali seemed more cheerful. Happier. More willing to smile. *Is she moving on like Chaitali? Am I to be left behind?*

"You certainly look the part," the man with the topknot said. "Come this way."

Shantanu didn't know what the man meant, but he walked inside anyway. To the left of the entrance, there was a visible auditorium, nearby construction noise blaring through the space. On the other side, picture frames of past productions filled the wall. Among them, David Auburn's *Proof*, which won a Pulitzer Prize, and *It Shoulda Been You*, directed by David Hyde Pierce. The man led Shantanu to a stairwell.

"Walk up two floors, make a left. The class will be in the second room down the hallway," Top Knot said. "Remember to 'Yes, and . . .'" He slapped Shantanu on the back with a force that sent Shantanu forward up the stairs, wincing at his knees aching with every step.

When he found the room, he understood what Top Knot meant by looking the part. About a dozen other people were in the class, eight of them appearing to be male, white, and just out of college, scrolling through their phones, all wearing jeans and a plaid shirt. Just like Shantanu, except for the skin color. Six of them had thick-framed glasses. Some of them had big bushy beards. There were rows of folding chairs facing the front in a wide-open space with nothing on the walls. Shantanu took a seat next to a woman, the only one who seemed to have not been born in the 1990s. She gave him an acknowledging look as he sat next to her.

Minutes later, the assumed teacher, a slender man, walked in wearing a plaid shirt, but with khakis.

"Hi, everyone! I'm Carl!" Every sentence seemed to be the embodiment of an exclamation point. "I'm excited for us to get started! Let's warm up! Can everyone gather in a circle?!"

The classmates all hesitated, but everyone got up and did as Carl asked.

"We're going to do some warm-ups!"

Carl pointed at one of the striking young women in the class, one who seemed like she was used to performing, and asked her to make an expression to the person standing next to her.

"This game is called 'Pass the Face'!"

The woman made an expression. The man next to her copied the expression and sent it on around the circle. It was a game of telephone, only with facial expressions. When it arrived at Shantanu, the older woman he had initially placed himself next to passed an expression of unmitigated rage, as if she were a monster jumping out of a closet. Shantanu mimicked her and did the same to his neighbor, one of the bushy-bearded twenty-somethings. And so on and so on the circle went. Shantanu felt ridiculous and yet, he was surprised to find himself laughing.

After the warm-ups, Carl had everyone sit in their seats.

"There are two concepts that make improv work!" Carl said. *Does he ever turn off?* Shantanu thought to himself. " 'Yes, and . . .' and 'Being honest.' 'Yes, and . . .' means that when your scene partner does something, you have to agree with the premise and then add something to it. So if your partner says he's a doctor, then you acknowledge that he's a doctor and you might say you're a patient. 'Being honest' means exactly what it sounds like: Don't *try* to be funny. Just be honest. Let's do some scenes! Two at a time, please!"

Carl began pointing at random duos to walk to the front of the room to perform brief scenes. He'd ask the class to suggest a location. "A classroom!" one person yelled. "A museum!" another one shouted. "A real estate open house!" the woman sitting next to Shantanu called out. The scenes seemed clumsy, but the teacher treated each one as if it were *Saturday Night Live* at its funniest. Carl yelled "Scene!" after a minute or so of each maiden try at improv with the same unwavering enthusiasm.

Shantanu's heart was beating rapidly when it was his turn to be paired off with the young woman. Carl asked the room for a suggestion of a location.

"A movie theater!" someone shouted.

"Movie theater! There you go!"

The woman effortlessly moved two chairs next to each other to face the audience and sat in one of them. *Yes, and . . . ,* Shantanu thought to himself. *If only Keya could see me now.*

"Hey, babe," she whispered, miming eating popcorn. The way she did it suggested she was totally in her element. "I can't believe they made *another Fast and the Furious.*"

Shantanu's mind was naturally analytical. His years as an academic kicked in. He synthesized the information he had in front of him, just as he would reams of data during office hours. Movies. "Babe." Popcorn. *Fast and the Furious.* But he was hesitant.

"Uh, yeah, me either," Shantanu offered.

"Thanks for going on date night with me, Harry," the woman said.

Harry. Harry? How can I possibly discuss a date with someone I barely know?

"You're welcome, uh, babe. You, uh, are a babe too." He remembered calling Chaitali "Chai" early on after they met. She loved it.

Shantanu heard some chuckles in the room. *Wait. Did I just make some people laugh?* Shantanu's date put her arm on his chair.

"Oh, honey, you've never used a pet name with me before!" the scene partner said.

A pet name? A pet name.

"Uh, pumpkin, do you mind keeping it down? I'm trying to watch the film," Shantanu said.

Shantanu heard a loud cackle from Carl.

"Of course, apple turnover."

"Scene!" Carl yelled. "Good job, both of you! That was the game! You recognized there was a punch line to be found in the pet name! Good stuff! Go have a seat."

Shantanu shook hands with his scene partner and walked back to his seat, feeling oddly elated. He wondered if this was what Keya felt like in *42nd Street.* His heart was still trying to escape his body, it seemed.

"Now we're going to break off into pairs again and practice more scenes!" Carl said. "Just get comfortable with 'Yes, and . . .' and 'Being honest.' Go for it! Do scenes about anything. Anything at all. Start from nothing and end in a different world. Remember to listen and build off your partner!"

The woman sitting next to Shantanu turned to him. Shantanu shrugged, and their partnership was formed. She was petite, with straight black hair pulled back by a green headband. She still had a puffy winter coat on over a colorful wrap dress and black tights, as if she was getting ready to leave at any moment, and orange mittens hanging out of the pockets. There was something distinct about her, a certain whimsical elegance that he couldn't quite figure out. Just from her green eyes and the way she was sitting—straight up, legs apart, elbow on one knee— Shantanu found himself drawn to her. He sat up straighter and ignored his back aches.

"I'm Catherine," she said with a hint of an Australian accent.

"Shantanu," he answered back. "I've never acted before."

"I have acted before," Catherine said, looking around the room. She had a sharp voice. "My most recent role was 'forty-three-year-old woman excited to do improv with a bunch of teenagers.'"

Shantanu laughed.

"My daughter gave this to me as a Christmas gift. Seems more like a punishment."

"Ha. I never had kids. Never got married either. Sounds fun, though."

Shantanu looked at the other pairs; many were very animated already, apparently well into their scenes. He decided to initiate. *Base scenes in honesty and "Yes, and . . ."*

"It's nice to meet you. Would you like to go to dinner?" Shantanu said robotically.

Catherine seemed taken aback.

"You're very direct. I would rather smoke pot right now."

"Oh."

Okay. Maybe she's a hippie? The kind I would see at that Rolling Stones concert? Okay, yes, and . . .

"You're free to join me," Catherine added.

Yes, and . . .

"Oh, sure. Yes, I would, er, like to smoke the gange. I have a pretty good, uh, supplier? We could go meet him right now," Shantanu said nervously.

Be honest and yes, and . . .

"Right now?"

"Totally. I, uh, know a guy down the street. His name is, uh, Grassy Green?"

"You don't want to wait till after class?" Catherine said. "And we don't need to see your dealer, silly. I got some at home. I live nearby."

Wait, what?

"Wait, what?"

"I mean, your daughter paid all that money for the class. You should at least stick through the first one."

"Are you not doing the scene?" Shantanu whispered, realizing maybe he'd missed some rule about initiations.

"Are we doing a scene?" Catherine said. "So you didn't just ask me to dinner?"

"I did!" Shantanu said, raising his voice, causing the nearest pair to look at him. "But I was doing improv! I was pretending."

"Ah." Catherine sat back in her chair, sighing.

"I'm sorry," Shantanu said. "I should've clarified that I was starting a scene."

Catherine guffawed.

"Shantanu, calm down, man," she said, further mystifying him. "I knew you were doing improv. I was just fucking with you."

"You're very confusing," Shantanu said, with a mixture of irritation and amusement. "I don't think I like improv very much."

"Nah, you're good, let's do a real scene," Catherine said.

Before Shantanu began again, Catherine held up her hand.

"It's too bad, though," Catherine said.

"What is?"

"That you didn't mean to ask me out to dinner," Catherine said. "If you actually were asking, I would have gone."

◇

"You've lost it," Mitali said, her head nuzzled on Neesh's chest. "How would that even work?"

Neesh reached for his T-shirt on the floor, which was in a pile with the rest of his clothes, along with Mitali's.

"You'd need, I'm guessing, twenty grand," Neesh said. "A producer. A director. Six cast members. Crazy doesn't mean impossible. You could do it at a black box theater."

"Where would we get twenty thousand? Or a producer? And any of the other things you mentioned? And who would come?"

"We'd figure it out," Neesh said. Mitali reached over to the thermostat next to her queen-sized bed and turned up the temperature before she buried herself more under the covers.

"You don't just *figure this out*," Mitali said. "You can't just put on a play. It's not like a television. You don't press a button and it turns on."

"Why?"

"What do you mean why?"

"Tell me why we can't do this," Neesh said.

"We can't! Who has the time for this? I haven't even seen a play! Not a professional one. Keya was the theatrical one. I'm not creative."

"You're a web producer. You write copy and shit. That's creative," Neesh said.

"That doesn't make me—who is that guy? The *Hamilton* dude," Mitali said.

"Lin-Manuel Miranda," Neesh said.

"Yeah, him. And you haven't answered the key question yet."

Mitali heard the wail of a police siren outside in the thick of night, speeding by her apartment. Whenever she heard one, she always tensed. An hour before Officer Giggenbach came knocking, Mitali saw a police car speeding by the Hillcrest Drive house. She always wondered if that was one of the cars responding to Keya. Now, most times she saw a police car, she wondered what life it was on its way to disrupt. What families were about to be split? Who would have to start thinking about a funeral? Who would have to start thinking about picking up the pieces? Would someone leave them on the ground and move on, or ignore them? Or both?

"What's the key question?" Neesh asked.

"Why? Why should we do this? What's the reason?"

Neesh pushed himself up, put his back against the bed frame, and brought his knees to his chest. He brought the comforter up to his chin and began chewing on it.

"Stop chewing on my comforter!" Mitali pulled it out of Neesh's mouth. It was characteristics like this that Mitali found amusing. But beyond that, Mitali found Neesh's reliability attractive. He always called when he said he would call. He never canceled on dates. Neesh was funny, but didn't *know* he was funny.

When Neesh looked at Mitali, he made her feel safe and cared for. She liked that he had taught himself origami at the rehearsal studio, and the joy he found in drumming. It was a kind of joy she had never found in anything herself. Mitali was able to be vulnerable around him. Sure, he seemed like a lost soul—he really had *no* friends? In *New York City* of all places?—but Mitali had begun to sense he was the type of person who revealed himself at his own pace, often when he didn't even realize. Those moments made Mitali feel a sort of accomplishment, that she had reached him when no one else could. Besides, Mitali felt lighter around him. And that lightness made her feel a way she hadn't in years, if ever.

"Well, did you read the play?" Neesh asked.

"Yes."

"And what did you think?"

Mitali's eyes drifted to the picture frame on top of the wooden dresser across the room. It was of her and Keya from when they were both in middle school. The frame was the only thing on top of the dresser, as if it was a shrine. She had her arms around her younger sister, on that shoddy lawn her father had long cultivated. Mitali's room was often a mess. But never the top of the dresser.

"Not that I have much experience with reading plays or anything, but I thought it was pretty good," Mitali said. "She was very talented."

"That's the reason," Neesh said. "It's raw. It has potential. But if we edit it the right way, it could be great. We don't need any other reason. There's your why."

"It is way more efficient, appropriate even, for us to take a big pile of money and light it on fire."

"Maybe that could be part of the second act."

"Why do *you* want to do this? Why do you care?" Mitali said.

He pondered it, and she reached up and stroked the stubble on Neesh's face. Neesh pulled the comforter back towards his mouth.

"There was a line in the play about cosmic forces," Neesh said. "It stuck with me. Cosmic forces. I loved it, man. Let me tell you. I feel them inside me. Last summer, before we met, I thought about blowing all my savings and renting a boat or some shit. And then just rowing until I couldn't go any further. Maybe some lifeguard would come rescue me."

"Jesus, Neesh."

Neesh sprang up.

"I didn't do it, obviously. I couldn't afford to rent a boat. But I feel that same connection to *this*." He turned to her, completely serious. "For years, I've felt insignificant, like I was floating from one day to the next. Just like Preethi. And then you came into my life. And then this play. I don't believe in God. But this play entered our lives to be put on. You know how? Cosmic forces. This is my rowboat. Sometimes—"

"The planets and stars align exactly as you need them to," Mitali answered.

She smiled, surprised at herself and slightly embarrassed for finishing Neesh's sentence.

"That's exactly right," Neesh said. "Honestly, I don't have much going on in my life. It's you and a desk. And I miss theater. This could be a way back in. And this could be something for us to do together. Or not. I don't know. Let's be the universe in ecstatic motion."

◇

Next to Shantanu's bedroom closet door was the slightly askew painting of New Orleans that he had purchased from a gallery after a stroll through the French Quarter. He had only been to the city once, for a conference years ago. Chaitali was delighted by the vibrant depiction of Bourbon Street and insisted on placing it right next to the closet so it could be one of the first things she'd see every morning. He paused briefly, and for the first time in years, he straightened it on the wall.

His closet was mostly empty, in part because it was meant for two people. There were two black suits. A hanger full of mediocre ties, including the Dilbert tie that Keya had gifted him once as a joke, to make light of his stiff nature. *Daddy Dilbert,* Keya called him as she made him try it on. It looked terrible. Then there was a plaid shirt. And another plaid shirt. More plaid shirts. *I have this many plaid button-downs?* Two pairs of jeans and four khakis. There was a trio of sweaters on the opposite end from the suits: all varying shades of mustard. It was missing all of Chaitali's floral dresses and *salwar kameezes.*

This was the first time since Mitali's college graduation that Shantanu remembered putting any effort into picking out an outfit. Even the commencement ceremony was easier because all he did was put on one of his two suits. But for a first date? Shantanu hadn't been on one of those in almost three decades. He settled on Plaid Shirt No. 3 and Khaki Pants No. 2. *Is a tie too much? A tie is too much. Is this even a date? It's just lunch before an improv class.* He had never ironed anything in his life, but these clothes sorely needed it. Shantanu would hang them up as he showered, he decided, and let the steam press the clothes into an appropriate condition for human interaction. Shantanu looked in the stained bathroom mirror like he looked in the closet, as if he was taking a long-overdue inventory.

"I guess steam only gets the wrinkles out of your clothes and not your face, huh?" he said to himself, a habit he'd picked up from spending so much time alone. He ran his hand over the bags underneath his eyes and then straightened to suck in his stomach.

"It's not great, but it's the best I've got," he told himself. His showers were getting longer by the week; the steam soothed his aching joints. Now, the steam was about to pull double duty. Before getting into his car, he knocked on Geoff Bocchino's door.

"Shantanu, do you know what time it is?" Geoff was still wearing pajamas.

"Time for me to smell like something that isn't a mid-life crisis," Shantanu responded dryly. Geoff came back with a bottle of Drakkar Noir that his son had given him.

"Happy hunting," Geoff said.

Now shaven and clean smelling, he sped up Route 18 towards New Brunswick. When "Gimme Shelter" by the Rolling Stones, his favorite song, came on 105.5, he turned up the volume.

As the Stones blared, his chest tightened and his breathing labored into a wheeze. Was he dying? He pulled the car over and shut off the radio just as Mick Jagger crooned the climax of the song. *It's just a shot away. It's just a shot away.* He missed his old life, that was all. The normalcy. Being *Daddy Dilbert.*

He thought back to his visits to Kalpana's condominium and her placing hands on his head, *Durga, Durga* now ringing through his thoughts.

He opened all the windows in the car and drew in deep breaths.

His phone buzzed. Shantanu checked. It was a text from Catherine.

Looking forward to lunch. Can I get a suggestion for a conversation topic? Anything at all for our next scene? I will "Yes, and . . ."

Shantanu slapped himself. *Get it together.*

◇

Shantanu had picked an Italian restaurant near the theater, Gianni's, that he'd been meaning to try for decades. Shantanu would often drive by the restaurant when leaving work, but it never occurred to him to stop and actually eat there. *Today will be all about trying new things.* Catherine was already waiting for Shantanu when he arrived. Her hair was curly instead of straight, but her green eyes seemed as penetrating as ever.

"I'm always early, don't mind me," Catherine said by way of greeting. She took her noise-canceling headphones off. Catherine reached for a hug, which Shantanu awkwardly accepted. For the last fifteen minutes, Shantanu had deliberated on how to greet Catherine and had not settled on an answer. There was no such difficulty, it seemed, on Catherine's part.

"You weren't wearing this cologne last week," Catherine said. Shantanu liked that her voice constantly sounded like she had just awoken from a nap, but he was slightly embarrassed by her cologne comment. "You're good. I've smelled worse," she added.

At the table, the waitress, with a smile that had to be inauthentic, asked if they wanted something to drink outside of water.

"I don't drink," Catherine said. She clenched a gray wool shawl closer to her. "It's cold in here. Any chance we can do something about the heat?"

"Of course," the waitress said. "And you?"

Shantanu was slightly relieved that Catherine didn't order alcohol.

"Water is fine, thank you," Shantanu said.

The waitress nodded and winked at Shantanu before walking away, to which Shantanu had to stop himself from rolling his eyes.

"For me, it's about the taste," Catherine said, her green eyes piercing enough that they seemed to bore into Shantanu. "I never liked the taste of booze."

"I don't drink either. Well, not anymore."

"Weed is much better," Catherine said. Shantanu didn't know how to respond. He had never smoked pot. She caught the look on his face.

"You'd think at forty-three, I'd be better at not saying awkward shit on a first date," Catherine said.

Shantanu smiled. She confirmed this was a date.

"I haven't gone on a first date in thirty years," Shantanu said.

"I've never gone out with an Indian guy," Catherine said.

"We're just like the brochure says, I promise," Shantanu said. "How am I doing so far?"

"Like you feel you shouldn't be here," Catherine said.

"I do want to be here," Shantanu said, caught slightly off guard.

"It's cool," Catherine said. "I've gone on dates with divorcés before. Sometimes there's guilt. Especially when there are kids."

Shantanu reached for the inquisitive nature within himself. This was the part that reflexively pushed him to question the illogical that had served him well in academia.

"But why are *you* here? I'm divorced. I'm on the wrong side of fifty. And I look like it too. You're none of those things."

"Are you asking me why we are going out?"

The waitress returned with glasses of water.

"What would you two like for lunch?" she said cheerily.

Catherine ordered the eggplant parm, Shantanu the spaghetti and meatballs, with red pepper flakes on the side.

"There's more than one way to age gracefully, man," Catherine said. "It takes a lot for someone our age to show up to an improv class. And you did it. Gift or not. Whatever shit you have going on, it tells me you're open to living life again. I like that. You could've regifted the class."

Am I that easy to read?

"Also, I looked you up," Catherine said. "Seems like you do some interesting work, Dr. Das."

"You what?"

"Not a lot of people named Shantanu in New Jersey, believe it or not. You come up on Google. We gotta update your headshot, though. Someone at the college must have a camera. You didn't google me?"

"No! I don't even know your last name."

"Yeah, you really haven't gone on a date in a long time. This is what we do today. I had to make sure you weren't the Rutgers Strangler or something."

"Well, I'm not the Rutgers Strangler," Shantanu said.

"That's exactly what the Rutgers Strangler would want me to think." Shantanu chortled.

"What would I find if I googled you?"

"Not much. My last name is Pullman, by the way. I'm not on social media, except for LinkedIn. I grew up in Perth. My dad was American, mum was Australian. Moved to California when I was fourteen. Came here to go to NYU for art history. What a waste of money that tuition was. I'm an event planner in the city, but I live here in New Brunswick."

"My therapist lived in Australia for a while," Shantanu said. *Did I really just say that?*

"You see a therapist?"

"Recently, yeah."

"How do you feel about that?"

"He asks me that all the time," Shantanu said. "That question never gets easier. How come you never married?"

Catherine took a gulp of water.

"There was this guy I was with for a long time. Maybe ten years. Have you ever heard of Nate Eyre?"

Shantanu shook his head.

"He's an artist. Did that big mural in Red Hook that the mayor loves. I thought we might get married, but it never happened. We were always on and off. On and off. On and off," she said, waving her fingers as if she was a conductor.

"By the time I had finally had enough of his shit—the cheating, the gaslighting, the jealousy—I was in my forties."

"Sorry."

"Nah, it's cool," Catherine said. "It's time for something else. No kids, though. Ran out of time for that."

"There's medicine," Shantanu said tentatively. "There's other stuff you can do."

Shantanu knew he was being intrusive.

"No kids for me. Some can end up giving you great Christmas gifts, like an improv class. Some end up like Nate: miserable, snake-bitten fucks. It's not for me."

Shantanu considered whether this would be the appropriate time to tell Catherine about Keya. *Is it too early?*

"Some end up another way," Shantanu said, feeling crass.

"What do you mean?"

"I take that back," Shantanu said, his breathing getting heavier. He closed his eyes and silently apologized to Keya. "I shouldn't have said it like that."

I didn't mean to bring this up. I'm not ready to do this. But how can I avoid it?

"Oh man," Catherine said in a low voice, looking away. "I know about your daughter. I found the article in the *Asbury Park Press*. Sorry."

Shantanu was not entirely surprised. He knew that a Google search of himself would easily turn up that piece. He wished he had someone's hands to hold. Even though he was divorced, he felt like his hands still belonged to Chaitali.

And yet, there were all those nights he was cold to her. Too drunk to take her hands. Too cold to make her feel welcome in his life. Too angry at himself to keep from being angry at her. Too remote to keep her from going to Jahar.

"Are you here?" Catherine cut in, snapping Shantanu out of his thoughts. Then she literally started snapping with her fingers. All Shantanu could see were her eyes, perpetually probing him. "If you'd rather think about your shit or whatever else, I can leave."

Shantanu was thrown off by Catherine's directness. Though another part of him—the indirect part—liked it.

"I am," Shantanu said. "I'm here. I guess I'm the one with the 'awkward shit' on a first date."

"We've all got pain, man. Just a question of what you're going to do with it," Catherine said.

"Can we talk about something else?"

"The chair recognizes the distinguished professor from New Jersey."

"What were you listening to when I walked in?"

"On my phone? Oh. *Exile on Main St.*"

Shantanu straightened up from his hunch.

"Say that again?"

"The Rolling Stones. Don't make me whitesplain the Rolling Stones to you."

"I *love* the Rolling Stones," he chimed in with a grin. "That is my favorite album. 'Rocks Off' is my favorite song. I love the horns at the end. I could talk about this for hours."

"We only have one before class. Let's use it wisely. You ever see them live?"

"Yes. In the nineties. Madison Square Garden. I took Chai—" Shantanu coughed. "I saw them live, yeah."

"I went in 1998. Best concert I've ever been to."

"I went to that run too! Best concert I've ever seen! Someone at work sold them to me for like five hundred dollars each. When my daughters weren't looking, sometimes I'd do the Jagger hip thrust. My neighbor Geoff has all the albums on vinyl. I used to go over and make him play them for me."

"Bet you can't do that hip thrust anymore, old man."

"You would win that bet. You should've seen my mother's reaction whenever I'd make her listen to 'Satisfaction.' She'd say, 'This feels like anybody could do this.' I'd say, 'Exactly!'"

Shantanu sensed a pulsating energy. He felt free. Younger. For the first time in who knew how long, Shantanu was awake, like a bear emerging from hibernation. Still, he was who he was. *Look at the data. This is almost assuredly temporary. She is sure of herself, and you are not. She is pleasing to look at, and you are not. You are hastily building a house of cards.*

Even still, as Shantanu was about to launch into more discussion, the perky waitress came by with their orders.

"I'm glad to see you guys are having fun!" the waitress said, before walking away.

"We are having fun, aren't we?" Catherine said. "All it took was you bringing up 'Mick Jagger Hip Thrust.'"

As Shantanu dug into his plate of pasta, he found himself silently wishing that the next hour would stretch as long as it could. Catherine reached across the table and took one of Shantanu's hands, much to his surprise. Across the room, their waitress, who was keeping a close eye on this date, smiled watching this interaction. When their hands touched, Shantanu felt . . . solace. Catherine was a stranger, and yet she felt familiar. She held his hand as if being distant was not an option.

◇

JUNE 2011

"A restaurant that isn't a chain?" Keya muttered as she typed "restaurants in Howell, NJ" into Google on the Das desktop computer. "Good luck to me." This was a tall order, as Keya pointed out to her parents. The spots in town that weren't chains were not really better than the spots that were.

"By the time we've driven by an Applebee's, Ruby Tuesday's, Chevy's, or anything else that is anywhere else, we'll be too tired to find something. It's the best thing Howell has going for itself: 'We Have Things You Can Find Everywhere Else,'" Keya quipped.

"Yes, but today is a special day," Chaitali rebutted.

For Shantanu and Chaitali, the familiarity of this middle-class New Jersey suburb was its appeal. Howell was a safe, uncontroversial suburb for families, the kind where adventure was rare by design, and that was the case particularly for culinary establishments.

So it was difficult, on the humid evening of Mitali's high school graduation, to pick a place to go for a celebratory dinner. It had to be within a thirty-minute drive so Mitali could attend a friend's party that night, which Shantanu did not want Mitali going to. After all, he had been eighteen once. He knew what went on at these things, but Chaitali convinced him otherwise.

"You have to let her go," Chaitali had said, as the names of Mitali's classmates were announced from a podium on the football field. She was using the flimsy graduation program as a fan.

"I don't have to like it," Shantanu had responded, wiping sweat from his face.

The family picked the Ivy House for a postgraduation dinner, which Keya found on Google earlier that day. As far as fine dining in Howell went, it was top of the class. It wasn't a chain. You could get a half-decent steak. It was a half-decent place to watch a football game on Sundays and guzzle down half-decent wings. In Howell, half-decent was the best you could do, so that was where the Dases went for a special dinner. The walls of the Ivy House were filled with pictures of Howell sports teams the restaurant had sponsored. Mitali was in one of the photos—a middle school softball team—which she excitedly pointed out before they were seated at their booth. Kalpana grimaced at the smell inside the restaurant.

"I should have just cooked," Kalpana grumbled. "It smells terrible in here."

"Those are ribs, *Shomadidi*," Keya said, laughing. "Have you ever had barbecue food?"

"Fifty years in this country and what I've noticed most is that Americans eat like pigs," Kalpana said. "I should open up my own restaurant. People would learn real food."

"We eat the pigs too," Shantanu said.

"*Eesh*," Kalpana said, as Chaitali pinched Shantanu.

After the drinks arrived—ginger ales for the daughters, a beer for Shantanu, iced teas for Kalpana and Chaitali—Chaitali raised a glass.

"We will not all get to be together very often when you leave for Rowan," Chaitali said. "We're very proud of you, Mitali."

"Here, here!" Shantanu said. "But, *sona*, are you sure you don't want to go pre-med?"

"Stop it, Baba!" Keya said. Shantanu put his arms up with a smile.

"You're next, Keya!" Mitali said, still wearing her navy-blue graduation gown. "Have you thought about what college you want to go to?"

"No. Maybe I'll go abroad or something. Or take a gap year," Keya said. "I think I'd like to become a writer."

"You have the grades to go to Harvard!" Mitali said.

"And be a snob? Thanks but no thanks, *didi*," Keya said.

"Can one of you please do something to get paid? You want to become a writer. Mitali hasn't even picked a major." Shantanu smirked. "Girls, our retirement homes won't pay for themselves."

"Speaking of which, Baba, I've saved up eight hundred dollars for a car," Keya said.

"You're too young for a car," Shantanu said.

"You said I can have whatever car I want with my own money," Keya said. "So I have my own money."

"You can't argue with the logic, Shanti. All that already from the ice cream shop?" Chaitali said. "Impressive."

"Mitali, now that you're officially a grown woman, it's time to talk about something more important: who you will marry," Kalpana said, immediately eliciting a horrified reaction from the two granddaughters.

"*Shomadidi*, no," Mitali said. "Just no."

"I'm happy to find someone for you," Kalpana said.

"No, no, no," Mitali said, covering her ears. "We are not talking about this."

"Actually, yes," Keya said. "Don't you think *Shomadidi* should pick?"

"What about that nice Justin boy from senior prom?" Chaitali asked.

"No, I can't hear you," Mitali said, fingers still in her ears.

"Neither of you need to date. Ever. Anyone," Shantanu said, recalling Amitava's restrictions on his social life as a teenager. He was easier on Mitali and Keya, Shantanu thought, but he had his limits. Shantanu waved his finger exaggeratedly.

"Maybe when you are both fifty and I am dead. Or if you finish medical school. Whatever happens first. Please just focus on your studies."

"You're being a Daddy Dilbert, Baba," Keya said, prompting laughter from the table.

◇

Mitali sat on her bed, staring at the lonely picture frame of Keya on her dresser. On her bed, there were several scattered note cards with bulleted, handwritten notes on them—Neesh's suggestions. Mitali also had a Word document on her MacBook Air, with more prompts in case she needed more data. From the frame, her eyes journeyed to the time on her computer: 6:55 . . . 6:56 . . . 6:57 . . . 6:58 . . . 6:59 . . . *I have no idea how this is going to go.* Until finally . . . 7:00 p.m.

Mitali clicked the Skype app using her keyboard and dialed two numbers she knew by heart. Soon, three dubious faces appeared on the laptop screen.

"Hi, Ma. Baba. *Shomadidi,*" Mitali said.

Shantanu and Kalpana appeared in the same box. They were together at her condominium. Chaitali was in her kitchen. All of them mumbled hellos.

"What's wrong, Meeti?" Chaitali asked.

"Nothing is wrong," Mitali said. "How are you guys?"

"You asked us to be here for a mysterious group video chat and we haven't spoken since Christmas. Of course I'm worried."

Seeing the concerned looks on her parents' faces reminded Mitali of that last family conversation with Keya, and it occurred to her that maybe her parents thought they were about to have another one on those same lines. *I wonder how they would react today. Surely, after what happened, it would be with kindness. But Keya thought that too.*

This talk was about something different.

"Baba, you look different."

"I do?"

Chaitali leaned closer to her computer's camera.

"Yes, Shantanu. You do. You're shaven. You got a haircut," she said. "You look good. And what sweater is that?"

Shantanu sighed. "It's new."

"You went *shopping*?!" Mitali yelped.

"You haven't gone shopping since right after you came out of the womb, and even then it was for another plaid shirt!" Chaitali joined in with her teasing.

In the background, Jahar moved about the kitchen, occasionally sneaking glances at the laptop.

"When you two are done, can we get to why we're here?"

Shantanu had a serious face, but if Mitali didn't know better, she thought she noticed the subtlest of grins pulling at the corners of his mouth, almost one of pride.

"My son looks fine," Kalpana said in an icy remark directed towards Chaitali. "He has always looked fine."

"Of course, Ma," Chaitali said. "I did not mean offense."

"I am not your Ma anymore—"

"Please, everyone, listen to me," Mitali jumped in. "Ma, Baba, the play that Keya wrote. I've been reading it. And it's really good."

Chaitali's lips pursed. Everyone was silent.

"I'd like to put it on. I've been doing some research. It would cost thirty thousand dollars for roughly three nights at a theater that seats sixty. We'd need to hire a director and six actors. Plus, rent out rehearsal space. And some extra money for flyers, that kind of thing. I need your help."

There was no reaction. It was as if she had hurled a concrete block against a brick wall.

"Did you all hear me?" Mitali said.

Still nothing. Finally, after what seemed to be an eternity of silence, Kalpana broke the quiet.

"*Bechara.* I miss her too."

This being the initial reaction immediately frustrated Mitali. She was prepared for there to be immediate resistance. But she found her *shoma-didi*'s tone to be patronizing. *Of course I miss her. But I'm serious about this.*

"What are you talking about?" Shantanu cut in. "What does that mean? 'Put it on'?"

"I know what I sound like. But I've looked into this. We'd essentially be renting out a theater, just like you would rent out, say, a conference room. Or a Chuck E. Cheese for a birthday party. And we would make the play happen."

Shantanu shook his head in disbelief. Chaitali was still expressionless, but she looked away from the camera and began rubbing her temples. Mitali thought of how Neesh had first broached the subject in her bed.

"Tell me why we can't do this," Mitali said.

"This isn't Chuck E. Cheese. There's a lot more that goes into making a play," Shantanu said.

"How do you know? You've never seen a professional one," Mitali shot back.

"Exactly. This is not logical. I don't know what goes into making a play. I just saw Keya in that one in high school. Also, that Broadway one. What was it, Chai?"

"It wasn't a Broad— Never mind. *Stomp.*"

"Right, that one. We couldn't even put that on. That's just a bunch of people bashing trash cans."

"Baba, you like data, right? You like when people do research? Let's pretend this is a dissertation. And I have to defend it."

And if that didn't work, she could always try guilt—she was, after all, their only remaining daughter.

Shantanu sighed. "How do we do this? What are the steps?"

"My . . . friend will help. But the first step is coming up with thirty thousand dollars. We can start a Kickstarter. We can find investors. Maybe we can reach out to some *mashis* and *kakus*. We can throw a fundraiser at the house. *Shomadidi*, you'd cook for that, right? Everyone loves your *batta* chicken."

Kalpana smiled, which put Mitali at ease, although she still wondered if Kalpana was being patronizing.

"Of course I would for you, *sona.*"

"Then what?" Shantanu said.

"While we're raising the money, my friend and I can work on the script. And reach out to potential directors and actors. We can put up ads. We'd have to find non-Equity performers."

"What is 'Equity'?" Chaitali asked. *Okay, so maybe Ma is on board?*

"The actors union. We couldn't afford them," Mitali said. "And then I can find a venue."

She reached for one of her note cards and flashed the handwriting to her camera lens.

"Look, here are a bunch to start: There's one at NYU. There are a couple downtown."

"You make it sound so easy," Kalpana said.

"*None* of this is going to be easy. But let's do it for her. Keya wrote a beautiful play. The least we can do is help bring it to life. You're right, *Shomadidi*. I *do* miss her. I can't bring her back. But we can do this *for* her."

"Is this for Keya? Or is this for you?" Chaitali said.

"It's for all of us," Mitali said.

Mitali could see Shantanu stroke his chin in thought.

"Baba, please. We all made mistakes with Keya. We'll never make all of it right. I can't do this without you guys. I don't want to."

Her father was considering the proposal. He just needed one more push. And then her mother would come along.

"Ma, do you remember that one year that Keya ran the snack stand at Durga Puja and made more money in six hours than it had at the rest of the puja combined?" Mitali said. It was only then that she realized her mother was wiping a tear away from her face.

"I do."

"This play would honor her. We owe it to her."

"Chai, what do you think?" Shantanu said.

Mitali couldn't help but notice that Chaitali had barely been looking into the camera. Judging from her demeanor, she found the whole conversation to be distasteful, infuriating, and traumatic all at once.

"I will have *no* part of this," Chaitali said with a sudden ferocity. "This play is not *ours* to stage. It wasn't even *ours* to read. I feel bad enough that I read it. I hope none of you read her letters. They were hers, not ours. They were private."

Now it was Mitali's turn to have her silence fill the video chat. She did not know how to respond, and her note cards didn't have the answers. She felt rejected, just as she did when Chaitali told her about the divorce. She felt a simmering rage about not being able to reach her mother— once again—like she could Neesh. She saw Chaitali's background—the nice house, occasionally Jahar fiddling about, and felt a new round of resentment for the new life her mother had built, and her unwillingness to be tied to her old one.

"The play should be buried. Everything about Keya should stay buried. And we want the whole world to know about our failures as a family? *My* failure as a mother? Those parents in the play are *us*. Why would we humiliate ourselves like that? And pay thirty thousand dollars for it? To relive our shortcomings day after day? Mitali, you are asking us to punish ourselves. We need to move on. As a family."

"As a family?" Mitali said, matching her mother's indignation. "How can you use those words? You left this family to start a new one. As if you were leaving for a new job. But wait! You still have your job at the library. It's just your family you swapped out."

"Mitali, *sona*, don't speak to your ma like that," Kalpana chided, but Mitali was heated by her mother's reaction.

"How dare you?" Chaitali said. "I've suffered too. And where were you when my suffering was at its worst? Keya would not have wanted us to wallow. And you don't call me either. Who is turning their backs on who?"

"None of us know what Keya would have wanted!"

"Exactly," Chaitali said. "So why go on this preposterous expedition?" Kalpana shook her head furiously at the laptop.

"Everyone, stop arguing," Shantanu said. "Just stop. I think we can all agree that Keya would not have wanted that."

Mitali and Chaitali fell quiet. In Chaitali's background, Jahar strolled by again, with a clear look of curiosity.

"Chaitali, you are right," Shantanu said. "Keya is not coming back, no matter how hard we try."

Mitali's face fell.

"A play like this would be extraordinarily difficult and has a high chance of failing," Shantanu said. "I'm just being honest with you, *sona*. I know how badly you want to do this. But how many people try to put on plays that even know what they're doing? I'm guessing a lot."

"I get it, Baba. I don't need the speech."

"But I'd be willing to help."

"*Kee?*"

"Yes, I would. However, Mitali, your mother brings up a good point. This play is not ours to put on. And it wasn't just Keya's."

Mitali's head jerked up. *Of course. How could I have been that stupid?*

"Shit," Mitali said.

"I ran into her mother at the store the other day," Shantanu said.

"Really?" Chaitali and Mitali said in unison.

"How did she seem?" Mitali asked.

"Honestly, I don't know," Shantanu said. "It was a strange conversation. But I'm willing to raise the thirty thousand dollars to do this. I can't make promises about whether I can get there. However, the play had a second author. And we need to find out what her intent was before we move forward."

"This is a bad idea," Chaitali said. "Mitali, I love you. But I can't be a part of this."

"It's okay, Ma," Mitali said, now regretting her harshness. Guilt could work both ways. Mitali may have been their only daughter, but Chaitali was Mitali's only mother, too. Still, her father—her amazing, confusing father; she found her affection soaring for him at that moment. It was then that Kalpana looked into the camera and muttered, "*Durga, Durga.*"

"So how do we get in touch with Pamela?" Mitali said.

Shantanu thought for a moment.

"I think I know where to find her."

◊

There was not much of a lunch rush at the Ivy House on this Saturday, so Shantanu was able to pick the exact same booth he sat in years prior, the night of Mitali's high school graduation. On his way in, he was pleasantly surprised to see the picture of Mitali's softball team in the exact same place. The plazas swapped out their shops often, Shantanu thought, but here was one place that still seemed familiar years later.

Shantanu had felt like a renovated home recently. He no longer woke to emptiness. Twice, in fact, he had woken up next to Catherine in her two-bedroom loft in New Brunswick. He didn't notice his emerging wrinkles as much. He was shaving more. Shantanu had energy he didn't recognize. *Thirty thousand dollars. Where will we ever get that? I don't have that kind of money. I can't go to the Bengalis for this. We're barely part of the community anymore. I stopped going to the pujas. And Ma is too old to be a fundraiser.*

A waitress came to pour Shantanu a glass of water.

"Excuse me, can I ask you a question?" Shantanu said. "Is Pamela here?"

"Pamela Moore? Yeah, you a friend?" the waitress asked suspiciously.

"Sort of. Do you mind getting her? I have something that belongs to her. I'll take a cheeseburger and fries, too," Shantanu said.

The waitress nodded, still eyeing him with caution. Shantanu was skittish. He wondered if Pamela's mother told her about their chance encounter a while back. He also wondered whether Pamela would even remember him. They hadn't spoken since before Keya died. Soon, a petite brunette woman in a ponytail appeared. She had a tattoo of a large dove on her left forearm and a streak of blue hair, accentuated by her all-black uniform.

"Hi, Deidre said you have something of mine?" Pamela said. Her voice was a bit on the thin and squeaky side. As she spoke, her lip and nose rings became more prominent. And then she fully registered Shantanu. Her face went from the mask of a professional waiter to displaying shock, which morphed into revulsion, and then back to shock. There was incomprehension mixed in too. From across the restaurant, Deidre was keeping an eye on the encounter.

"Hi, Pamela." Shantanu saw the look on her face and found it unsettling. If he was apprehensive about seeing Pamela after all this time, surely she would be that and more. They had both been different people when they last encountered each other in what seemed like a lifetime ago. He should have expected this reaction, Shantanu thought. Once again, he had drastically misread the situation.

"I don't know if you remember, but I'm Shantanu."

"I remember who you are, Mr. Das," Pamela said, her voice cool. "How can I help you?"

Suddenly, Shantanu missed the cheery waitress from his first date with Catherine.

"I was wondering if we could talk," Shantanu said.

"I don't think that's a good idea." Pamela shifted to an angry whisper. "Can I get you a drink?"

This was the reaction that Shantanu had expected from Pamela's mother, and it made him wilt on the inside.

"No, it's okay," Shantanu said. "I came here to speak to you."

"You wasted your time."

"I saw your mother a while ago at the grocery store," Shantanu said, desperate to keep the conversation going. "She said you worked here."

Pamela suddenly looked panicked. "Did you tell her anything?"

"No, of course not."

Pamela breathed a sigh of relief. "Okay. Well, let Deidre know if you need anything."

Pamela turned to walk away.

"I found the box," Shantanu said. "The one with the notes. And the play."

She stopped in her tracks.

"I don't know what box you're talking about. Take care, Mr. Das," Pamela said in a hard whisper. She walked away, faster than she arrived.

NINE

If Neesh's eyes were open—*truly* open—he would have recognized the high tides creeping towards him. They were stalking the former drummer slowly but surely, waiting for the right moment to drown him when it was too late for him to see.

He was back at Jared's apartment with another, larger envelope. This time, he was grateful to be there since he didn't have air-conditioning at his own apartment. In the six months since he'd run into Sandeep at Jared's, Neesh had become much more proficient at selling fake commodities. He was either at concert venues with fake tickets, running falsified checks on Jared's behalf, or walking around the city trying to find hourly work. He was most successful at the first two, not so much the latter.

"Neesh, my man, this is good," Jared said, as he counted the bills again on the bed. "I'm already at two grand? Damn."

"Yeah, it's good out there," Neesh said, slightly ashamed at how skilled he'd become at cheating and that it was paying off. Neesh didn't admit it to Jared, but he was terrified: at the prospect of getting caught and at the thought of accepting his life as a petty con man. He could have tried cleaning up the mess he made, but instead, he had doubled down and created a bigger one. Though with all the cash coming in, he hardly realized this. He was not as worried about paying rent anymore. Neesh, somewhere deep inside him, still distrusted Jared and Sandeep, but he ignored his misgivings. *They've made the most of being dealt unfair hands*, Neesh convinced himself, regardless of whether it was true or not. They had come through for him in a way his father never did. And besides, they seemed sure of themselves and their plans. Most importantly, Neesh had no other choice, at least from his vantage point. Neesh sold himself a story about this life—that he needed this—and it pushed him to be as close to at peace with his choices as he had ever been.

Neesh lost himself in these thoughts as he admired the bookshelf against a wall in Jared's studio. It was stacked with classic titles like *The Great Gatsby* and *Lolita*.

"Those are from the old store," a preoccupied Jared said.

There was a knock on the door, which interrupted Neesh's thoughts. He swung it open and saw Sandeep there, standing next to a man almost as tall and burly as him, but with a buzz cut and tattoos up the length of his arm.

"Yo, bro." Sandeep greeted Neesh with a knuckle pound and a hug. Jared still hadn't finished counting bills.

"Is that you, Hector?" Jared said without looking at the doorway.

"Yeah, man," Hector said. "It's good to see you."

"Hector, this is Neesh. Neesh, meet Hector," Sandeep said.

"You're the drummer," Hector said. "I heard you were on Broadway. I've always wanted to act."

Neesh and Hector shook hands. Hector walked over and sat in the reclining chair next to the windowsill with the picture frame. There was also a vase with obviously fake roses. *Is that new?* Neesh had never seen them before.

"Bro," Hector cackled. "You fake everything in life, and you can't even get real flowers?"

"They never die," Jared said as he finished counting. "Neesh, Hector is a security guard over at Javits."

"The convention center?" Neesh said. "I bet you see some interesting stuff. Expos and all that."

"We *all* do," Sandeep howled, holding his stomach.

"What's so funny?" Neesh said.

Sandeep and Jared exchanged looks. Jared nodded at Sandeep.

"There was a baseball card convention there the other day, like a month ago," Sandeep said. "And we went and ripped it."

"The biggest one in the city," Jared said.

"You stole from a baseball card show? What do you need with baseball cards?"

"See, this is why we didn't tell you," Sandeep said. "You would've rained on our parade. They're worth thousands. And of course, we weren't alone."

Sandeep winked at Hector, who grinned. Hector, it turned out, was adept at distracting multiple dealers at a time so that Jared and Sandeep could slip cards off the table. The three of them devised a system so that Hector could warn them when the other security guards were lurking nearby. And sometimes, Hector would take cards himself and hand them off to Jared and Sandeep, who wore multiple layers of shirts to discard, for the cameras that would inevitably catch them in the act.

"We didn't lift enough high-value stuff to make it worth it," Jared said. "We'll be lucky to get a thousand max for those. A Mike Mussina rookie card isn't exactly high-dollar stuff."

I'm not that *kind of thief,* Neesh thought to himself.

"Yeah, that's not my thing," he told the group, even though no one had asked. He was mostly talking to himself.

"I know," Jared said. "It's not our thing either. A one-off. We've got to do smarter shit than straight knockoffs. Hector, what did you want to see me about?"

"Are you sure about this being a one-off thing? Because there's an antiques expo coming to Javits next month. And let me tell you: this will be prime. It's going to be much bigger. More opportunities."

"No." Jared was firm. "Too much risk."

"Everything you do has risk," Hector said. "This is just a different type."

"What will be there?" Sandeep asked.

"Lots of shit," Hector said. "Furniture. Dishes. Ceramics. Watches. Jewelry."

"That *is* risky," Sandeep said, but Neesh caught the glimmer of temptation in his eyes.

"We couldn't take big stuff, obviously. But we could lift the smaller stuff, throw it in a backpack," Hector said.

"Did you say an antiques convention?" Neesh interrupted.

Hector nodded. The other three men in the room continued their conversation, but Neesh's mind drifted to being held at gunpoint, when his father did nothing but gaze at him with indifference. Those shattered dishes mattered to his father more than his son's well-being. When Neesh once asked his mother why his father was like this, she said that he considered their store his greatest creation. A way for him to defy all the people, including in his own family in India he had little use for, who had doubted him. Nothing else was as important to him, and she had accepted that.

And Neesh remembered how grudgingly Jigar came to his college graduation, only agreeing to do so at the urging of his mother. The gleeful way he withheld money to help Neesh with his move to New York. And the slaps. There were so many slaps.

Neesh went to expos just like these with Jigar, and watched his father deftly underpay or mark up trinkets to be sold. There was the one in Milwaukee, when Jigar sold a cracked gold locket to a pair of unsuspecting newlyweds. Jigar told them that while it was impossible to know for sure, he was "almost 100 percent positive" that the locket's provenance stretched back to the estate of David and Peggy Rockefeller.

Of course, Jigar had purchased it from another dealer who said that the crack came from him dropping it, and that while it was possibly from a Rockefeller collection, his own investigation showed that to be highly unlikely. Nevertheless, Jigar profited.

And it occurred to him: *I'm exactly that kind of thief.*

"Let's do it," Neesh said. "I want in."

The room fell silent.

"What?" Jared said.

"Let's take shit at the antiques expo. I know how they work. I know how to talk to the dealers."

Hector smiled, while Sandeep and Jared were not sure how to react.

"Why would you want to do this?" Jared asked, incredulous.

"My father always wanted me to get into the antiques business," Neesh said. "I can think of no better way."

"You're fucking nuts, Neesh," Sandeep laughed. "You didn't even want to be associated with us a while ago, and now you want to lead the charge to rob a convention center?"

"No way we're doing this," Jared said. "We're going on a rip because you hate your dad?"

"Call it fair market value," Neesh said, looking out at the East River view from Jared's window.

◇

Three lines is customary for something like this, Neesh told himself as he walked into the cavernous Javits Convention Center, stuffed at the edge of Manhattan's Hell's Kitchen neighborhood. He was briefly intimidated by its see-through glass exterior. The only hindrance to seeing the interior was the windowpanes, which made the building look like a series of cubes stacked on each other, with the blinding sun's reflection shooting back at pedestrians walking by. Neesh was already sweating. He had a backpack on, which was searched, and a security guard had run a wand over his body. Neesh was the last of the group to arrive. Jared and Sandeep had already been in the center, walking the aisles to scope out potential victims. Hector was keeping watch, walkie-talkie and all, near a stall for a merchant from Kansas City.

The targets, as the four of them had laid out, would be the smaller booths, the ones with one or two people running them. They would operate in pairs. If Neesh was at a booth, Hector, as a security guard, might approach the dealer and engage him or her in conversation, particularly about threats to steal. He would ask the dealer if they'd seen a man matching a certain description. Surely, dealers would want a thief caught.

While that conversation was happening, Neesh was to grab what he could and disappear into the crowd. Elsewhere, Jared and Sandeep would try something similar. One of them could start an argument with a dealer over price, something not uncommon at these events, while the other stole what they could. It's what worked at the baseball convention. The goal was to take small trinkets—jewelry, watches, figurines, and the like—and get away before the dealer noticed something was missing. They would target corner booths, out of view of security's line of sight, provided Hector was right about there being some blind spots. All of them were to wear inconspicuous clothing: thick glasses and a hoodie. Neesh had purchased hair pieces for Jared, Sandeep, and himself, in case surveillance cameras did catch them in the act. Holding the wigs took Neesh back to his *Rock of Ages* days, which only made him more sure he wanted to do this.

Neesh wove through the crowd for an hour to observe the layout. He had already seen a map that Hector provided the night before, but he was taken aback by the dozens of booths that seemed to line every row. Soon, it was time to make his move.

He found Hector standing next to a row of booths near the bathroom. Hector was wearing a walkie-talkie on his chest, along with a connected earpiece. They made eye contact. Hector moved his eyes to the row nearest him. This was the signal: *These patsies are yours.*

Neesh walked up to an elderly couple manning a table. The sign in front read MILLSTONE WATCHES. The address underneath said their store was located in Old Bridge, New Jersey. Neesh eyed the couple. They looked like the type Neesh would give fake checks to on a different day. There were no other customers standing at the booth, but plenty at the surrounding ones. *Perfect*, Neesh thought.

"Hello, son," a man with warm, friendly eyes said as Neesh approached. "Have a look at our watches?" On the table, there were several rows of pocket watches in glass cases.

"These ones are all made of gold," the man said. "Over there, silver."

"Can I take a closer look?" Neesh said.

The man unlocked two of the cases, and Hector made his approach.

"Excuse me, have you seen a white male wearing a turtleneck, maybe in his fifties, walking around?"

Neesh's hand began shaking, as the couple headed for the front corner of the table to talk to Hector. Neesh could hear Hector tell the couple that they were on the lookout for this turtleneck-wearing man. Apparently, he had ripped off some booths, from Hector's telling. Neesh reached for the door of the gold case, with his head turned away, his eyes on the lookout for nosy witnesses. He fumbled picking up several of the watches.

Some of them fell to the table, but Neesh was able to hold on to four and slip them into his backpack. He shut the door and reached for the keys, which the man had left on the table, and locked the case. His eyes darted left and right. It was time for him to disappear. He speed-walked to his left into the crowd.

Neesh was amped. He walked quickly by other tables and noticed that neither those manning the booths nor the customers strolling by were watching, so he grabbed more things. Sometimes they were worthless: pens, mugs, badges, business cards. But there were some successful lifts: a bronze pocket mirror, some gold pendants.

At the end of the row, Neesh saw a sight that caught his breath. It was a booth, not unlike the others, but there was more jewelry on this table than the others. A man who looked to be in his forties and a young boy were sitting behind the table, unbothered by any customers. The boy appeared to be playing some sort of video game as Neesh approached them.

"Hello, *bhai!*" the man said. His jolly tone reminded him of someone, as did his bald head. "We have everything you need right here. And for you, a discount. After all, you look like my son in five years. Isn't that right, Chittesh?"

Chittesh giggled at Neesh.

"No, *bapuji*. He's so big! I'm only seven!"

The man turned back to Neesh.

"He's named after my father. My name is Madhar. Madhar Gandhi," the man said. He ran his hand through Chittesh's hair. He put his hands up with a wide, exaggerated smile. "I know what you're thinking. Gandhi! But no relation! It would have been much easier to get a U.S. visa if I was related to *the* Gandhi. Don't you think? Are you Gujarati?"

Neesh nodded and began to feel dizzy. His breathing got heavier. Neesh was breaking the cardinal rule Jared had set out: *Keep moving. Don't stay in one aisle for long.* He didn't notice multiple figures headed towards this table, nor the hand that Madhar had extended for him to shake. Neesh stuffed the arm of his sweatshirt into his mouth and his leg began tapping the floor.

"*Bhai*, are you all right? You look flushed and you haven't said a word!" Madhar said. "Would you like some water?"

Neesh closed his eyes and saw the man with a gun to his head in Jigar's shop, felt his terror. He opened his eyes to see the young Chittesh eyeing him strangely. *Madhar is much leaner than my father*, Neesh thought.

He recalled being at similar booths growing up with Jigar, and the stress that Jigar wore on his face.

"Can we go now, *bapuji*?" Neesh would ask after hours at an empty stall.

"No, *dikro*, I have to sell more," Jigar said. "It was always silly of me to leave real estate behind. To build something of my own. It was supposed to be easy in this country. Nothing is easy for people like us."

Nothing is easy.

"*Bhai*, sit down. Sit down here." Madhar brought his own chair to the side of the table and guided Neesh to sit. Neesh did as he was told. Chittesh brought over a bottle of water.

"Good boy, Chittesh," Madhar said. "*Bhai*, your eyes don't look right. Perhaps we should call a medic."

"Excuse me, sir, can you come with us?" a man said suddenly. Neesh looked up to see a man with broad shoulders wearing the same polo shirt and earpiece that Hector was wearing, standing over him, apparently a colleague or one of Hector's supervisors. Hector stood next to him with a worried look. Down the aisle, even with the dozens of other attendees, Neesh could make out the elderly couple he had ripped off, staring intently at him.

"Are you a doctor?" Madhar said.

"No, sir," the man said.

"Then you can leave," Madhar said, his tone becoming more aggressive. "He's not bothering us."

"Can I get a look inside your bag?" the man said. Neesh looked at Hector's red face and his eyes conspicuously avoiding contact. Neesh realized the jig was up. The tide had come. All he could do was protect Hector now.

"Ah, of course," Madhar said. "A person darker than you *must* be a thief. Would you like to look through my things too? You should be ashamed of yourself."

"Uncle, thank you," Neesh said. "But I must go."

Madhar gave Neesh a look of confusion. And then, for a brief second, a flash of hurt.

As Neesh got up, he heard a gasp in the crowd.

"NOBODY MOVE!" Jared suddenly appeared with a gun pointed at the air.

Most of the attendees started running. But those nearest to the Gandhi table froze. Some nearby kneeled on the floor with hands up. Madhar ran for Chittesh and threw himself in front of his young son. Hector looked at Jared with horror.

"What the fuck?" Neesh muttered. He felt the same terror that he did back in high school at the store.

Where is Sandeep?

"Run," Jared directed Neesh. "Get out of here. GO!"

"I'm sorry, Uncle," Neesh said as he turned and bolted. He left the bag behind.

The bolt didn't last for long. Neesh heard a scream behind him. The security guard standing next to Hector had tackled Jared to the floor. As Neesh turned to look, Hector was half-heartedly helping pin Jared down. And then Neesh himself was thrown to the floor. All he could see was a glimpse of blue.

"Stay down. You're under arrest," Neesh heard a gruff voice say from somewhere above him. His face was pressed into the concrete.

In his most fearful moments, Neesh pictured his downfall to be with guns drawn. Someone in a suit, maybe an old white guy named Todd or something, would surely stroll up casually with a cigarette in his mouth, armed with just a sarcastic quip like on television.

"Mr. Desai, looks like you're going to need one of those checks cashed for a lawyer," Neesh imagined Todd would say. And then he would be perp-walked in front of cameras for the world to see. The headlines the next morning would read DISGRACED FORMER BROADWAY DRUMMER ARRESTED.

There was no Todd with a sarcastic quip. Neesh stopped struggling. He had enough. Neesh closed his eyes and pictured his first night playing *Rock of Ages* and the standing ovation after. It was the best day of his life. As he was picked up off the floor, Neesh saw the faces for the first time of the two expressionless officers carrying him outside. The activity of the expo began to return to normal, although many of the attendees still had their eyes on him. Past the officers, Neesh could still see Madhar holding a crying Chittesh.

And he heard his father's voice: *Soon, I'll fill my warehouse with the world. What will you do?*

◇

"You have some powerful friends," said the man sitting across from Neesh at a table in the Tenth Precinct. The windowless holding room was chilly and bare. It was nothing more than concrete. Neesh was thirsty, hungry, and tired. He had been booked, fingerprinted, and photographed. But that was hours ago. *Or was it?* Neesh had no idea.

"I do?" Neesh asked. "What time is it?"

The man, wearing a gray suit and a tie, looked at his watch. He looked tired as well.

"It's a little after nine," he said.

"Jesus," Neesh whispered. He just wanted to go to sleep. "So who are you?"

"I'm your lawyer," the man said. "Jerome Padilla."

Jerome pushed the thin frames he was wearing up the bridge of his nose.

"I don't have a lawyer."

"Ah. Well, you do now," Jerome said. "I'm a lawyer at Falcone and McKinley."

"How much do you charge?"

"Typically, six hundred dollars an hour."

"I can't afford that."

Jerome reached for his briefcase.

"I work with your friend Sandeep's father," Jerome said. He looked at Neesh with a combination of bemusement and pity, something Neesh didn't appreciate. "He asked me to take this case pro bono. I owe him some favors, so I said yes. And here I am."

"What does Sandeep have to do with this? I thought he got away."

"Got away with what? From my understanding, he had no idea a robbery was about to take place," Jerome said, prompting an incredulous look from Neesh.

"The prosecutor doesn't know what you're going to be charged with yet. They're going to get your buddy Jared for second-degree robbery. A Class C felony. Normally, they would charge him with first degree, but he was actually carrying a toy gun."

"No shit."

"Apparently, he snuck it in using a secret pocket in his backpack. Now for you, they're looking at a felony too. The police think you were in on it with Mr. Rupp, which changes things."

Upon hearing this, Neesh wished he had used his one phone call to get in touch with his mother instead of his father. But he had decided to call Jigar, hoping that for once, he would receive his pity. With each press of a button on the phone, Neesh became more anxious. On the second ring, Jigar picked up the phone. As Neesh explained what had occurred, with a preamble about how he knew Jigar would be angry, Neesh heard a click on the other end. Neesh had never felt so alone.

"Okay."

"Okay? That could be years in prison."

"Yeah."

"Is that what you want?"

"I don't care."

"Yes you do. I won't let you not care. Professionally, I can't. Legally

either, for that matter. Sandeep told me today that you have other information on Mr. Rupp's operation."

"Why did you speak to Sandeep?"

"Because he asked his father for help. Apparently, from Sandeep's telling, Jared physically threatened you into going to the convention today.
He manipulated you into taking part in other schemes, which you have
information on, he said. Check cashing?"

"I was threatened?"

"Yes. And if that's the case, I can get this knocked down to a misdemeanor. You'll have to pay a fine, but it's a misdemeanor. You'll have to
be willing to testify, but it's much easier to restart your life with a misdemeanor instead of a felony."

Jerome bent his head towards the table to get in Neesh's line of sight.
But Neesh refused to make eye contact.

"Neesh? Is it true? Was Jared into other stuff?"

The thought of restarting seemed attractive to Neesh. But to do so
would require another lie. Another scam. *Why did Jared bring a gun in
the first place?* But Neesh realized: Jared waved the gun to instinctively
protect him. *He could have run. He could have let me take the fall myself.
But he didn't. All those monthly rent payments. Jared really has gone out
of his way to look out for me. He tried to save me, even after I fucked up
by straggling at one booth for too long.* When it came down to it, Jared
had been selfless at many turns with Neesh when he didn't have to be.

"Do you hear me?" Jerome said louder.

"I'm thinking."

*But why did Sandeep turn on Jared? To save me? Why did he call his
father? Who am I to him?* Neesh was tired. He was too exhausted to think
anymore. Neesh wanted it to be over. He wanted to be far away from
Sandeep and Jared. He wanted never to see Jerome again. Life wasn't a
meritocracy. Jared made the dumb decision to brandish a gun. And to run
scam after scam after scam. He didn't think about his victims. This was the
bridge Jared had built for himself.

"Okay."

"Okay, what?"

"I'll say whatever."

"Is it the truth?"

"Yeah."

Jerome was satisfied. He rubbed his eyes and wrote some notes on his legal pad. Jerome got up to walk to the door, but before he left, he turned back to Neesh.

"Oh, I almost forgot," Jerome said. "Sandeep's father wanted me to deliver a message to you." He took out a folded note from his breast pocket and slipped it to Neesh. The paper read, *Stay away from my son. If you don't, a misdemeanor isn't all you'll have to worry about.*

TEN

S hantanu, wearing a matching set of Rutgers University sweatpants and sweatshirt, wheezed as he rounded the corner of Hillcrest Drive. It seemed like everything below his waist was in pain: his knees, an ankle, and both shins throbbed. He was drenched in sweat, made worse by an unexpectedly warm day outside. Finishing his first jog in a decade proved more difficult than anticipated, and he was especially irritated by several younger runners who simply flew by him. Shantanu could not even enjoy his new oversized noise-canceling headphones, ones that Catherine recommended, or the Rolling Stones live album he had never heard before.

As he returned to his driveway, he was surprised to see another car there, a beat-up green Ford Escort with the windows down.

As Shantanu stepped onto the pavement, he bent over to catch his breath.

"You definitely aren't a runner."

He saw a streak of blue hair.

"Pamela." Shantanu could only get that out before laying down on the yellowish lawn.

"Do I need to call a doctor? Or a track coach?" Pamela said. She opened the driver's-side door and stepped out, revealing tattered jeans and a black hoodie.

"Do I look like someone who runs a lot?" Shantanu said, his eyes staring up at the sky. It was mostly clear, but he could spot some clouds in the distance. "A thirteen-minute mile. I used to be able to do this in eight." Shantanu pushed himself up and leaned on his elbow. "Before you were born, of course. What are you doing here?"

"I came for the box," Pamela said sternly.

Shantanu adjusted to a sitting position.

"Would you like to come inside?"

"Just the box."

"Of course. It's inside. I'll go get it. Do you mind if we sit on the front steps and talk? You don't owe me that, of course."

Shantanu and Pamela made eye contact. He smelled of sweat and unexpected desperation. He still felt a weight on his shoulders, which would not be lost no matter how many runs he went on.

"I can come inside," Pamela said.

Shantanu didn't mean to breathe a sigh of relief but couldn't help himself. He limped to the door and let Pamela inside.

"Can I get you something to drink?" Shantanu called out as he headed to the kitchen, while Pamela went to the living room. "How about, uh, hot chocolate?" Shantanu threw open a cupboard. It was empty. "Never mind. Orange juice?" He opened his fridge. Again, mostly empty. "Oops. I don't have any orange juice. Do you want milk? I have milk. Are you a fan of Froot Loops? I really need to go shopping."

"Mr. Das, water is fine," Pamela called back from the other room.

"Call me Shantanu," he said as he poured two glasses of water.

Shantanu had brought the box back up to his bedroom, essentially to keep him company as he went to sleep. Now he went upstairs to retrieve the box, and also changed into one of his plaid shirts.

"We never read the notes," Shantanu said to Pamela, as he handed her the box. Pamela was sitting on the floor of the living room, her back against the wall. This wasn't completely true, as Shantanu well knew, but at the moment, he just wanted to open a dialogue. "Mitali said it wasn't our place."

"It wasn't." She paused. "This house is different. Is Mrs. Das home?" Pamela asked, as she thumbed through the box, her hands plunging through the piles of notes as if in a shallow lake. "Where are all your *things*?"

"We . . . didn't work out," Shantanu said. "She still lives in Howell, though."

Pamela gave him a sympathetic glance, which raised Shantanu's hopes for a détente.

"I thought this box was lost," Pamela said, unfolding a letter and beginning to read. On the outside, there was a heart with the words "Die Hard *Is* A Christmas Movie" written on it. "She was beautiful. I loved her."

"I know."

Pamela's face remained hard.

"No, you didn't. You had the chance to accept her. And you didn't."

Shantanu knew he looked ashamed. And he was. He was familiar with feeling this way.

"You are right, Pamela. We made a mistake. One that we'll live with forever. I would give anything to take it back."

Shantanu ran a hand against the back of his head, mopping the still visible sweat off his forehead along the way. The weight of the conversation was a gravitational pull that sent Shantanu to sit on the couch.

"There were so many times after that I wished I could trade places with her. We all did."

"We were both supposed to tell our parents the same night. I chickened out. Keya was the brave one," Pamela said. She began reading one of the notes out loud.

"Hey!!

My mom won't stop badgering me about college. She thinks I should be doing more volunteering and joining National Honor Society and all that shit. They're not happy about the acting-school thing. In a couple years, I won't care what they think. I won't have to. ICE CREAM LATER!!! I LOVE YOU!

Pamela"

Pamela's face softened. Shantanu got up and walked to the kitchen to get tissues. He realized he did not have any, so he opted for a paper towel roll that was in one of the cupboards.

"The night she, you know," Pamela said stoically. "That night, she was on her way to my place."

"She was?"

"Yes. She spent a lot of time with me."

"How angry was she with us?"

Shantanu steeled himself for an answer he didn't want to hear.

"I don't know if 'angry' was the right word. Hurt. Bewildered. So was I. She felt she let you guys down."

Shantanu closed his eyes. Here he was, going for runs, thinking about his girlfriend, his improv classes, this new life he'd built around himself. But watching Pamela thumb through the papers brought his old one rushing back to the forefront. He felt like he was reliving the night Keya had died all over again.

"I found out about Keya from Jackie. Giggenbach's daughter," Pamela said.

"The police officer?"

"I'll never forget it. One minute, I was in my room expecting Keya to knock on the door. We were going to watch a movie. She *loved* watching movies. We'd spend hours talking about scripts. Did you know that?"

"I did. A little."

"The next minute, I got the call, and she was gone. I stood there in my bedroom. I thought I was in a movie; that someone was going to yell "Cut!" and I could go back to living real life. But that never happened." Pamela thumbed the notes in the box, but her eyes were fixated on the carpet. Her voice became a mumble. It looked as if Pamela was speaking to herself as much as she was to Shantanu, which made him feel like an intruder in his own home. "Reality just hits you, man. And then I wailed and wailed. My mom and dad were pretty good that night, actually."

"Pamela, did you ever tell your parents about you and Keya?"

"No. You didn't say anything, right?"

"No."

"Good. No one knows except Deidre from work."

"How long were you and Keya together?"

"A year? Maybe longer? We had big plans. Go to college near each other. Maybe in New York. I was going to try and become an actor. I'd audition for Tisch or something," Pamela said, reaching for her glass of water. She barely took a sip before putting it back down. "She hadn't quite figured out what she wanted to do. But she could've done anything. She was so good in *42nd Street*. And she had never acted before. Once she was gone, I felt like I lost a part of me. I'm sorry. I'm ranting."

"Please don't be sorry," Shantanu said, his own tears welling up. "I've always wanted to know."

Shantanu went to the kitchen to refill their water glasses, although only his needed refilling. When he returned, Pamela's face was again emotionless as she unfolded more letters.

"I miss her. I used to love how she'd read random Wikipedia pages to me. She loved Snapple facts. Who loves Snapple facts?"

"The play, *The Elm Tree*," Shantanu asked gingerly. "Do you remember it at all?"

"Yes." Pamela mustered her first smile of the visit. "We started writing it shortly after *42nd Street*. We thought it might be a good way for us to come out to everybody all at once. Especially after what happened with Keya's grandmother, when she walked in on us. But the car crash happened. I deleted my version of the play. This is the only copy. I don't remember a lot of it, though."

Pamela began flipping through the play.

"I don't know much about plays, but it's lovely," Shantanu said.

"You read it?"

"I'm sorry, we couldn't help ourselves," Shantanu said. "What did you intend on doing with it?"

"Huh?"

"The play. You never finished it."

Pamela leaned back.

"I think we were going to pitch it to be a spring show for senior year."

"So you both wanted it made."

"It wasn't a homework assignment, if that's what you're asking."

Shantanu took another gulp of water. He had stopped sweating.

"I have a question for you," Shantanu said. "And I don't know how to ask this. But—I have struggled ever since Keya was taken from us. It gives me some solace that she had you to share these feelings with. But really, it should have been us. I failed as a father. And I failed as your best friend's father. And I don't know how to make it right. But *The Elm Tree* feels like a way I can honor Keya."

"What do you mean?"

"It was Mitali's idea. Do you remember her? I was wondering what you thought about staging the play. I'd come up with the money. We could put it on something called Off Broadway."

Pamela looked at Shantanu with a look of pure incredulity.

"'*Something* called Off Broadway'?"

"Yes," Shantanu said. "We wouldn't do it without your permission. And in fact, you should finish writing it. We'll put it on for an audience. We could share your story with them."

"So you'd produce it?" Pamela asked.

"Is that what it's called? Yes, I'd produce it," Shantanu said. "Mitali will also help. She has a whole plan and everything."

"Do you know anything about theater?"

"I know *Stomp*," Shantanu said.

Pamela grimaced and turned her palms upward.

"You don't just produce a play. Plays aren't pears to be picked on a tree in a backyard."

"I know."

"People that do this for a living fuck it up all the time," Pamela said. She began to get angry. "My— Our play isn't some vehicle for you to feel better about your own fuckups."

"That's true," Shantanu said, sounding desperate again. "I don't blame you for being skeptical. This is something to do because you and Keya created something beautiful. Let me do this for my daughter, and for you."

He could see Pamela was still fuming. Shantanu could see that even with Keya gone, she was fiercely protective of her and what they had.

Maybe this was what Keya loved about Pamela; why she felt safe around her. *Pamela provided it to her unconditionally, unlike me.*

"Plays aren't cheap, you know that, right?"

There was an easing in her features. She looked contemplative. The door was open, just a crack.

"I'm going to sell this house, and I'll draw from my retirement fund if I have to. That should get us thirty to forty thousand. This won't be easy. But I'll figure it out if you let me."

Pamela began flipping through the pages again.

"I haven't read this in a long time," she muttered. "If my parents ever read this, they would disown me."

"Why haven't you told them?"

"In case they react like you did."

Shantanu impulsively rubbed his cheek, as though he had been slapped.

"If Keya was here, she would yell at me," Pamela said. "*'Someone is offering you tens of thousands of dollars to finish writing a play we wanted to put on!'*"

"She is here," Shantanu said. "Both of you are, in those pages. You just have to finish it."

She stared at him, as if meeting this challenge. And then she abruptly closed the box and headed for the door.

"Thank you for the water, Mr. Das. I will think about it."

PART 2

PART 2

ELEVEN

"You haven't come around much recently," Dr. Lynch said. "You look good. You're sitting up straighter."

"I am?" Shantanu shuffled in his seat, the familiar brown task chair. "I've been going on some runs. The woman I'm seeing, Catherine, she makes me eat celery. She tells me it's good for digestion."

Shantanu glanced around the room.

"Is that new?" he asked.

"Which thing?"

"Well, you pick."

Dr. Lynch was wearing a blue turtleneck that Shantanu had not seen before. But beyond that, there was a shelf where the Grant Hill poster used to be. It was lined with Yankee Candles.

"Ha, yes," Dr. Lynch said. "You've noticed the candles. I'm trying something new. Those are all autumn scents."

"It's July."

"It's fall somewhere."

"No it's not."

"Have you been to Seattle? It's always fall there," Dr. Lynch said.

Shantanu was wearing Plaid Shirt No. 5 and Khaki Pants No. 1 to this appointment, his first in several months.

"So where have you been?" Dr. Lynch said. "Was it something I said?"

"Not at all," Shantanu said. "I sold my house and moved in with my mother. I'm taking a leave next semester."

Dr. Lynch raised his eyebrows. "Is everything all right?"

Shantanu looked down at the hardwood floor, deep in thought.

"Actually, yes," Shantanu answered, over the whir of the air conditioner fighting off the ninety-degree weather outside. "My mother is totally fine. Well, she's old, but fine. I needed some money for something."

◇

Shantanu had received the call two months prior, while he happened to be at Catherine's apartment. She paused the movie they were watching: *Top Gun*, one of her favorites, and one that he had never seen.

"Mr. Das." Shantanu heard a high-pitched woman's voice on the phone. "It's Pamela."

Shantanu mouthed to Catherine that it was, indeed, Pamela. He could scarcely believe it, as he scampered as quickly as his body would let him to the hallway. When she left his house with the box, he assumed he would never see her again. He figured that Pamela had humored him by considering participating in the play.

"How did you get my number?" Shantanu asked in a hushed tone, so as not to disturb the neighbors. Catherine said that at this building, neighbors complained if noise from the next apartment rose above silence.

"Keya gave it to me once," Pamela said. "I think we were going to prank call you or something."

"Ah."

Shantanu paced the hallway, as neither of them said anything at first.

"I'm on break. I don't have much time," Pamela said. "I've been thinking about what we talked about."

Pamela had been reading the play repeatedly, she said. And before she said anything else, Shantanu knew that Pamela was in.

"Every day, the first thing I've done in the morning is read this play," Pamela said. "I've read it on lunch breaks. Sometimes I read it at night, at three a.m. after the restaurant closes. I've made copies. I have it practically memorized, at least what's on paper."

"And what do you think?" Shantanu said expectantly, his heart racing.

"Are you really willing to sell your house?" Pamela asked.

"And a limb," Shantanu said. "An arm. Not a leg. Some toes, maybe."

Pamela let out a faint laugh.

"I can't help but feel—" Pamela began. "I keep thinking about why we wrote the play."

"Really?"

"I can't spend the rest of my life like this. I've been an empty shell."

"I know the feeling," Shantanu said.

"Lately, I've felt *something* reading the lines. I feel familiar to myself. At home. Because I was at home with *her*. And fuck, we were good writers. Sorry, Mr. Das, for the language. Actually, no, I'm not."

Shantanu felt a pressure in his chest, as if his heart were about to collapse in on itself.

"I need to tell my parents. And I need your help."

"About the play?" Shantanu was momentarily confused.

"No."

And Shantanu understood.

"You want to use the play as it was intended."

"Yeah."

"Are you sure?"

"I'll never be sure. But they can't react any worse than you did, right?"

Shantanu stopped pacing.

"Mr. Das, sorry." Pamela sounded stricken.

"It's okay," Shantanu said. He had said these same things to himself, but it still stung when it came from someone else, particularly Pamela. "First things first, finish the play in the way you want. Then we'll figure out the rest."

"Why are you so willing to do this?" Pamela asked.

Shantanu stood up straight. He thought back to the toaster and his inability to go near it.

"For Keya."

"Wrong answer," Pamela said.

"Sorry?"

"For me too."

◇

"So, you sold the house? Just like that?" Dr. Lynch said, the hint of a grin on his face.

"Just like that."

Shantanu had, indeed, sold the house, just like that. He made a handsome profit, too, even though they'd refinanced the house to help pay for Mitali's college, and the lawn's unwillingness to be perfect had lowered the property value. Shantanu cursed himself for not putting in the sprinkler system. Kalpana was delighted to hear that Shantanu would be living with her once again.

"This is how Bengalis are supposed to live," Kalpana squealed, when Shantanu asked if he might be able to move in temporarily. "*Bechara, choto bhala mothon hobe.*"

"Don't baby me, Ma. Please," Shantanu pleaded, but he knew it would be to no avail. And soon, he would have to tell her about Catherine, a conversation he was not yet ready to have. There would be some nights when curries made for dinner would be left in the fridge because he would be at Catherine's. The thought made Shantanu chuckle: he had just turned fifty-three and still felt he had to hide his girlfriend from his mother.

Mitali seemed equally galvanized when Shantanu told her that Pamela had given the go-ahead for the play, and that she would finish the end. When the subject of money came up, Mitali had already devised a list of several ideas to recruit investors and raise funds. Shantanu told her it would not be necessary; he was finally selling the house, as he had long planned. And in fact, he had already called Brendan, the agent who sold them the property, to begin the process. Decades later, Brendan's hair was still curly, and his energy was still off the charts.

"But what if we can't make this happen? You sold the house for nothing! *Our* house!"

Shantanu did not expect Mitali to show any sort of longing for her childhood home.

"Not for nothing," Shantanu said. "For Keya. For Pamela. And for you. Let's figure out what to do with your things. And besides, it's long been time for me to downsize."

They didn't tell Chaitali about the sale of the house or that Pamela was going to write the play. Chaitali had made her point clear—she did not want to be involved. So it was Mitali alone who helped Shantanu with the move. He didn't tell her about Catherine. This was to their disadvantage: having done so might have recruited an extra body to help with the move. If there was a moment that saddened Shantanu, it was packing Keya's room. They did it wordlessly, as if this was a sacred ritual. There were so many other drawings Keya had scattered throughout the room that they had never discovered before. After they finished, Shantanu looked at Mitali.

"I feel guilty doing this without your mother."

"Me too, Baba."

Seconds later, there were tears flowing from both of them as they embraced each other.

But overall, Shantanu was not particularly sad about leaving this house behind, and he knew Mitali wasn't either, until the day came when Shantanu had to give the keys to the new owners: a young couple with a newborn baby.

"We'll take good care of her," the husband told Shantanu.

"A sprinkler system is like Rogaine. You stop watering it and it stops growing."

"Baba, let's go," Mitali chided, although Shantanu could see a mixture of sadness and regret on her face.

They drove away slowly, watching the house edge out of view in the rearview mirror.

"So this woman, Catherine. Why won't you tell your mother about her?" Dr. Lynch asked.

"I'm not sure," Shantanu said. "I'm a fifty-three-year-old man. She's younger. By a decade. She's smart. Fearless. Sure of herself. I don't know why she finds a past-his-prime anthropologist interesting. She's dated artists and musicians. We don't have much in common, other than a love of the Rolling Stones."

"You're worried she's going to get to know you more, find you boring, and leave? Right after you tell your mother."

"I don't know what I'm worried about."

"Maybe that's what she likes about you. That you're a stodgy old professor winding down your career. For once, she gets to be with someone who isn't on a hamster wheel. Maybe she can be the interesting one in the relationship."

"I know humans. Humans aren't meant to stay in one place, especially when there is not a reason to stay. Millennia of observed behavior tells us that."

"You have to consider the fact that you're as deserving of love as anyone else is," Dr. Lynch said. "One of the biggest mistakes I see couples make is that one partner is often putting the other in a position of having to convince them that they are actually in love. That they are as invested as the other side. That they are *in*. Every day is a battle to show worthiness, even though the war is already won. This kills relationships."

In another life, Shantanu thought, Dr. Lynch would have made a great actor. He had a talent for delivering convincing monologues.

"My point is that you are more interesting than you realize, Shantanu," Dr. Lynch said. "We all are. It's up to us to realize in what way and accept that we are. Since we first met, you've taken an improv class, begun dating, sold your house, and moved in with your mother. Now you're using the money you made from that to put on your daughter's play when you know absolutely nothing about theater. Do you see a future with Catherine?"

"She doesn't want to get married."

"Do you?"

"I never thought in a million years I'd have to think about that question again," Shantanu said.

"If life went exactly as we thought it would, there wouldn't be a need for anthropologists," Dr. Lynch said. "Or therapists, for that matter. Our paychecks come from the unexpected, my friend."

◇

Not the best of my ideas, Catherine thought as she and Shantanu climbed into a booth at Fiorello's, a glitzy, busy Italian restaurant near Lincoln Center she had picked out. *It'll work, though.*

Shantanu's naive enthusiasm at the notion of this dinner, a rare trip to Manhattan, convinced her this would be worth it. When Catherine made the reservation weeks ago, he immediately looked deep in thought and pressed a nearby pen to his temple. It was as if he had come across an unconfirmed study he had to verify but which he hoped was academically sound, an expression Catherine had come to know and appreciate. She saw it when she came across Shantanu hunched over his laptop, typing in "how to produce a play" on Google, and taking extensive notes on a wiki-How page that boiled down the process to fourteen easy steps.

For much of Catherine's life, she had run in circles full of overly confident men. It was almost routine that at gallery openings, younger male artists holding champagne glasses would pester her in a practiced way and wax poetic about how Warhol and Pollock were defining influences, as if she didn't know who they were. *It was always Warhol and Pollock. Never someone interesting.* And then would follow some variation of: *Hey, we should discuss this more over coffee,* in a tone that suggested it was an honor for Catherine to be invited to discuss art with this talent.

She'd often whisper something pithy in response like, "I'm not high enough for this shit. And Pollock was just a lukewarm Siqueiros. Thank you, though." And the men would watch her walk away, their prey escaping their grasp.

Catherine radiated her own confidence, which was what those men found attractive, until they didn't. She always found that men loved that she didn't take any shit, but would be frustrated when that included *their* shit. She was proudest of starting her own event-planning business and growing it to oversee multiple employees. And she had plans to expand. Catherine was never one to let others define what she could and could not do: Not the men she dated. Not even her older brother in California with whom she'd had a falling-out after he found out about her abortion in her early twenties, and who had said her life would be meaningless without children.

Catherine's least proud moment stretched over a decade: letting herself take shit for the first time, and then time and time again, from Nate

Eyre. Nate was a talented, self-destructive painter with crippling anxiety who had trouble meeting deadlines. He also had a penchant for romantic gestures, as Catherine found out from the other women whom he was seeing during their relationship.

But it didn't deter her from trying to make their relationship work, in part because Nate encouraged her to pursue her business ambitions, but not much else, like a social life. Catherine also had enough confidence in herself that she could make Nate see the good in himself and stay there. What was event planning if not solving problems? Nate was a problem to be solved, an attractive, creative one at that. Catherine's friends called her a "fixer"—someone who wanted to patch the holes of others. Those friends had another not-so-secret name for her: enabler. It was only after Catherine and Nate split that she realized Nate encouraged her business ambitions because he saw her as a future ATM.

And here was Shantanu. He wasn't unlike many she had come to know over the years, in that he was vulnerable and willing to go broke for the sake of art. But he was a different type of partner. He didn't care about art per se. He cared about making things right for his daughter. He cared about guilt.

And he seemingly cared about her. "Seemingly" was the operative word, because after Nate, Catherine had no use for certainty anymore. She had sensed a pain bubbling under the surface in Shantanu from the moment she met him at the improv class. He wasn't as attractive as Nate, but she found his earnestness arresting, nonetheless. Shantanu was older, a bit out of shape, and yet she found him intriguing. She didn't know how long this would last. But in the meantime, she would help make this play happen.

"Have you ever told Mitali or your mother about us?" Catherine asked Shantanu. "I don't suppose I'll spend nights at your mother's apartment."

"It's complicated, Catherine," Shantanu said. "I worry that Mitali still harbors hope that Chaitali and I will get back together someday. I don't want her to be as angry at me as she's been with her mother. And as for *my* mother, I don't know how she will take it. My father was always traditional.

I fear that she might be upset about us not having plans to get married. We don't divorce in my culture. Not really."

Catherine found a familiar irritation being stirred inside her. Once again, a man was putting the feelings of others in front of hers. *But why am I even thinking like this? I don't want to get married. Or have kids.*

"So you want this to just be an affair until one of us gets sick of the other," Catherine said. "That's cool with me. I'm having fun. I just want to make sure we're on the same page."

Shantanu extended his hand. She declined to take it.

"Please don't be angry at me," Shantanu said. "Are you bothered? If it is—"

Suddenly, Shantanu was interrupted by a towering figure over the table.

"Ms. Pullman, my dear! I didn't expect to hear from you. You look ravishing."

The voice was loud, and each word was spoken with a dramatic flair. Shantanu was startled to see a lean man with white hair and a white beard. He was wearing a perfectly pressed gray sports jacket over matching pants and a white dress shirt with no tie.

"Thank you for keeping my seat warm, sir," the man said to Shantanu. "I'll take a whiskey on the rocks and some menus."

Shantanu looked at Catherine, confused, while she rolled her eyes.

"Shantanu, this is Jerry Santucci," Catherine said.

"A pleasure to meet you," Jerry said. "Now, if you don't mind. We have a lot of catching up to do."

"Jerry, this is Shantanu," Catherine said. "He'll be joining us."

"Excuse me?" Jerry said. He looked aghast. "Why?"

"Because we have a play that we'd like you to direct," Catherine said.

Jerry pursed his lips as his eyes moved from Catherine to Shantanu. "I've been hoodwinked."

"Did you not *tell* him?" Shantanu glared at Catherine.

"I didn't." Catherine motioned for Jerry to sit next to her. "Because I knew he wouldn't come if I did."

"You're damn right about that," Jerry said, but he took a seat anyway. "You used to be a lot more fun, Cat. How long has it been? Twenty years?"

"About that," Catherine said. "I'm sure you preferred me in my twenties. You do have a taste for younger women."

"Indeed I do. You had spunk," Jerry said. "A special spunk. The mouth of a Greek goddess. And I liked it. You were different. You should've married me when I asked."

"The solo backpacking trip to Europe sounded more fun, frankly," Catherine said fiercely. She could sense Shantanu's discomfort at the conversation, as he shifted in the booth. "And that's when I knew we were a bad idea. Although I suppose the age difference should've been a red flag. And that leaving the country seemed like a better idea than continuing to see you."

I should have told Shantanu more.

"Besides, if I didn't leave, you wouldn't have focused on *Waiting for Godot*. Wasn't that your second Tony?"

"It was," Jerry said longingly. "It was my favorite one of the three."

Jerry turned to Shantanu.

"Cat and I met when I hired her as an art consultant," Jerry said. "Her taste was impeccable. Now forgive me for my language, sir. But why won't someone tell me what the fuck I am doing here, if not to rekindle an old romance? I guess it could be for the whiskey. I still haven't forgiven that drummer Gary Whyte for turning me on to it back then."

Catherine took out a copy of *The Elm Tree* and slid it to Jerry. He pushed it back.

"I haven't directed anything in ten years," Jerry said. "I'm retired. I don't even do Broadway anymore. Why would I do this?"

"Because it's good," Catherine said. "And you can make it great. We want to do it Off Broadway for three nights."

"Flattery?" Jerry said with mock surprise. "That's not like you. Who wrote it? Let me guess: one of the New York Theatre Workshop's 'rising stars.' Or is it one of your friends at the Public? Who are you trying to elevate? Is it him?"

Jerry sneered and pointed at Shantanu, who did not know how to respond.

"It is being fleshed out, but it was written by two people that were in high school at the time," Catherine said. "We haven't cast it yet or found a venue. You're the first person we're approaching."

"You want me to direct a *high school play*?" Jerry said. He began to look under the table and all around. He stopped a flustered waitress as she walked by. "Excuse me, dear. Have you seen any marbles? It appears that my dear Cat here has lost hers."

The waitress flashed a smile and continued walking.

"I was sitting on *a beach* the other day," Jerry said. "A beach! Do you know the last time I sat on a beach?"

Catherine and Shantanu both shook their heads.

"*The day before!* The day before! That's the best part about being retired!"

"You *retired* because of the bad reviews your last several plays got," Catherine said, unimpressed. "Let's not treat me like an idiot. You don't 'do Broadway' anymore because no one wants to work with you. You haven't worked in ten years because the box office receipts didn't justify your attitude. Calling the *Times* theater critic to curse him out on the record didn't help. I'm giving you a chance to come out of the cold."

"Simmons called *Lamps in Brazil* 'pedantic,'" Jerry spat. "I'll never forgive him for that. The bastard." He sighed. "But yes, Cat, you are correct. I've had creative differences."

"Show them they were wrong," Catherine said.

"Who are these high school students to you?" Jerry said. "Why should I give a shit—pardon me—about some wannabes?"

Shantanu slammed his water glass on the table, startling Jerry.

"Don't talk about my daughter in that way," Shantanu said.

"Your daughter—"

"His daughter wrote the play. She passed," Catherine said faintly. "She was eighteen."

Jerry stared at Shantanu, his wrinkled face easing. And he looked down at the packet in front of him.

"Good sir, I apologize for my tone," Jerry said, looking chastened. "But the stage is not a place for charity. I'm an artist. I'm not going to compromise the integrity of what I do out of sympathy."

"Very well," Shantanu said. "I will not beg you. My daughter deserves better than that. Thank you for your time."

Shantanu abruptly stood up and stormed out the exit. Catherine waited a beat and followed him. She found Shantanu outside stewing.

"What the *hell* are you doing?" Catherine said.

"What am *I* doing?" Shantanu said. "What was this? Why wouldn't you tell me what I was walking into?"

"I'm trying to make something happen for you," Catherine said. "Something no one else in your life can make happen. I need you to shut up and roll with this."

"He called Keya a 'wannabe,'" Shantanu said.

"He's eccentric. He's a jerk. But he's good," Catherine said. "Now, get back in there."

"Absolutely not," Shantanu spat. "Did you think I would be comfortable with this? Me just having a casual dinner with your ex-boyfriend?"

"'Boyfriend' is a strong word. It was more of a mutual crossing of paths when I felt like it."

"Yes," Shantanu said. "I'm sure that's *much* different from a boyfriend. Is that what I am too? A 'mutual crossing of paths'?"

"You're jealous? Of him?"

"I'm nothing."

Catherine felt her face get hot.

"All men are the same. You're so insecure. You think that if you had something to worry about, I would bring you to dinner? Get ahold of yourself."

"The way he talked about Keya. You wouldn't understand how that feels."

"I'm doing something *for* your daughter and *for* you. Learn how to accept a favor. No matter how awkward it is. Do you trust me?"

"I don't know."

"Do you trust me? If you don't, I'm walking away. And I'm not coming back."

Shantanu remembered Dr. Lynch's words about fighting battles when the war was already won.

"I won't beg."

"Do you know how to direct?"

Shantanu was distracted by the fountains going off outside Lincoln Center.

"No."

"Then beg if you have to. I'm going back inside."

Catherine turned around and disappeared into the restaurant. Shantanu trailed after her.

"I understand you're overqualified," Shantanu said, almost through gritted teeth, after he sat back down at the table. "But I think you'll find that the writing is better than most high schoolers'."

"Everyone has a baby they think is beautiful," Jerry said. "I promise you, sir, not all babies are beautiful. Most aren't, in fact."

"Look," Shantanu said, his patience wearing even more thin. "You do this play. If it's not good, you go back to your life of sitting at the beach with your reputation exactly where it was. If it *is* good, think about what that means for you. You turned a high school play into a brilliant work of art. What director wouldn't want that on his résumé?"

"My résumé is *very* good, sir," Jerry said.

Shantanu turned to look at Catherine.

"I've done all I can do," he said. "I've had enough."

"That's *it*?" Jerry said incredulously. "You're going to take no for an answer?"

"I am," Shantanu said. "As the producer of this play, I will only work with a director who is excited about the project."

Catherine briefly had a look of pride on her face as Shantanu stood up again.

"This world has changed, huh?" Jerry said. "Sit back down, my good man. You mustn't lay down that easy. In the old days, Harold Prince would ask me every day for a year to do *A Streetcar Named Desire*. He'd send me unhealthy amounts of gin. Flowers. And more, if you catch my drift. And now, you leave after a couple minutes? Wine me! Dine me! This way I didn't put on this blazer for nothing."

Shantanu looked at Catherine, who nodded at him. He sat back down.

"I'll read the play," Jerry said. "You seem like a good man and a non-moron. And because Catherine is asking me to. But first, where is the damn whiskey? And then you can tell me exactly what you want to do with this."

◇

The knights wore resplendent colors as they paraded around on horses, effortlessly trotting around an indoor dirt field while carrying lances that looked to be bigger than the knights themselves. The spotlights made the bright cloths that covered the horses themselves even more visible. The soaring string music played in the background, as one of the knights addressed the roaring crowd in an exaggerated British accent. The voices that cheered back were mostly of a higher register, since there were many children sitting in the roughly fifteen hundred seats.

Soon it was time for the queen, who was standing next to an elevated throne on one end of the theater in the round, to make her move.

"Forget not that I have inside me the blood of kings," the queen, who was wearing a majestic robe, said. "Come, come, my friends. Let us raise our cups. To honor!"

The audience raised their cups. This meant that the children raised their juices, waters, and sodas. Mitali and Neesh raised souvenir cups with beer in them.

"To honor!" they both yelled.

"Happy birthday!" Neesh excitedly yelled in Mitali's ear, causing her to recoil. "Sorry!"

Mitali took another sip of her beer.

"I can honestly say I've never had a birthday like this," she said.

"You've always wanted this, right?" Neesh said.

"Wanted what?"

"To go to Medieval Times!"

Mitali snickered, prompting a look of doubt on Neesh's face.

I emptied my bank account so I could rent the car and buy the tickets.

"What made you think that I've always wanted to go to Medieval Times?" Mitali said.

"The play! The line from *The Elm Tree*. Keya's character said that you told her that you had never met anyone willing to take you here. Did you not tell her that?"

"Oh, Neesh. That's just a line from the play. I don't know why that was—"

Neesh's face grew hot.

"I love this," she said. "It's the best birthday present ever. To honor!"

"To honor!" Neesh repeated, as they both raised their glasses.

Some of the children nearby shushed the couple. Mitali mouthed an apology to them, as well as to their disapproving parents. The last time Neesh did coke was in his twenties, when he was in his scamming days. But sometimes he wished he had it at the ready. This was one of those nights.

"It's my birthday!" Mitali said to the little girl, who was likely around eight, sitting at the seat closest to her. "I'm twenty-six!"

"Mine too!" the girl said in response. "Look!"

Mitali looked down at the floor, where a horse draped in a purple cloth was on his hind legs performing tricks at the behest of a knight.

"Do you think that horse wants to be doing this?" she whispered to Neesh. "Just doing whatever he's told?"

"Nah," Neesh said. "That horse was meant for bigger things. But one way or another, we've all been that horse."

The show ended with all the characters riding around the dirt field and giving one last goodbye to the crowd. As the audience filed out, Neesh and Mitali stopped at a gift shop so that he could buy Mitali a plastic crown. As he handed the cashier his credit card, Neesh hoped that there would be no other purchases on the way home. The card was close to maxed out.

"For chivalry!" Mitali shouted in the parking lot as she put the crown on.

"For chivalry!" Neesh repeated.

Neesh liked driving at night, something he rarely did as a city dweller. It was something he did quite a bit as a high schooler, particularly after altercations with his father. Neesh would grab his mother's car keys and drive aimlessly for hours at a time. He didn't have a cell phone then, so there was no way to reach him. Tonight, the highway was mostly empty, giving him a chance to collect his thoughts. He turned his head and saw Mitali's eyes drooping. Her crown was sliding off her head.

"This was a good birthday," Mitali muttered. "Now I'm tired."

"Good," Neesh said.

Mitali was too tired to say anything else and fell asleep. Neesh turned on an episode of *The Moth*, but his mind drifted. *Is there any hope of a long-term future with Mitali?* The other day, Mitali had asked Neesh about the possibility of going away on vacation for a week. Neesh said it would be tough to get days off in the summer from the studio. The summertime, Neesh told Mitali, was the studio's busy season. There was no busy season, Neesh knew, but he couldn't pay for flights. And he was too ashamed to admit it.

Neesh worked for hourly wages and was barely able to make rent. He had no other career prospects. He could play with another band, but none of the competent ones had a need for a drummer, and besides, Gary Whyte had surely soured his name in the industry. But he fantasized about *The Elm Tree*. He would not be onstage for the show, of course. But maybe if he could help put it together, it would be a path to something, *anything* else. Neesh didn't know what, but he felt something on the horizon. The universe was in ecstatic motion.

"Hi, Baba!" Mitali said suddenly, holding her phone in her palm. Neesh hadn't heard her wake up. He was able to make out the voices on the other end.

"Happy birthday, *sona*. I'm here with *Shomadidi*. Ma, ready? One-two-three."

Shantanu and Kalpana proceeded to sing a very off-tune version of "Happy Birthday." Mitali held the phone away from her ear so that Neesh could hear more clearly.

"Thank you for the card and the spa day," Mitali said. "I'll put it to good use. Ma sent me one too. You all have to get more creative with your gifts."

"How's your mother?"

"I missed a call from her," Mitali said. "I'll get back to her later this week."

"Listen, I actually do have another birthday present for you," Shantanu said. "The director, Jerry. The famous one. He said he is interested in directing the play. He wants to see the final version, but he said he liked what he read."

"Really?!" Mitali yelled, causing Neesh to look at her with a mixture of alarm and excitement. "How did you manage that?"

"Honestly, it was all Catherine. She set it up," Shantanu said.

"Who is Catherine?" Mitali asked, sounding curious.

"You've never mentioned a Catherine," Kalpana said.

"No one. She's someone I know in New Brunswick. A friend," Shantanu said.

"Oh, like another professor or something?" Mitali said, this time with a hint of suspicion.

"Yeah, or something. That's right," Shantanu said. Neesh had done a lot of lying in his life. He was virtually certain Shantanu was not telling the whole truth here, but he wasn't going to say that out loud. "Now we work on finding a venue and setting up auditions. Do you want to take the lead on that?"

"Sure," Mitali said. "Actually, it's funny. Remember where you took improv classes? Neesh helped me with the list of venues and said that the George Street Playhouse might be a good place to do this."

As soon as she said that, Neesh could see Mitali wince.

"Who is Neesh?" Shantanu said.

"You've never mentioned a Neesh," Kalpana chimed in.

"No one. He's a friend. Here in New York."

Did I just get friend-zoned? Neesh thought. *Have I always been there?*

"Okay," Shantanu said.

There was silence on both ends of the line.

"Well, look. Happy birthday, again. Are you out with friends?" Shantanu said.

"Yeah, friends. Listen, Baba, my phone is dying."

"Go celebrate and we'll talk during the week."

"Thanks, Baba."

The call ended. Mitali turned to Neesh, who was chewing on his shirt, which he had pulled towards him with one hand, the other on the steering wheel.

"I haven't told them about you," Mitali said, looking apologetic. "I should. We just don't talk about this kind of stuff."

"It's cool," Neesh said. "We all have secrets."

"Oh yeah?" Mitali said. "What are yours?"

"I don't know how to ride a bike," Neesh said.

Mitali gasped.

"I'm serious," Neesh said. "I had no one to teach me."

"I'll teach you," Mitali said. A silence hung in the car before Mitali spoke again. "Do you have any thoughts on where you want to be in five years?"

"Why?"

"I feel like we always talk about what we're doing now. We never talk about the future."

Neesh switched lanes and rolled down the windows to let in some air. He let that question run through his mind like the breeze through the car: *What does five years from now look like to someone who can't see five minutes ahead? How can I think about the future when I've failed in the past and I'm barely holding on in the present?* The road was empty, just the way Neesh liked it. No cars to serve as an obstacle as he wound his way home.

"In five years, I'd like to feel full," Neesh said. He looked over at Mitali and saw that she had drifted to sleep again. In the darkness, Neesh was able to hide his relief. After returning the rental car, Mitali and Neesh walked back to his apartment. She was energized by the nap, and she ran up the front stairs of a nearby apartment building, spreading her arms wide while facing the sidewalk, her face triumphantly looking into the sky.

"*You* are the universe in ecstatic motion!" Mitali yelled. Other nearby pedestrians looked alarmed but kept walking. Neesh was amused. He had never seen Mitali like this. The alcohol had helped, surely, but she seemed less troubled with each passing month of their relationship. So was he, for that matter. But Neesh had the same feeling he had when he spent time with Jared and Sandeep, the notion that his life was a game of Jenga, and at any moment, the tower of wooden blocks could come crashing down, no matter how fun it was in the moment.

"Jerry Santucci is a big deal," Neesh remarked when Mitali rejoined him. "Well, he *was* a big deal. But he has a bit of a reputation. Still. Some real name recognition there. He did *Waiting for Godot*. We need to figure out a venue right away. His name should help."

Secretly, Neesh's stomach was doing backflips. Keya wasn't his sister. He didn't know Pamela. He had never met Mitali's family. All he had done was read the play. He wanted it to get made as much as anybody else. And Jerry Santucci could help make that happen.

When Mitali and Neesh got back to his apartment, Mitali was the first to open the door and stumble inside.

"You must be Hector," Neesh heard Mitali say. His breath caught in his throat. "Hi! It's nice to meet you. I'm Mitali."

Neesh nervously followed Mitali inside. He and Hector almost never spoke. They barely had seen each other in their years of living together, which was borne out of desperation: Hector needed a place to stay after being evicted from his last apartment. Neesh happened to need a roommate.

"It's a pleasure to meet you," Hector said. He picked up the remote and muted the television. "I've heard about you."

"How is it that in nine months I've never met you?" Mitali said. Neesh bit his bottom lip. His right leg tapped restlessly as Mitali took a seat on the couch.

"I work a lot of nights," Hector said, laughing. "And I stay at my partner's place in Manhattan a bunch."

"I thought Neesh said you wanted to be an actor," Mitali said.

"I do," Hector said. "I audition during the day. But no bites yet."

"We're making a play! You should come be a part of it! We'd have to cover up your tattoos, though."

"Why don't we go watch a movie in my room?" Neesh suggested. He didn't want any more crossover between his past life and his current one.

"No, I want to get to know your roommate!" Mitali insisted. "I don't think you've ever told me. How did you guys meet? Craigslist or something?"

Hector was about to answer, but Neesh cut him off.

"Through some friends."

"So you *do* have friends," Mitali said. "How come I never get to meet them?"

"I spend all my free time with you. And they're not my friends anymore."

"You're being rude," Mitali said.

"I'm sorry."

Hector viewed the whole exchange with raised eyebrows. His unkempt face was full of amusement.

"I can tell you how we met," Hector said. Neesh was still behind Mitali, so she didn't see him putting the knuckles of his fist in his mouth. "We used to rip shit together back in the day."

" 'Rip shit'?" Mitali said.

"Steal."

Hector's lips twitched, as if he was about to smile, but no smile came. He sounded serious. Neesh bit the knuckles of his fist so hard that his skin became red. He made eye contact with Hector. In Neesh's eyes, there was pleading. In Hector's, there was indifference. If eyes could shrug, Hector's would have done so. Outside, a dog began howling. But Mitali's cackle cut through the noise.

"You're funny!" Mitali burst out laughing. "Good one."

Hector let out a laugh of his own, and Neesh uncomfortably chuckled along.

"It was nice to meet you, Hector," Mitali said as she rose from the sofa. She headed for Neesh's bedroom.

"Let's do this again sometime," Hector said.

Neesh went to the bathroom to get a bandage for his knuckles.

◇

"I have something to ask you," Mitali said to Neesh a week later, after a movie. Neesh tensed. Were the Jenga blocks about to come tumbling down again? "I told my dad and grandmother about you. And they'd like to meet you. Would you want to come to dinner with them?"

This took Neesh by surprise. In an instant, he felt some sense of relief. Maybe Mitali saw him as something more than a temporary occupant in her life. Why else would she have told her father about him? He felt a rush of affection for Medieval Times. *What a great idea that was.* But he also felt strange. Something was officially going right in his life for the first time in a long while, and he did not know what to do with that information. Neesh didn't have note cards that told him what to do in case of happiness.

"Uh," was all Neesh could say.

"It's totally fine if you feel uncomfortable doing that," Mitali said. Neesh could see her trying to be casual about the invite, but this was clearly a bigger deal than she was letting on. He had learned that she often put up a front whenever something anxiety-inducing came up; this notion that she was unflappable and emotionless. But the way she was looking at him—the infinitesimal nervous twitch of her eyebrow—told him this was something more.

"I'll go," Neesh said. "If you want me to. I just wasn't expecting it. I was worried that—"

Neesh stopped. He didn't want to ruin the moment.

"What?" Mitali said.

"Nothing."

"What?"

Neesh exhaled.

"It's just that when your dad was on the phone the other day, you called me a friend."

Mitali reached for Neesh's hand, but her face was expressionless.

"Did that bother you?"

"It was clarifying."

Neesh felt a squeeze on his hand.

"Neesh, I lo—" Mitali stopped. Neesh could feel sweat on her palms. She looked away. Neesh couldn't see her eyebrows. "You're not a friend."

Not knowing what else to do, Neesh looked away as well.

"Dinner will be great. Maybe. I don't know. You're not a friend either. I never know what to say in these situations."

He squeezed her hand back harder. This dinner would be notable for Neesh, too. He had never met a significant other's parent before, not to mention one he mostly knew through his portrayal in an unfinished play co-written by his deceased teenage daughter.

And this was more than meeting Mitali's father, someone Mitali talked about in warmer terms than she did when she first started dating Neesh. It turned out that his suspicions about Mitali's father and the woman he overheard him referencing on the car ride were correct. Mitali had relayed that another woman would be at the dinner, along with her grandmother. She didn't know much about the other woman, but her name was Catherine, and she and her father were seeing each other.

"Should I be there for this?" Neesh said. "Shouldn't you meet your dad's girlfriend, you know, one-on-one?"

"As I said, you're not a friend. You're my—" Mitali searched for the right word. "Person."

◇

The dinner was scheduled for August, shortly before Labor Day: a double date, plus one, at Gianni's in New Brunswick, the restaurant where Shantanu and Catherine first went.

Mitali could see that Neesh was anxious on the day of the dinner when he arrived at the Port Authority for the bus—twenty minutes early, so he could practice how he might approach the evening. This was confirmed when he showed her the note cards he had spent hours writing out for conversation topics, which he had stuffed in the pocket of his khakis. Neesh didn't have a suit, but he did have a clip-on tie that he wore over a plaid shirt, which was tucked into his pants, an uncommonly formal outfit for Neesh. At first Mitali found Neesh's out-of-the-box preparation to be charming, as she often did, and she chose to make a mental note to buy Neesh some real ties.

The problem was that shortly after getting to the bus station, Neesh realized he had left his wallet at the studio. He briefly considered just leaving it at the desk, something Mitali encouraged. But he needed his license. Neesh sprinted back to the studio, which incensed Mitali, who stewed on the bus ride to New Jersey. The couple was an hour late to the restaurant.

"I'm a fuckup," Neesh said apologetically on the bus. "I'm sorry. But I really need you to help me fill out more of these note cards."

Mitali did.

When Neesh and Mitali finally arrived, no one at the table seemed irritated, as Neesh hurriedly shook everyone's hands. Mitali gave Kalpana a *pranam*.

Neesh's plaid shirt was not too dissimilar from the checkered button-down Shantanu was wearing as they sat down. Same for their pants. Kalpana wore a sari.

"This is an auspicious occasion!" Kalpana said in a raised voice.

Neesh had his first question for Shantanu ready and memorized for as soon as he sat down.

"Mitali tells me you like the Rolling Stones," Neesh said, a bit robotically. Mitali knew that Neesh had rehearsed this. "I too like the Stones a lot too."

"You like the Rolling Stones?" Shantanu said, his voice light.

"We *love* the Stones," Catherine said.

"His baba wouldn't let him go to concerts as a child," Kalpana said.

"He's also a drummer," Mitali said.

"*Was* a drummer," Neesh said. "I used to drum for a Broadway show."

"How come you don't any longer?" Shantanu asked.

"I . . . Things didn't work out," Neesh said. "I was just a substitute, and I went to do something else with my life. Although to be honest, I'm still trying to figure out what."

"You're our own personal Goopy and Bagha!" Kalpana exclaimed. "The misfit musician!"

"Goopy and . . . I'm sorry?" Neesh looked confused as he reflexively put a straw wrapper in his mouth. Mitali squeezed Neesh's knee under the table, and Neesh put the wrapper down.

"*Goopy Gyne Bagha Byne,*" Shantanu said. "It's her favorite film."

"Although, they were *bad* musicians in the film, *Shomadidi*. Neesh is good!" Mitali said.

Mitali's day job involved *selling* things. Promoting them. She wanted to do the same for Neesh with her father and grandmother. Her *shomadidi* was right: this was an auspicious occasion for her. A year ago, she would never have been able to foresee this kind of dinner or the notion of introducing a boyfriend to her family. But there was someone else here, which made for what Mitali couldn't help but think was an odd dynamic. Mitali secretly wanted this dinner all to herself; all about her and Neesh.

"*Shomadidi*, I have to ask. Were you surprised when Baba told you about Catherine?" Mitali said. Kalpana turned to Shantanu and spoke as if she was making a grand pronouncement.

"*Babu*, whenever I've put my hand on your head and prayed, I've wished for your protection and happiness," Kalpana said. "*Durga, Durga.* Just those two things. For many years, I thought Chaitali was the answer to that prayer."

Catherine didn't react to the mention of Mitali's mother.

"And she was for a time," Kalpana continued. "But who is to say that prayers don't have multiple answers? Durga herself has ten hands."

Kalpana now looked directly at Catherine.

"Now, I get to meet you," she said. "Shantanu said you've studied art. I'm going to teach you about the best Bengali painters."

Catherine nodded and smiled. *How is she so calm?* Mitali thought to herself.

The dinner also served as a production meeting. Shantanu told the table that he had gone to the longtime executive director of the George Street Playhouse, at Mitali's insistence, to ask if *The Elm Tree* could be staged there now that Jerry was signed on to direct. Carl, Shantanu's improv teacher, had set up the meeting with the director, whom Shantanu described as an older, curt woman named Hannah Caldwell. Hannah was putting together the theater's winter season. She was skeptical at first, Shantanu said, even after reading Pamela and Keya's rough draft.

"Well, did she say yes or not?" Mitali said.

"She said, 'We don't usually put on plays here for inexperienced parents who want to throw their kids a bone,'" Shantanu recounted in a mimicking voice. "'This is a place where Broadway shows do out-of-town tryouts. We need to fill seats.'"

"*Eesh!*" Kalpana hissed.

But Shantanu said he made his case: It would be one weekend, and he'd fund the whole thing. And the great Jerry Santucci was attached to direct.

"'Jerry? I haven't seen him in years,'" Shantanu said, again mimicking Hannah.

"Those improv classes turned you into an actor, Baba," Mitali said.

"She looked impressed," Shantanu said. "Hannah said that we would likely not make any money off this. I told her I'm not doing this for profit. But Jerry's name got her interested. She said it would help with marketing."

"I can see it now," Catherine said. "Jerry Santucci's return to greatness comes via a high school play."

"I think he sees it that way too," Shantanu said.

"Is he still a jerk?" Mitali asked.

"Jerry? He's motivated," Catherine said.

The news of the venue animated the dinner table. Neesh volunteered to be the set designer, citing his experience working Off Broadway. Mitali would coordinate any marketing that had to do with the show. They would post ads online for auditions, for which they would all be present. In terms of creative choices, that would be left to Pamela and Jerry. Kalpana said she would offer her prayers every day. Catherine would handle costuming. They all agreed: any proceeds from the show would go towards creating a scholarship in Keya's honor.

"It feels strange not to be preparing for the classroom," Shantanu said. He excused himself to go to the bathroom. Kalpana said she had to go as well.

"You look like a strong man," Kalpana said to Neesh. "Would you like to escort me? I have more questions for you. I want to get to know my future grandson-in-law."

Shantanu was taken aback. Mitali turned beet red in embarrassment. *Shomadidi, what the fuck? I couldn't even say the words "I love you" to him the other day.* Neesh shrugged and offered a polite smile before he rose from his seat, and went to Kalpana's chair. Kalpana got up and slid her arm around Neesh's. They shuffled away, leaving Catherine and Mitali alone at the table.

"It must be strange for you that I'm here," Catherine said to Mitali.

Mitali picked up the fork next to her plate and twirled it. *You have no idea.*

"I never pictured this, no," Mitali said. "To be honest."

That was more aggressive than I meant for it to be.

"Someone white with your father?"

This is going in the wrong direction.

"That's not what I meant," Mitali said. "I've just always pictured my mother here."

"If it makes you feel any better, I feel like an intruder."

Catherine sipped her water.

"Why *are* you here exactly? It's one thing to date my father. But you didn't know my sister. You don't have to take part in this."

"Your father is a good man in a world full of bad ones. And when I'm in, I'm in. I'd like to lighten his burden."

"Does he lighten yours?"

"Yes."

"Good."

Don't forget. Baba deserves this as much as you do, Mitali scolded herself. If anything went awry in life, Mitali had Neesh, someone who, for the first time, she hoped to have unabashedly on her side. *Why shouldn't Baba have the same?*

Mitali spooned some more ravioli into her mouth.

"My mother moved on. It's only fair that my father does too. I haven't seen him this . . . *something* in years. Whatever you've done, you've done it right," Mitali said.

Mitali pictured her mother somewhere down Route 9, separate from all of them. In Jahar, Chaitali had found what Mitali had in Neesh and what Shantanu had in Catherine, she only found it sooner. In a way, Mitali thought, Chaitali had given them permission to do so. *Maybe I should be thankful to her for that, instead of angry.*

"'Happy' is the word you're looking for," Shantanu said as he sat back down. He gave Catherine a kiss on the head. Mitali did her best not to blanch.

"*Sona*, are you angry with me?" Shantanu said.

"No, Baba," Mitali said. "This will just take some getting used to. I'm still working on it with Jahar Kaku."

"Neesh is a good man," Shantanu said. "Thank you for introducing us to him."

"I'm glad you like him," Mitali said. "He's a sweetheart."

"I wish he had a job that paid more, though," Shantanu said.

"Shantanu," Catherine said.

"Baba, please, not now."

Shantanu put his palms up in surrender.

"He's a bit awkward," Shantanu said. "Tell him to relax."

"When did you become so cool, Baba? Do you remember your nickname, Daddy Dilbert?"

TWELVE

Pamela was sick to her stomach as she looked down the row of chairs lined up at the conference table on one end of the room. There was Shantanu, who for some reason was wearing a suit. He had remarked several times that this was the same room he had taken improv classes in. He appeared to be resting his eyes. Mitali was next to him, as was her friend Neesh—Pamela still wasn't sure why he had such an interest in the play, but they both pored over a stack of note cards and discussed them in hushed tones. When Pamela asked what was on them, Neesh held them up: the squiggly lines were a to-do list. Among the notes: "Set designer." "Press." "Program design." "Posters." "Sound guy." But the rest of the words on the note cards simply blurred in front of her.

On the far end of the table, Jerry Santucci, wearing a baseball cap, T-shirt, and jeans, loudly sipped his coffee while scrolling his phone, looking indifferent. Catherine was leaning against a wall next to Jerry, flipping a lighter in her hand, probably listening to nervous actors and actresses in the hallway practicing their lines for the third and final day of auditions. Pamela had seen the group in person over breakfast before the first day of auditions. That was her first time meeting Neesh, Catherine, and Jerry. She had known Mitali from when she was growing up, but their interactions were brief, so she barely remembered her. At first, Pamela was struck by how much Mitali looked like Keya. The eyes were similar. Mitali had a slightly more defined nose. They greeted each other with an extended, silent hug.

One moment made Pamela snicker that morning. Neesh seemed distressed that he was not wearing a suit like Shantanu, who was sitting a few feet away from him. Neesh felt the need to address this and did so by telling Shantanu, "I like your suit. I don't own one, but if I did, it would look like that." Shantanu took the compliment in stride, but Mitali gave him an odd look.

For the last several weeks, each of them separately had gone out to post flyers advertising the auditions. Mitali got word of the auditions onto theater message boards. Jerry sent word to some agents and acting teachers he knew. Shantanu emailed professors at Mason Gross, the performing arts school at Rutgers University, and at Tisch, the one at New York University.

Pamela had already vomited this morning. An entire weekend of hearing her lines read out loud was overwhelming, as was this group of mostly strangers doing all this work on behalf of something she had helped create.

This was her first time throwing up since the night that Pamela had mostly finished rewriting the play, right around the family's Labor Day dinner, after receiving a call from Jerry. One section was still vexing her: the ending.

"My god, you sound tiny," Jerry said, as a way of greeting. "This is Jerry Santucci. Do you know who I am?"

Of course, Pamela knew exactly who Jerry Santucci was. He was the kind of director who theater-obsessed high schoolers knew, even though he hadn't produced anything of note while Pamela was coming of age. Jerry didn't wait for an answer.

"Your play has potential," Jerry said. "I like how you have the two families onstage together in the second act. It needs more cleaning up on the front end so I can block it correctly. I can't make some of these set changes work. Good thought on having this Ms. Kanoople character never appear. I need to understand more about the Preethi and Kate relationship. Write more scenes at the tree. What do they want to do with their lives? Figure out your ending. Do the girls reconcile with the parents? Do the parents accept them? I also think we shouldn't have multiple acts. Let's make this seventy-five minutes flat, one act. Sound good?"

"Are you asking me what I think?" Pamela said. She glanced at a cardboard mount next to her bedroom door, which had several Playbills tacked on it.

"No, not really."

"Okay, then."

She hung up the phone. It was ten o'clock and Pamela began to furiously type. She could not believe this play that she and Keya wrote so long ago—one that she had almost forgotten about, or rather, tried to forget about—had notes to incorporate from a Tony Award–winning director.

Pamela wondered what Keya would say about all of this. And her ferocious typing immediately stopped. She recalled the night Keya had that ill-fated conversation with the rest of her family, driving to the Moores' house immediately afterwards. In her room, Pamela cradled Keya's head in her lap.

"This is exactly how my grandmother held me after *42nd Street*," Keya had said, her hands clutching Pamela's.

"I can't believe your dad recommended therapy," Pamela said. "It makes me so mad."

"I don't understand. All of this. Any of this," Keya said. Her face seemed like it was made of stone. She looked up at the ceiling, as if she were trying to talk to the whole world and not just Pamela. "Do you think he's right?"

"No fucking way," Pamela said. "No. Fucking. Way. Dude, you don't think that, do you?"

"I don't know," Keya said. "My dad said, 'You are a great many things. You aren't this.' I'm only his daughter when it's convenient. And Mitali. Why was she so mean? What was she talking about with grandchildren? My mother sat there and barely said anything, except something about the community. This sucks."

"What are you going to do?"

"I don't know. I guess I could run away to my grandmother's. But she wouldn't like it."

"You could come here," Pamela said.

"Please. We knew your parents wouldn't approve of us, with all the 'sin' bullshit they spew. But my parents? They're supposed to be the understanding ones. They weren't supposed to react like *this*."

Pamela looked forlorn.

"If your mom and dad were like that, imagine mine?"

"We'll never know, will we?"

Keya slammed her fist on the rug. But she hit the floor too hard and shook her hand in pain.

"Ow!" Keya yelped.

"I've never seen you do *that*," Pamela said. She began to gently run her fingers through Keya's hair. Keya closed her eyes as Pamela eased her tension.

"I chickened out tonight. I'm sorry," Pamela said. "Roger might throw me out. He'd accuse me of being depraved. Janine wouldn't believe me if I told her. She talks all the time about how she can't wait to see me walk down the aisle like she did, with some dumb 'hunk of a man' next to me. And you know how she is about church. And yeah, sin. She barely likes who I am now. I couldn't go through with telling her. Someday soon, I promise."

"It's okay," Keya said. "Doing it the same night was always a fantasy. It's something we wrote in a play. Nothing more. Who knew, though? Chaitali, Shantanu, Janine, and Roger are all cut from the same boring, backwards cloth."

"Keya."

"This didn't go the way we planned."

"Keya, one day we'll live together," Pamela said. "We're eighteen. Maybe even next year. We'll get a dog. We'll both star in shows. Or I'll direct. You star. Who gives a shit? We'll move to Hollywood. Or New York. Or anywhere. We'll leave them all behind."

"I don't want to leave everyone else behind," Keya said, again at the ceiling. "I want them to want to come *with*. I thought they would, without question."

Keya mumbled something to herself.

"What are you saying?" Pamela said.

"*Durga, Durga*," Keya said. "Something my grandmother says."

She sat upright and looked Pamela square in the eyes.

"Have you always known? That you, you know—"

"That I liked you? Not always, no," Pamela said.

"When did you know?"

"One day, I was looking at you. In Spanish class with Mr. Ritter, maybe. And it hit me—*bam!*—that I think about you all the time. And I thought that I wasn't supposed to obsess over one person so much. But I wanted to spend all my time with you. And I realized there was something more."

Pamela paused.

"Okay, your turn."

Keya stroked her chin.

"The roller-skating rink, last year. Raquel fell and skinned her knee. You couldn't move fast enough to go help her up and then you guys held hands as you went around the rink, because that klutz couldn't skate. I was enraged but I didn't know why."

Pamela reached for Keya's face and pulled it close to her. Right as her lips were about to connect with Keya's, there was a soft knock on Pamela's door. Pamela threw Keya off her, causing Keya to hit Pamela's desk. Several textbooks fell off. Janine opened the door. She looked worn down.

"Keya, dear, will you be staying for dinner?" she asked.

"Uh, can I?" Keya asked, rubbing the back of her head.

"Of course," Janine said. She looked at Pamela. "Your father just called. He won't be home for dinner. Again. Some supplier meeting in the city. Again."

Pamela and Keya exchanged looks. Pamela's mother noticed the textbooks on the floor.

"What was that crash I just heard?" Janine asked.

"Nothing, we're just talking about—" Pamela looked at Keya desperately.

"Boys?" Keya said. "Yeah, boys."

The room felt painfully quiet, empty.

"If God wills it, you'll both have the same thing that I have. Companionship is just so important," Janine said softly, before she closed the door behind her.

As the sound of her footsteps evaporated down the hallway, Keya whispered to Pamela, "Do you think by 'companionship,' she means that senior Brandon you dated when you were a freshman?"

Pamela immediately pinched Keya on the shoulder, eliciting a playful yelp.

"Get the papers. It's time to write more of the play," Keya said.

"Can't we just work on my computer?"

"No! You know how much I prefer to work off handwritten notes. This is why I print everything out!"

In the room set aside for auditions, Pamela wished that her co-writer was there, scribbling on a notepad, so she'd feel less alone. And even with the team in the room with her, Pamela felt she was taking a large part of this journey by herself, something she was never meant to do. She considered how her parents would react to what she and Keya had written. Would they know this was based on her real life? How explicit could she be? *I have to do this. I should've done it that night. That is who Keya was. This is who I am.*

◇

Shantanu was dozing off. The days of auditions and weeks of coordinating them had him running on fumes. The lumpy mattress at Catherine's didn't help either.

Jerry leapt up from his chair, disrupting the relative silence of the audition room and jerking Shantanu awake. A startled Neesh dropped the note cards that he and Mitali were looking at. Everyone in the room turned to look at Jerry, who had previously been scrolling through his phone.

"Before we start day three of the Mediocre Audition Revue, I've spent the last week coming up with a partial solution," Jerry said.

"Partial solution to what?" Shantanu said.

"What part of 'Mediocre Audition Revue' did you just not understand?"

"They haven't been bad," Shantanu said. "The younger actors have been strong."

"Thank you. And how many Tonys have you won?" Jerry said.

This attitude, not to mention Jerry's general presence, grated on

Shantanu. But Shantanu had come to terms with needing him. Without Jerry, *The Elm Tree* would still be in a box in the attic.

"We talked about this," Catherine cut in. "Jerry, go easy."

"Dr. Das, I'm trying to make a play here. I want to be impressed by these actors. And I haven't been impressed. Do you let your students turn in C-quality work? And then they get to be called doctors?"

"What's your solution?"

"Well, this is the benefit of being a three-time Tony Award winner."

"How many times is he going to mention his Tonys?" Shantanu heard Mitali whisper under her breath.

"The other day, I called my friends Toby Barone and Francesca Kazakoff."

Shantanu greeted the names with blank stares.

"Toby Barone and Francesca Kazakoff. They've been on Broadway. Several times. They worked with me on a couple plays. I sent them Pamela's play. And I've convinced them to play Kate's parents."

Again, a blank stare.

"Do you know what this means? We have Broadway performers attached to the play. Professionals! They said no at first, but once I promised not to throw anything during rehearsals, they agreed to consider it. I just got an email from both of them saying they're in. And I've gotten them to agree to just above the Actors' Equity minimum! You know how I did it? I used my charm."

"We said we weren't going to use Equity actors," Catherine said.

Shantanu sighed. "What is the minimum?"

"They'll do it for three thousand dollars each a week. So I'll probably need two weeks of rehearsals. Plus the three show days."

Shantanu ran through calculations in his head.

"The cast of six would cost fifty thousand dollars, give or take. Plus we have ten thousand dollars for everything else," Shantanu said. "Neesh, how much would we need to build a set with?"

"I could get used furniture. An old backdrop. I have to figure out the tree," Neesh said. He picked up one of his note cards off the ground. "I think I could do it for ten thousand dollars. We would need some stage-hands."

"We're still short," Shantanu said. "We'd probably need an extra ten thousand dollars in production costs. Maybe twenty thousand dollars. I already sold my house and I need to find a new place. I'll go broke if we continue at this rate. Plus we have to pay your fee, Jerry. Where will we get the money?"

"Waive my fee," Jerry said. "I don't care. I *have* money. I'm trying to get back into the business. We need this to be good. We can hide the fact that amateurs are behind this if we put professionals out front."

Shantanu looked at Pamela, who was raising her hand to speak.

"Pamela, you don't have to raise your hand," Jerry said.

"I have a thousand or so saved up," Pamela said.

The look on Pamela's face reminded Shantanu of Mitali's determination when she initially broached the idea of the show. There was a resolve in her eyes, just as there was in Shantanu's when he asked her to finish the play.

"I'll find the money," Shantanu said. "I have money left over from the house. I'll just have to live at Ma's longer. Surely, every man dreams of that in his fifties. Let's start the audition."

"Baba," Mitali said.

"Don't worry," Shantanu said. "I'm the producer of this show. This is my job. What should we do about auditions today? What about the people auditioning for Kate's parents' part?"

"I'll keep them in mind for my next show," Jerry said dismissively. "Let's begin."

Catherine went out to retrieve the first prospective actress of the day. When she brought her in, Mitali let out a loud gasp.

THIRTEEN

"Chaitali?!" Shantanu quickly pinched himself. She was wearing a blue floral dress, one that used to hang in Shantanu's closet.

"Ma!" Mitali, who had just reorganized the note cards, was holding them in such a way that her stack fell apart all over again. Catherine went back to the corner where she had been standing. She looked unsure of herself, which was a rare sight.

"Mrs. Das," Pamela said. "We weren't expecting you. What are you doing here?"

"I'm auditioning," Chaitali said. "For the part of Preethi's mother. These are still open auditions, correct?"

"For this role, yes," Jerry said. "There aren't many, if you'll excuse me for saying so, people of your descent in theater. I think there's three Indian women in all of Hollywood. All of them are named Mindy Kaling."

Jerry seemed proud of himself for that joke.

"What do you mean 'auditioning'?" Shantanu was still in shock. "Is this a practical joke?"

"The part of Preethi's mother," Chaitali said. "I want it. Who better to play it than the woman it is based on?"

"I'm sorry, who are you?" Jerry said.

"She's his wife," Pamela said.

"*Ex*-wife," Shantanu corrected. Catherine raised her eyebrows.

"Oh dear," Jerry said, suddenly realizing the situation.

"I thought you said you didn't want to be a part of this," Mitali said.

"I changed my mind," Chaitali said. "Shall I start?"

"Do you have a headshot? And a résumé?" Jerry said.

Chaitali reached in her purse and took out a piece of paper, with a picture clipped to it, and handed it to Jerry.

"This says you're a librarian," Jerry said.

"That's correct."

"I meant an acting résumé," Jerry said.

"That's the résumé I have," Chaitali said.

"Have you ever acted before?" Jerry said.

"Over the summer, I took classes at the Barrow school in New York."

Jerry nodded. Mitali and Shantanu looked on in disbelief.

"What will you be performing for us today?"

"A section from *The Elm Tree*. A play by my daughter and Pamela Moore. Two young playwrights."

Pamela gave the slightest hint of a smile, as Chaitali walked towards the table and handed Mitali a copy of *The Elm Tree*. It was the rough draft.

"We've been asking actors for specific scenes from the show or comparable monologues," Jerry said. "This isn't the one for that part."

"This is what I have prepared," Chaitali said tersely. Jerry looked down at the table and shrugged.

"You kept a copy this whole time?" Mitali said.

"If you don't mind reading the lines for the character of Preethi here," Chaitali said.

Chaitali pointed her finger at the page and handed the papers to Mitali. She did not wait for a yes as she backed into the center of the room and faced the conference room table. She had no papers of her own in either hand. Mitali began.

PREETHI

Come in.

PREETHI'S MOTHER

Preethi, are you okay?

PREETHI

How do you think I'm doing?

PREETHI'S MOTHER

I don't know. Do you want to come down for dinner?

PREETHI

I never want to eat dinner with you again.

As she read that line, Mitali's voice cracked, but she recovered.

PREETHI'S MOTHER

Can we discuss?

PREETHI

What's there to discuss?

Chaitali's delivery was practiced and commanding. Her eyes never left Mitali's face.

PREETHI'S MOTHER

We are who we are because we are Bengali. If my mother knew that America would corrupt her granddaughter like that, she would have stayed in Kolkata. All your *mashis* and *kakus*. They would never accept us anymore if we let this continue.

PREETHI

Let what continue?

PREETHI'S MOTHER

What you told us before.

PREETHI

You can't even say it.

Chaitali's eyes closed, as if the line wounded her in the reading. She balled her fists, before releasing them.

PREETHI'S MOTHER

There is nothing to say. Don't be cheeky, little one. You have great things ahead of you. You need to focus on your studies. Not these childlike fantasies. Do us proud. Do our culture proud. Don't indulge in these distractions.

PREETHI

Do you love me? No matter what?

In the next line, Chaitali seemed to summon as much compassion as she could.

PREETHI'S MOTHER

You are my daughter.

PREETHI

That doesn't answer my question.

Then came a stern response:

PREETHI'S MOTHER

You are my daughter. That means you have responsibilities too.

PREETHI

Do I have your love?

PREETHI'S MOTHER

Earn it. Get the grades we expect of you. Practice the singing. Show us respect. And then the answer is yes.

PREETHI

You don't love me.

Chaitali turned away from the table and whispered to herself, "Of course I love you, Keya," but the whisper wasn't soft enough. Everyone in the room heard. She turned back to the table. All the eyes were transfixed on her. But she met them with a steely gaze.

PREETHI'S MOTHER

Sona, there are bigger things than you on this planet. One day, you'll be old enough and you'll understand.

The stage directions called for Preethi's Mother to leave the room, bringing the scene to an end. Chaitali stopped and waited for a response from the creative team. The silence lingered, but Chaitali looked unfazed, almost defiant. Neesh shuffled his note cards. Pamela turned her head towards Shantanu and Mitali, who had their eyes still glued to Chaitali. Catherine still looked unsettled. But Jerry was the first one to speak.

"Thank you. We'll let you know if we need anything else."

Chaitali walked to the table and took her copy of the play. She looked around the room and walked out, leaving a stunned silence in her wake.

"Why don't we take fifteen?" Shantanu said, staring at the doorway.

"We just started the day," Jerry protested.

"Fifteen." Shantanu got up and started to chase after Chaitali.

"Fine," Jerry said. "Hey, Shantanu, one thing before you go."

Shantanu stopped at the doorway.

"She's got raw talent. But she's not going to work for this."

Shantanu put both hands in his pockets and looked down the hallway, where dozens of people were waiting to audition.

"Yeah, I know."

◊

Shantanu's knees ached as he ran out the front door of the George Street Playhouse and caught up to Chaitali, who was standing on the sidewalk outside with one hand on her bowed head.

"I have a headache," Chaitali said.

"Do you want to sit down? There's a bench right there," Shantanu huffed.

Chaitali said yes. The two walked over to the bench on the sidewalk. Chaitali reached into her purse and took out an aspirin, as well as bottled water.

"When did you learn to act like that?"

"We're Bengali. We're known for being artists."

"I'm serious."

"I told you. I've been taking classes."

"You were very good."

"Thank you."

Chaitali took another swig of water. She offered the bottle to Shantanu, who declined.

"We can't give you the part," Shantanu said. He watched as buses and cars zoomed by on the street. "Jerry said—"

"It's okay," Chaitali cut him off. "You have quite a professional operation going in there. I looked up that guy Jerry. How were you able to get such an accomplished director?"

Shantanu looked from the street into Chaitali's eyes.

"The woman in there on the left. Catherine. She connected us."

"Ah," Chaitali said. "Is she another theater person or something?"

"She's . . . we're seeing each other."

Chaitali looked back into Shantanu's eyes. She looked hurt.

"I'm glad."

Both of them went back to watching the cars go by.

"You seem different," Chaitali said. "You've lost weight. You're energized. You're wearing a suit."

"I am."

"It's a good look on you. Reminds me of when we met."

"Yes."

"Who was the other guy? The younger man?" Chaitali said.

"That's Neesh," Shantanu said. "Mitali's boyfriend. Yes, she has a boyfriend now. He's quite nice. Dedicated. We might be grandparents yet."

"She never told me," Chaitali said. "She didn't return my call on her birthday."

"She should have," Shantanu said. "Why did you come here?"

"I miss Mitali. I miss our family. And once I saw that you were intent on doing this, I didn't want to be left behind."

"What about all that stuff you said about how this wasn't ours to do? And exposing our family?"

Chaitali clasped her hands together. She kept her eyes straight ahead, as did Shantanu. In that moment, Shantanu wished they were in one of the cars, driving away from the playhouse to somewhere, sometime, else.

"I kept thinking that there might be another Bengali family of four out there. And maybe seeing this play would make them think differently. Maybe I—we—could atone for our mistakes."

"Maybe."

"That scene I performed. She thought I didn't love her at the end. Or that my love was conditional."

"She thought the same of me."

"She didn't write a scene with just you, though."

Shantanu looked at his watch.

"I have to head back. Would you like to come? Watch the rest of the auditions?"

Chaitali put her palm on Shantanu's cheek, before removing it.

"I'm glad you've found something, Shanti. And someone," Chaitali said. "You wear a theater producer well. Tell Mitali to call me sometime. Let me know what you need help with. We are here for you. I hope you can make this better than *Stomp*."

"How are things with Jahar?" Shantanu said.

Chaitali stood up. Shantanu followed suit.

"I'm here in part *because* of him."

A pause.

"What did you do with Keya's things? That were at the house?" Chaitali said.

"Storage," Shantanu said.

"Will you take me there someday?"

Shantanu nodded, and Chaitali turned and walked down the street. He watched for a bit before heading back inside. As he turned around, he saw Catherine leaning against the front doorway watching them.

◇

"Chaitali?" Jahar poked his head into the kitchen, where Chaitali sat drinking a hot chocolate and reading *Jane Eyre*. "Picked that one up off the shelf, I see."

"Yes," Chaitali said. "I haven't read this one in a couple years. I like to pick it up every now and then. Did you have lunch? I can make you something."

"No, no, sit," Jahar said. "I have something to give you. Our wedding anniversary is approaching."

"It's not for a couple months," Chaitali said, putting her book down on the table, which was covered by a linen tablecloth with a plastic sheet layered on top. One of the few things she had inherited from her upbringing. "And do we celebrate that kind of thing?"

"What did I say when we married? 'There is no shame in love,'" Jahar said. "This year we are going to celebrate. And this can't wait."

He reached into the pocket of his jeans and took out an envelope. Chaitali delicately tore the seal off and took out the papers inside.

"What is this?" Chaitali said as she unfolded Jahar's gift. She read from the paper: "The Barrow Group."

"It's an acting school in New York," Jahar said.

"Excuse me?"

"An acting school. Where you learn to become an actress. My stepdaughter gave me the idea."

"Mitali told you to get me this?"

"No," Jahar said, taking a seat at the table next to Chaitali. "She gave Shantanu improv lessons. I'm giving you acting lessons. They start next week."

"But why?" Chaitali said. "I have no interest in acting. I don't like public speaking."

"You used to sing at pujas, did you not?"

"That was years ago. And it was in a group. And it was because I felt it was what I was supposed to do."

"It counts," Jahar said with a soothing smile. "The reason you should take the class is so you can audition for that play." Chaitali hit her mug on the table, spilling hot liquid.

"Are you losing it?"

"Perhaps," Jahar said. "But I've seen you recently. Walking around in a daze, as if Durga herself hit you over the head. You haven't been present, ever since that call with Mitali, Shantanu, and Kalpana."

"I told you why," Chaitali said. "I don't think that play is a good idea."

"Yes," Jahar said. "You don't want the world to see your flaws."

"This was way more than a 'flaw.'"

Chaitali burned her tongue on the hot chocolate from an aggressive sip, which caused another slight spill on the table.

"You felt you had already lost your family when you and I got married," Jahar said. "Do you remember that?"

Chaitali stayed quiet as she went to retrieve a paper towel.

"Now your daughter and ex-husband are about to embark on a new journey. And once again, they're doing it without you," Jahar said. "Don't let them do that."

"It's not a journey I need to take with them," Chaitali said as she wiped the mess clean. "The journey ended that night when the officer came to our door."

"I'm not so sure you believe that," Jahar said. "Just because Keya passed doesn't mean she can't still do some good in this world. Shantanu and Mitali believe that too. And if in that process, you have to confront your own blemishes in the world, so be it."

"I don't know that Keya would have wanted this," Chaitali said.

"I'm going to suggest something you may not like: Is it possible that you are *hoping* that Keya wouldn't have wanted it?" Jahar said. "I remember Keya when she was a tiny tot. She was fearless. Always a pitbull. She always loved expressing herself. In some ways, the play is an expression of who she was. Why not help with that?"

Chaitali looked out the window at the backyard, populated by the lush green grass she had come to love. The blades moved slightly with the breeze.

"Jahar, you are the new chapter in my life," Chaitali said. "Why should I reopen these old wounds?"

"Look at this as a new chapter rather than an old one," Jahar said. "And it's a chance to bring you closer to Mitali. I lost my son years ago. But it's not too late for you."

"This play won't even happen," Chaitali said, holding the papers in her hand again. "What do any of us know about putting on a play?"

"Shantanu is a smart man," Jahar said. "Maybe that's why he sold the house. To raise money. Look, all I ask is that you give this class a try. Worse comes to worst, when we see plays in the city, you can snobbily whisper notes in my ear."

Chaitali took the last sip of her hot chocolate.

"Keya would have a good laugh about me taking an acting class."

"That is reason enough to take it."

◇

Neesh was distracted at the front desk of Electric Smash, which was within a small office connected to a separate, even smaller office. His eyes were fixated on a blank piece of paper in front of him, where he had sketched out a tree with wide leaves hanging off scores of branches. The pen he had used to draw the tree was a shell of its former self thanks to Neesh's chewing. He took out a calculator and began plugging in numbers, trying to determine how much foam he would need to build an elm tree on a budget. *I'm going to have to spend some time hiking and get some real tree branches to attach to the foam,* Neesh thought to himself. *I have to do this on a budget. Can I buy a fake elm tree? One that could fill the whole stage? That's the size Jerry wants. How will I ever get the right amount of lights for this? Do I light it up like a Christmas tree?*

"Excuse me," a woman holding a guitar said from the other side of the desk, opposite a counter. Neesh didn't hear her. The woman coughed, but still couldn't get Neesh's attention. She rapped her knuckles on the desk. "Neesh, are you there, buddy?"

This shook Neesh away from the paper.

"Sorry, Griselda," he said apologetically. Griselda, now in her sixties, had more gray in her hair to mix with the red. Where there used to be cigarettes sticking out of her jeans, there were now Tic Tacs. She handed Neesh the guitar.

"Room D left for the night. The Fourtones. I told them they could settle up next week. That drummer Chris spilled some coffee. Can you take care of it before you leave?" Griselda said.

"Sure," Neesh said. "Even though Chris isn't a good enough drummer for me to clean up his coffee."

"I knew you'd say that," Griselda said with her gravelly-sounding chuckle, followed by a cough.

Neesh rolled his chair over to the water cooler. Griselda looked relieved when he handed her a cup of cold water.

"Thanks," she said, swallowing in one gulp. "Don't get old, Neesh. Things get harder."

Neesh got up to make his rounds, something he did at the end of all his closing shifts. In every room, his tasks included rolling up XLR cords, moving amps back to their normal position, cleaning up spills and ashes, repositioning drums, and otherwise making the rooms ready for more musicians the next morning. The cycle was steady and mindless. The only enjoyment Neesh got from this job for the last seven years was being around Griselda and sitting down with a pair of sticks at high-quality drum sets after everyone had left. She was the closest thing he had in the world to a friend. The one place he wouldn't play: room C. That was where he used to jam with Jared and Sandeep.

"Don't leave yet," Griselda said. "I have to talk to you."

Neesh sat back down on the beat-up office chair. Its leather seams were ripped. Yet Neesh had sat on this same chair every work shift since his first one. Griselda never wanted to buy a new one. She preferred to put any extra money into studio upkeep, and Neesh never asked for new furniture. Griselda pulled up a plastic folding chair next to Neesh.

"I have to tell you something," Griselda said.

"Oh fuck," Neesh said, suddenly looking worried. His leg began to bob up and down.

"What?"

"You're laying me off. I know business has been slow, but can I take a pay cut instead?" Neesh said.

Griselda laughed again, followed by a cough.

"I'm not laying you off," Griselda said. "I'm laying myself off."

"What does that mean?"

Griselda looked at her empire.

"Johnny and I started this place thirty years ago. I still remember we started with two jam rooms in Flatbush. Then we came here. But it's hard doing this by yourself, you know?"

Griselda took Neesh's hands.

"The truth is that my health isn't getting any better. I've gotta start planning for the next world."

"Oh, fuck off. What are you saying?" Neesh said.

"I'm selling this place to some old friends," Griselda said. "I got a good price. Finalizing the paperwork now. I've earned a vacation, don't you think?"

Neesh leaned back on the creaky chair and put the chewed-up pen in his mouth.

"Of course," Neesh said. He looked at the tree sketch on the table. "Am I going to be okay?"

"Generally? I don't know," Griselda said. "You're much too good of a drummer to be sitting here opening doors for other drummers. But as far as this gig goes? I've asked the new group to keep you on. They seemed open to it. You've never been late or called out sick in all these years. You've done really well here, and I told the new guys that."

"Thank you."

"No, thank you. You're a sweet guy. And you made my life easier around here."

The doorbell buzzed.

"Maybe one of the Fourtones left something here?" Neesh said.

"No," Griselda said. "One of the new owners is about to come by with some more paperwork. You want to meet him? You might as well."

Neesh nodded and hit a button on the desk to unlock the front door, which was down a hallway and out of sight of his desk.

"Gary Whyte! We're in here!" Griselda yelled.

The pen fell out of Neesh's mouth.

"Gary Whyte," Griselda said. "Great drummer. You'll like him. He's one of the buyers."

Griselda didn't notice the pained look on Neesh's face.

"Grizzles! You got that whiskey I asked for?" a voice shouted from out of sight.

For a moment, Neesh held out hope there was a different drummer named Gary Whyte who happened to be buying the studio. But it wasn't. *The* Gary Whyte appeared opposite, holding a manila folder. He did a double take, as if he couldn't comprehend the sight in front of him, while Neesh tried to avoid eye contact, feeling the same. Gary Whyte's white hair was thinner than the last time Neesh saw him. The spikes were gone. Now he had a buzz cut, which accentuated the wide black spectacles on his face.

"What could you possibly be doing here?" Gary Whyte said to Neesh, irritated.

"He works here," Griselda said. "This is Neesh. He's the guy I told you about. You know each other?"

"Yeah, I know him," Gary Whyte said. "*This* is the guy you want me to keep on?"

"All drummers know each other, huh?" Griselda said. "I'm going to the copy room. I'll be right back."

Griselda took the folder from Gary Whyte, who came around an adjacent door that led to where Neesh was sitting behind the desk.

"Jesus," Gary Whyte said, as Griselda walked away. "Of all the fucking people."

Neesh kept his eyes on the tree sketch.

"Do you know how much trouble you caused me?" Gary Whyte said.

"I don't," Neesh said. "You never took my phone calls."

"Pit musicians get to where they are by word of mouth," Gary Whyte hissed. "I *vouched* for you. And you were high at performances. High! Do you know how bad you made me look? How much shit I had to take from conductors? I couldn't recommend anyone else for a while. God," he laughed, "you were such a dumb fucker. You blew a golden ticket."

Neesh wished Griselda would come back soon with the papers. He could hear the copy machine whirring from down the hall. He sighed.

"I was," Neesh said. "You can drop the holier-than-thou act, though."

"What?"

"I was a dumb fucker," Neesh said. "And I'll live with that the rest of my life. But you act like you've never been around drugs before in your line of work."

"I had the decency to be subtle," Gary Whyte said.

"Well, I didn't."

Gary Whyte grimaced.

"It wasn't just the coke, was it?" Gary Whyte said. "I heard about Javits too."

Neesh finally looked directly into his eyes. His breathing got heavier.

"Yeah, I know about that," Gary Whyte said. He seemed to relish telling Neesh this. "Your arrest made the *New York Post*. Are you forgetting? I knew it was you as soon as I saw it."

Neesh remembered the blurb tucked into a corner on the inside flap. It had haunted him. Neesh took the sketch off the desk and put it in his backpack. He began thinking of all the job applications he was about to begin filling out. How many background checks would he fail? And he wondered about his bank account. He could go maybe two weeks without work.

"It's getting late," Neesh said.

"Young people," Gary Whyte said. "This is what happens when you give them things."

Neesh sprang up. With every movement, the chair squeaked loudly.

"I'm sorry for what I did," Neesh said. "I'll stay on here until you take over. Then I'll go find something else."

"Does Griselda know?"

Neesh said no.

"You never told her."

"She never asked," Neesh said. "And she needed someone."

"Yeah, she did," Gary Whyte said. Neesh could hear Griselda's footsteps coming down the hallway. He stepped out the office door and began to head for the exit. Again, he would not meet Gary Whyte's gaze. But Neesh realized he forgot something. He quickly turned around and went back to the desk. He stepped around Gary Whyte and picked up a note card with "You are the universe in ecstatic motion!" written on it and stuffed it into his backpack.

Griselda returned and handed Gary Whyte's folder back to him. She was holding a bottle of whiskey in the other hand.

"You guys getting cozy?" Griselda said. She reached for a stack of paper cups on the desk and poured the smooth, brown liquid into three of them.

"Life is a weird labyrinth, G," Gary Whyte said as he took his cup.

He pointed at Neesh, who hesitantly took one as well.

"He reminds me of Johnny," Griselda said. "Every spring, Neesh comes over and replaces my storm windows. He's a good egg. I was just telling him that I asked you to keep him on."

Gary Whyte held a cup in the air.

"To Johnny. A great guitarist. I feel his ghost in here still."

Griselda and Neesh followed and sipped from their cups.

"He drank a bit too much," Gary Whyte said. "Especially at the end.

I stopped coming around here afterwards. I'm glad I'll be spending a lot more time here next month."

"And I'll be on a boat somewhere. Maybe the Long Island Sound," Griselda said. She took another sip. "And Neesh?"

Gary Whyte examined his cup and then Griselda's beaming face.

"I trust you, Grizzles," Gary Whyte said. "If Neesh wants to be here when we take over in a couple weeks, he'll have a job."

Neesh took a longer sip from his cup and leaned back, causing a familiar crunching noise to emanate from the chair.

"Thanks, Gary Whyte."

"Don't thank me. Thank Griselda."

FOURTEEN

P amela was used to Saturday evenings at the Moore household being nothing but still. The dozens of framed family photographs that lined the main hallway outside her room only served to increase the artifice that concealed this family as being tightly connected. One end of the hallway met the kitchen, which served as a throughway to the living room, a layout that irritated everyone in the family (however, not so much that anyone complained too loudly about it). The other end of the hallway met Pamela's room. The pictures progressed from the kitchen end to Pamela's room as a sort of museum exhibit of the Moores through the years: black-and-white photos of Janine and Roger from their wedding night. Then their honeymoon. Pamela as a toddler in a bathtub. A group photo from her baptism. A seven-year-old Pamela in a full, pink ballet costume at her first dance recital. A twelve-year-old Pamela singing in the church choir. At fifteen, the smiling Moores at a family reunion in the Poconos, surrounded by several cousins Pamela had only met a handful of times. The last photo before her room was one of all three at her high school graduation, Pamela unsmiling. There had been one photo Pamela had insisted Janine take down: the one of Pamela in her all-black stagehand outfit after *42nd Street*.

Janine was rarely home on weekends nowadays. She was usually at a banquet here, a fundraiser there, or something to do with the town council. The mayor had put in her ear that perhaps she might make for a compelling council candidate in the upcoming election. A combination of boredom, self-regard, and loneliness seemed to have kept the idea in Janine's head. Roger still spent most of his time at the furniture store. He was either there, or at an apartment in Manhattan where he would sometimes stay if he needed to meet with a supplier in the city.

When Pamela was growing up, she craved attention and adulation from her parents. There were the hours after many ballet classes when she would make Roger watch her pirouette repeatedly, and he would grunt his approval with his eyes poring over a newspaper. Pamela didn't even like ballet that much, but she kept spinning. Janine was the more effusive one in her praise, making her daughter play a scale on the clarinet over and over again for the neighbors.

"She has musical genes," Janine used to say, followed instantly by, "I was a singer in high school."

Pamela was once again hunched over her laptop in her bedroom, which was littered with printouts of *The Elm Tree* covered in her handwritten notes. Jerry hoped to begin rehearsals for the play within a matter of weeks with the auditions completed. And Pamela had yet to come up with an ending. Returning to the play now felt different. She was older. She was more alone.

Jerry had sent her an email with instructions: "Make a choice: Do you want there to be a happy ending or a sad one? Do you want the characters, particularly the parents, to be redeemed or villainous to the end? The question you have to ask yourself: Do people fundamentally change or not? In the universe you've created on this stage, only you know the answer to that."

Pamela did not, however, know the answer, and was becoming increasingly stressed about her writer's block. *Keya never had writer's block*, she thought to herself. *Or blocks of any kind. She'd write essays as if they were toys to be played with and, eventually, conquered.*

She picked up one of the printouts of the play off the ground and began reading the last scene she had written for what had to be the hundredth time that day, from her count. She didn't hear her door slowly swing open or see Janine, dressed in an elegant pantsuit, hovering just feet away from her. When she did, she jumped.

"Mom!" Pamela said. "You scared me."

"Your door was open," Janine said.

"What do you want?"

"Hello to you too. Your dad is home tonight. I made chicken caccia-tore," Janine said. "Do you want to have dinner with us?"

"I'm good," Pamela said, turning back to her notes.

Janine looked disappointed.

"What is all this?" she said.

"Just something I've been working on," Pamela said, without looking at Janine.

Janine hunched over to pick up one of the papers, causing Pamela to leap from her seat to block her from doing so.

"Is this the Magna Carta?" Janine said. "What are you hiding?"

"You've been watching political speeches, huh?" Pamela said, hastily picking papers up off the floor.

Janine looked embarrassed and turned back down the hallway. Pamela shoved the papers into her desk drawer.

"What time is dinner?" Pamela called out. She heard her stomach grumbling and felt guilty for snapping at her mother.

"Twenty minutes" was the answer from the kitchen.

Pamela looked back at the laptop and considered the document. She needed to take a break, and chicken cacciatore, the only dish Janine cooked expertly, would be a welcome distraction. She stared at the laptop for a few minutes more, searching for answers that wouldn't come, and headed to the kitchen, ignoring the pictures gaping at her as she walked by. Roger was already sitting at the table, scrolling through his phone, in a bathrobe and sweatpants, while Janine set the table. Pamela went to help her, and Janine snuck her a look of gratitude.

After Janine spooned chicken thighs coated in red sauce onto their plates, they all clasped hands and prayed. Usually, on the rare occasions that the family would eat dinner together, Pamela would space out during prayer. Tonight, though, she asked for the strength to finish the play.

"Hon, Pammy is working on some secret project in her room," Janine said, as she sipped a glass of wine.

"Is that right?" Roger said distantly.

Janine poured herself some more wine. *Fuck this guy*, Pamela thought.

"Speaking of secret projects, Chuck told me that I should start attending Board of Education meetings again and start getting to know the higher-ups there," Janine said. "It would help if, you know, I decide to go for town council."

"Is that right?" Roger said again.

"Yes, it is right, Dad," Pamela snapped. "That's what she said."

Roger's mustache twitched.

"You can give me lip when you have your own place to live."

"Roger, please," Janine said. "Maybe we can do a game night after dinner?"

"I can't," Pamela said.

"*I* can't," Roger said. "I have to head into the city to check on a shipment."

"A shipment?" Janine said tersely. "A shipment. You have to go yourself to check on a shipment. This late at night."

The three of them were rarely together as a family, but when they were, the conversations were usually tense, repetitive. Janine would express dismay about Roger spending this much time at work and what she saw as needless overnight stays in Manhattan. To which Pamela always wanted to say, *"Bless your heart, Mom. How do you not see what he's up to?"* Roger carried himself like being at home was a dismaying notion anyway.

"This way I can be at the store in the morning," Roger said. "I'm too tired for bullshit tonight, Janine."

This was the end of the discussion.

"I'm writing a play," Pamela announced.

"Huh?" Roger replied, either as a statement or question.

"It's a thing with actors onstage. Where you say a bunch of scripted lines to tell a story," Pamela retorted sarcastically.

"He knows what a play is, Pamela," Janine said. "What play?"

"We start rehearsals soon," Pamela said. "It's being directed by Jerry Santucci. Toby Barone and Francesca Kazakoff are in it. They're Broadway people. Do you know them?"

Both of her parents shook their heads. Pamela stabbed the chicken on her plate with extra gusto.

"Honey, this is wonderful! That's why we rarely see you anymore. What's the play about?" Janine said.

Pamela hesitated.

"It's . . . it's about a friendship between two girls," Pamela said.

"That's it?" Roger said.

"It's based on me," Pamela said. "Us, really."

"'Us'?" Janine said.

"Well, my experience growing up," Pamela said. "And I'd like you to come see it. It's in December."

"I'd like to read it first," Janine said. "Don't we? Roger?"

"Nah," Roger said flatly. Then he looked up from his plate and at Janine, who was glowering at him. "What? It's her play. If she wants us to read it, we can. If she doesn't, she doesn't. Besides, what do we know about plays? It's not like we can give any feedback. Unless a sofa has a speaking part."

"Well, forgive me for wanting to know how I'm portrayed," Janine said.

"Is this about you running for office?" Roger said. "It's a play, not a campaign ad. And this town council thing isn't real. I wish you'd stop pretending it is."

"What will a play about our family show?" Janine asked. "Dinners like this? Arguments? Or will it be us ignoring each other while living in the same house, the nights you're even here?"

Pamela regretted coming down for dinner. *Why did I even just tell them about the play?* Though a part of her knew she wanted them to be proud, unconditionally. She wanted them to be open to the possibility that this play would let them into her world.

"The answer is no," Pamela cut off her bickering parents. "I want you to experience it the same way everyone else will."

Janine opened her mouth as if to argue more, but stopped.

"Well, I never wanted you to go to acting school, but I've prayed for years that you find something. Or someone," Janine said. "And if this is how God is answering me, so be it. We'll be there, of course. Won't we, Roger?"

Roger thought for a moment. He made eye contact with Pamela for the first time.

"Of course," Roger said.

This exchange made Pamela hopeful that her parents would be open to the play's message, and who she was. Who she actually was. Maybe. Maybe she had misjudged them. Maybe age had softened them, even if they had hardened towards each other.

"How did this even happen?" Janine said with a hint of jealousy. "This is an impressive thing. I didn't know you had this in you."

"I served the right customer one day at work. Keya's dad, Mr. Das. He's been helping me."

"Shan-TAN-oo? I ran into him once at the store. He darted away from me. It was a bit strange."

Pamela snickered.

"That sounds like Mr. Das."

◇

"Baba, of all the things you could be eating here, you're eating *that*," Mitali scolded Shantanu, standing in the high school cafeteria. Shantanu unwrapped more of the Hershey bar and took a larger bite. "You were doing such a good job eating better."

"When Keya used to run this snack bar, I tried to make her sneak me candy for free," Shantanu said, wiping chocolate off his lips. "She'd never do it. Catherine isn't here today, so I get to cheat."

"At least have a bite of my *shingara*," Kalpana said, as bread crumbs flew out of her mouth. "It's Durga Puja! They'll be gone soon."

Shantanu surveyed the room and saw so many of his old acquaintances dressed in saris and gold pajamas. He had not seen most of the attendees here since Keya's funeral, which made him feel like he had just emerged from a time machine. He felt a bit strange in his suit. So much had changed for him since he was last in a room like this. The Shantanu that used to come to these gatherings with Chaitali at his side would not recognize himself. Nor would the one a year ago before he found the box in the attic.

"It's been so many years," Pallavi, one of the elders in the room, said as Kalpana paraded Shantanu around as if he was a returning hero. As Shantanu offered Pallavi a *pranam*, she said, *"Thumi kothai cheele?"*

"I've been busy, *mashi*," Shantanu said.

"We miss your Keya running around here," Pallavi said, gripping her walker tightly as she put a hand on Shantanu's face.

"I do as well, *mashi*," Shantanu said with practiced solemnity.

"Don't be a stranger. Strangers forget what comfort feels like."

"Of course."

Even being part of this community was a generational inheritance. It started small but began to expand when Kalpana and Amitava's generation found each other decades ago. Many had moved to the area for work, rich as it was with engineering jobs and other fields attractive to new immigrants. Sometimes, finding other Bengalis took a leap of creativity. Shantanu used to overhear Amitava using the phone book to find people with Bengali last names. He would call them to introduce himself. Soon, weekends were filled with dinner parties with almost complete strangers. Looking around the room at the generations of Bengalis, he felt grateful for the community his parents had helped build, proud even. There were the older ones, like Pallavi, who were born in India. Shantanu was among the first in the room to be born in the United States. And then there was Mitali's age group to carry the torch.

Kalpana, now walking with a cane, began her own conversation with Pallavi as Shantanu turned back to Mitali.

"I feel strange."

"I felt that way last year," Mitali said. "You get used to it."

"Neesh couldn't make it today?"

"He's working," Mitali said.

"When does your mother get here?"

"She said she and Jahar Kaku will be here in a couple minutes. They got caught in traffic."

Strange as it was to be back at a Durga Puja celebration, it was also familiar. Shantanu still was not sure how Kalpana and Mitali convinced him to make the trip this fall. He had withdrawn from the other Bengalis once the drinking started and his marriage ended. Divorce made for good gossip, and there was no better place to gossip than a puja. Still, somewhere deep inside him, he had missed it, and how many more of these would he be able to attend with Kalpana by his side? Besides, there was business related to *The Elm Tree* to be done.

"There you guys are." Pamela appeared next to the Dases. "I thought I lost you. The bathroom wasn't easy to find."

"Would you like a piece of chocolate?" Shantanu said.

"No thanks, Mr. Das."

"Either you call me Shantanu or I call you Ms. Moore. You pick."

"Okay, Mr. Das," Pamela said with a defiant smile. Shantanu couldn't help but laugh. "So this is Durga Puja, huh?"

"Sure is," Shantanu said.

Pamela eyed the imposing Durga figure in the corner.

"This is cool," Pamela said. "Keya used to talk about this. She showed me a dance she was practicing once."

"She wanted to bring you that last year," Mitali said.

"Really?" Pamela said. "She never told me that."

"She really did," Mitali said.

Mitali considered the room as silence hung between the three.

"I should've been a more present older sister," she finally said.

Shantanu pretended to absentmindedly gaze around the room.

"I'm sure you did your best," Pamela said. Shantanu could see her eyes steel.

"I never told her I was happy for her. You know, that she found you," Mitali said. Pamela looked away. "I should have. 'I'm happy for you' was the right thing to say. And I never got to do it."

"Yeah."

"Did she ever say anything? Before she, you know," Mitali said.

"She loved you. But I can't forgive you on her behalf," Pamela said.

"I know."

"But she would have loved us doing the play."

"It's not enough, but we're glad you're here right now," Mitali said.

Shantanu, having had enough of his room survey, addressed Pamela. "Are you nervous?"

"I'm not great at public speaking," Pamela said.

"Don't worry about it. The crowd will be full of Bengalis. Most of them will be talking to each other and not paying attention to the stage. Or paying attention to each other, to be honest," Shantanu said. "Do you see all those *kakus* over there?"

Shantanu pointed to a corner, where several men seemed deeply engaged in conversation while holding cups of coffee.

"They're probably arguing about politics and sports," Shantanu said. "And the thing is: none of them know anything about politics and sports. But they definitely disagree on it. Bengalis are the world's greatest experts on things they know absolutely nothing about."

"I heard that."

Shantanu recognized Jahar's voice, and his back stiffened. The group turned around and saw Chaitali and Jahar standing there. Chaitali was wearing a glittering red sari, while Jahar sported a gold dhoti.

"Jahar," Shantanu said. "Chaitali. That sari looks familiar."

"It's similar to the one I had made for Keya when she performed here," Chaitali said.

"That's right! I found a picture of it in the attic."

Chaitali walked over and gave Mitali a hug. She clutched her tightly.

"Purple is your best color," Chaitali said.

"Thank you, Ma," Mitali said. "Will you be performing tonight?"

"Very funny, Meeti," Chaitali said.

She turned to Pamela.

"When I heard you were coming, my heart leapt."

"Thanks, Mrs. Das," Pamela said awkwardly.

Finally, Chaitali shifted her attention back to Shantanu.

"Can I talk to you in private?" Chaitali said.

"Of course," Shantanu said.

"I'll let you two catch up," Jahar said. "Mitali, I have a cigar for you if you want it. Might as well begin celebrating Christmas early."

He waved to Mitali and walked away, while Chaitali guided Shantanu away from the group.

She reached into her purse and handed Shantanu an envelope.

"What's this?" Shantanu asked, feeling the outside of the envelope.

"It's from Jahar and me," Chaitali said.

Shantanu gently tore open the envelope. Inside was a check made out to Shantanu for twenty-five thousand dollars. He stared at the blue piece of paper and let out a soft gasp.

"What *is* this?"

"I heard you're preparing for rehearsals. And Jerry made the production more expensive."

"I can't accept your money. This is too much, Chai," Shantanu said. "Is this Jahar trying to flaunt his wealth at me? I'll never be able to pay this back."

"Shanti, please," Chaitali said. "A part of this is from my savings. This is us doing our part."

"How did you even know I needed to come up with more money?"

"I had a hunch," Chaitali said.

Shantanu turned to look at Mitali, who was talking to Pamela, with one inconspicuous eye on her parents.

"She shouldn't have done that," Shantanu said.

"Mitali didn't ask," Chaitali said. "We talked after my audition. She told me about the Broadway actors. I can add numbers as well as read, Shanti."

Shantanu continued shaking his head.

"You've done a great thing here," Chaitali said. "Let us help. Let *me* help. For Keya."

Shantanu put the check back in the envelope and stuffed it into his suit's breast pocket.

"Before opening night, we'd like to have all of you over for dinner.

Catherine. You. Neesh. Mitali. And your mother, if she is willing to come," Chaitali continued. "She looks as active as ever."

"That sounds like the strangest gathering," Shantanu said. "But I've missed your cooking."

Shantanu and Chaitali made eye contact, and both smiled.

"Shanti, in another world . . ."

"In another world," Shantanu said.

They looked away.

"Are you prepared for tonight?" Chaitali said.

"Are you?"

◇

That evening, Shantanu, Chaitali, Mitali, and Pamela were huddled backstage in the high school auditorium. The program had already begun. The opening act was a revue of several spirited classical dances by young Bengali girls, followed by one of the adults singing a Bengali song solo on the harmonium, "Ruum Joom Joom Joom." She was energetic enough that the room, only about three-fourths filled, began clapping along to the beat of the song. Then there was a solo *tabla* performance.

"Vikas really hasn't lost his touch," Shantanu said. "His hands still move like that?"

"Didn't you try to get him to teach me *tabla*?" Mitali whispered.

" 'Try' is the operative word," Chaitali said.

Vikas's hands were a blur on the dual drums. The baby powder on his hands created a small cloud around the *tablas*. The audience roared, as the remaining seats became filled. Vikas finished his performance and addressed the audience.

"Thank you for coming, everybody," Vikas said. "Hopefully, all of you will have a chance to taste my wife's *rasgullas* in the cafeteria this weekend. I'd like to introduce some special guests who have something they want to tell you. Please give a hand to the Das family."

The group walked onstage to a podium. Shantanu's palms were sweating as he took out a piece of lined paper. There was scattered applause from the seats. In the dark, he could make out Kalpana sitting in the front row. She gave him a reassuring smile.

"My name is Shantanu Das," he said into the microphone, but spoke so loudly that there was feedback. Pamela stepped in and motioned for Shantanu to lean away.

"Sorry about that," Shantanu continued, softly this time. "My name is Shantanu Das. It's been wonderful to see so many familiar faces today. As some of you know, we lost our younger daughter, Keya. She used to perform here on this stage. Last year, we found a play that she and her friend—our friend—Pamela wrote."

Shantanu stepped away from the microphone and Mitali took his place.

"I'm Mitali. Keya was my sister. We've been working hard to stage the play," Mitali continued, reading off Shantanu's paper. "And while nothing will ever bring her back, this play is an illustration of who she was. And who we were."

Chaitali took Pamela's hand, and then Mitali's, as Shantanu went back to the microphone.

"The play will run from December thirteenth to the fifteenth at the George Street Playhouse in New Brunswick. We would love for you to come. All the proceeds will go towards a scholarship in Keya's name. Thank you."

There was no reaction from the crowd. Shantanu cleared his throat.

"That's it," Shantanu said.

Kalpana clapped as loud as she could, and others followed her lead.

As the group arrived backstage again, Mitali said, "As long as there are hundreds of *shomadidis* out there, our play will be a smashing success."

Shantanu was still looking out at the audience.

"There's only one *shomadidi*."

◇

Mitali rolled her eyes for what seemed like the hundredth time that hour.

"Where the *fuck* are Toby and Francesca?" Jerry yelled. "When I say a fifteen-minute coffee break, I don't mean twenty-five minutes."

"It's been ten minutes," Mitali said, looking at her cell phone. "And you asked them to get you a coffee too."

Jerry glared at Mitali, who was sitting near the front row of the George Street Playhouse auditorium on the third day of rehearsals, next to Neesh. Both of them were vigorously chewing on their own pens about two weeks before opening night. Shantanu had gone to pick up Kalpana, who had insisted on making Bengali food for the cast for lunch.

"This is not what I need from an assistant director," Jerry said.

"I'm not an assistant director," Mitali replied.

"I know," Jerry said. "Your father made it clear he didn't want to spend the money to hire one."

Mitali turned back to her laptop, where she was reviewing the cover of the show's playbill, which she designed herself and was getting ready to send to the printers.

"Neesh," Jerry said. He didn't get an answer. "Neesh! I don't have time to say your name twice."

"Yeah, sorry, Jerry," Neesh said, looking up from his phone. "I'm just looking at couches on IKEA."

"I changed my mind on that," Jerry said. "These ones are fine. Where did you get the blue one?"

"Yard sale," Neesh said. "Sidewalk sale, more like. Brooklyn. Mitali told me Keya picked out a blue one for her grandparents once, so it felt appropriate."

"Fine," Jerry said dismissively. "Did you get it fumigated? You know what? I don't want to know. And nice job with *that*."

He motioned to the stage, where an oversized elm tree loomed in front of the backdrop. Its trunk was made of a circular plywood frame, which Neesh painted a deep dark brown, along with etched-on black lines to detail the outer bark. The trunk was reinforced by a steel pipe. The tree's leaves were fleshed out with layers of brown and orange tissue paper combined with a series of camouflage nets. Neesh had spent days assembling the tree in pieces. Mitali had never seen anyone work at such a manic pace before. He had transported most of the set pieces himself in a rented U-Haul. Mitali, Shantanu, and Pamela helped him assemble the set.

"I'm not sure that people will know that it's an elm tree," Jerry said, putting one hand on his chin.

Mitali saw Neesh look discouraged and opened her mouth to say something.

"But it doesn't matter," Jerry said to himself, much to their relief. "The tree is a metaphor. A safe space. That looks safe. And autumnal. It's fine."

Jerry began to flip through his notepad, which was filled with black scribbles. Mitali leaned over to Neesh.

"By the way," Neesh whispered, "I'll be a little late to Thanksgiving. The new owner asked me to stop by. He's officially in charge now, so I don't want to piss him off."

Toby and Francesca returned holding a mocha latte for Jerry. Both of them carried themselves with the air of people who could not be bothered by the insecurities of those surrounding them. They were both unintentionally wearing matching black turtlenecks. But Toby's had crumbs on his: a result of Francesca buying him a croissant for his half-birthday. Sixty-two was six months away, she revealed upon their return.

"Did you go to the Starbucks in Yellowstone? Christ," Jerry said, taking the cup from Toby.

"I'm going to boot your ass to Yellowstone if you keep talking to me like that," Francesca said.

"I'm going to get you decaf coffee," Toby added.

"Don't do that," Jerry said. "Either of those things. Let's gather, everyone. EVERYONE! GATHER!"

Toby and Francesca made themselves at home in front-row seats. The rest of the cast came to the front of the stage.

There was Sheila Robinson, the twenty-three-year-old woman from Shantanu's first improv class, who was playing the part of Kate, based on Pamela. She was Shantanu's first scene partner. When she walked into the audition, Shantanu looked almost as surprised to see her as he was Chaitali. Shantanu and Sheila never spoke outside of improv, Shantanu had said afterwards, but he had always suspected that she was a more seasoned performer than a typical level-one improv student. She had previously studied acting at Carnegie Mellon University, which endeared her to Jerry, who had done several workshops there. Her audition was, as Jerry called it, "spirited," which was high praise coming from him, and he added that Sheila just needed an opportunity.

Next to Sheila was Swati Roy, a junior at Rutgers who had just transferred into Mason Gross after deciding that the pre-med program wasn't for her. She got the part of Preethi after auditioning on a whim. Swati had very limited acting experience, having only been in one high school musical, as an ensemble member in *Bye Bye Birdie*. But her audition left the panel, except for Jerry, speechless, and there were only seven young South Asian auditioners to choose from. Jerry wanted to hold another weekend of auditions for the part, but relented at Shantanu's insistence.

"Why do you want to do this play?" Shantanu had asked Swati before she left the audition room

"Preethi reminds me of myself," Swati said.

Mitali knew right then that the part was hers, especially once she thought to herself in response, *You remind me of Keya*. There would be no need for callbacks, Shantanu told Jerry. The director wanted to fight back, Mitali could tell, but Jerry knew a losing battle when he saw one, and deep down, he didn't think a better actress for the part was going to audition.

The part of Preethi's mother went to Seema Gopal, a fifty-five-year-old actress from Jackson, New Jersey, who had retired from the profession a decade before. She was looking for something to occupy her time now that her two children had moved to the West Coast. She had been on television once: as a defense lawyer on *Law & Order*, where she had three lines in a 1997 episode. Coincidentally, Francesca had appeared as a witness on a later episode in the same season, one of dozens of television credits for her.

Much to Mitali's amusement, auditions for Preethi's father were the most difficult to sit through for Shantanu, who watched a dozen or so South Asian actors perform monologues to ostensibly end up in a part based on him. None of the performers satisfied Shantanu, including one that Jerry liked: Sudip Banerjee, who had been in several Off-Broadway plays. He was drawn to the audition out of necessity. Sudip was having trouble getting parts. His monologue—one from the father in a play called *Framed Fracas* by a young playwright named Terence Whitling that won a Drama Desk Award—was the only one out of all the auditions that caused Jerry to snap his fingers at its conclusion.

"How weird to see all these men come in and try to be you," Mitali leaned over to Shantanu and said after Sudip left. "And Ma. And Keya. They all come in thinking they know us."

"*We* don't even know us," Shantanu whispered back.

But Sudip impressed Jerry enough to get the part. And now he was one of the six gathered around the anxious director as he addressed them.

"We have to get everything blocked by the end of Sunday," Jerry said, scribbling more lines on his notepad. "Especially who is moving what set pieces. You need to all be off book as soon as possible, given our truncated schedule. And most importantly, for some of you to deliver your lines as if you give a shit about what you're doing. I'm begrudgingly giving you guys tomorrow off for Thanksgiving."

Francesca and Toby rolled their eyes, while the rest of the cast looked alarmed. Swati timidly raised her hand.

"Mr. Santucci," Swati said.

"Jerry. Actually, Jeremiah according to my mother," Jerry said. "Although, she's dead now so I guess I have final say."

"You said we have to be 'off book,'" Swati said. "How can we memorize the end of the play if we don't know what happens?"

"Ah, a good point," Jerry said. "Everyone, take your places for the start of the show. I need to speak to Pamela."

◇

The cast headed backstage, while Jerry strolled over to Pamela, who, upon hearing Swati's question, pulled her sweatshirt hood over her face.

"Pamela," Jerry said. "Pamela, Pamela, Pamela. Swati is right. You have exactly two days to fucking decide the last two scenes of this godforsaken play. Is that understood?"

"I don't know what I'm doing," Pamela said, tugging the hood again. "I don't think I can do it."

"Does this look like school to you?" Jerry said. "Do your job so I can do mine."

"I can't," Pamela said. "I stare and stare at the play and nothing comes out. My parents are going to see this. And I'm going to have to answer their questions. They know it's about them. And what will I do after that?"

Jerry sat down next to Pamela.

"This isn't writer's block," Jerry said. "This is fear."

"Yes," Pamela said.

"I will not let you fail," Jerry said. "I will not let us fail. Because if you fail, then I've failed. And I've already had too many of those."

Jerry's facial expression eased.

"If you fuck this up and you don't finish this play, you have the rest of your life to write another one and figure it out," Jerry said, a slight smile coming to his face. "I don't have that kind of time. So fuck your fear. Figure it out now."

"Fuck my fear," Pamela said. "That's your advice?"

"Kid, it's the best I got," Jerry said. "It worked for *Godot*. When I directed that show, Nolan Sullivan had terrible stage fright."

"This isn't *Waiting for Godot*," Pamela said.

"Not unless you finish the play it's not."

Jerry held out his hand and Pamela clasped it briefly.

"You may be scared," Jerry said. "So was Keya. I could tell from reading these scenes. Don't kid yourself: great art comes from fear. Now go write."

FIFTEEN

Neesh walked into the studio and found it unnervingly empty. There was mostly silence in the hallway, usually only the case at opening or closing times of the studio. But the sounds of two speakers in the office playing a live Allman Brothers album wafted towards him. The walk down the hallway towards the reception desk used to be Neesh's favorite part of the job. There were pictures of famous acts onstage—Def Leppard, Joan Jett, Bruce Springsteen, and many others—mounted to the walls. When Neesh first started the job, he still harbored dreams that he would be in one of the frames someday. Those dreams dissolved as the mundanity of the desk set in. Near the end of the hallway, there was a black-and-white picture of Daryl Hall, John Oates, Griselda, and Johnny with big grins in room B. Everyone except Griselda was holding a guitar. Griselda held drumsticks.

Gary Whyte was sitting at the front desk, looking through invoices, and motioned that Neesh should sit down.

"Thanks for coming in," Gary Whyte said, swiveling the office chair around. "I've got to order a new one of these for the office. Seams bursting and all. Do you have plans later? Why are you in a suit?"

"I'm going to New Jersey to spend Thanksgiving with my girlfriend's family," Neesh said. "Do you need me to work today?"

"Actually, no," Gary Whyte said.

"Okay," Neesh said. "So, see you tomorrow?"

"I should clarify," Gary Whyte said casually. "I don't need you to show up to work ever."

"What?"

Gary Whyte reached for Neesh's note card with Rumi's words written on it and handed it to him. Neesh had placed it there again in its usual spot.

"I believe this is yours."

Neesh didn't grasp what Gary Whyte had said. He put his clip-on tie in his mouth. His palms immediately began sweating.

"I don't understand," Neesh said.

"You're fired," Gary Whyte said, maintaining his even tone.

"But you told—" Neesh whispered.

"Griselda," Gary Whyte said. "Yeah, I was there. I own the place now. I needed to get the deal finalized. And I didn't want to piss off the departing queen."

"Why are you doing this?" Neesh said. "I'm good at this. I've contributed a lot to this place."

"What did you think was going to happen?" Gary Whyte said impassively. "You were a thief. You lied. How was I ever going to be able to trust you? How do I know you didn't rob Griselda?"

"But that's not fair," Neesh said in a high-pitched tone.

"Fair?" Gary Whyte said. "This is life."

Neesh opened his mouth to protest. Gary Whyte put his hand up.

"Enough," he said. "It's done. I have to finish looking through these. Leave, before I call security. Happy Thanksgiving."

Neesh's heart was beating rapidly. He saw Gary Whyte's lips moving but could not hear anything he was saying. He got up and strolled to room C, which could not be seen from the front desk. He walked in, grabbed the high hat from the drum set, and tossed it across the room, causing the sound of a resounding crash. He bolted out before Gary Whyte realized what had happened, and ran down the stairs towards the Port Authority. He had a bus to catch.

◊

"This is the strangest Thanksgiving of my life," Catherine said in the driver's seat of her 2012 Ford Fiesta. Shantanu sat in the passenger seat. He was estimating the amount of trees per square feet on Route 18.

"Why is that?" Shantanu said absentmindedly.

"We are going to your ex-wife's house," Catherine said.

"Good point," Shantanu said.

The cooler between Shantanu's legs smelled of cranberry sauce and a pumpkin pie. Rather than put it in the trunk or the back seat, Shantanu wedged it in front of him so he could ensure it wouldn't spill. It was something his mother would do. That very moment, he wondered what Kalpana was packing into Tupperware containers as they were headed her way.

"Thank you for coming today," Shantanu said. "Jahar and Chaitali are making an effort. And it would be nice to have Mitali not have to choose between us."

Catherine kept her eyes on the road and didn't answer.

"I've never asked you. What did you do for Thanksgiving before you met me?" Shantanu said.

"Nothing," Catherine replied.

Shantanu waited for her to elaborate, but she did not. He went back to counting trees on the highway. His mind drifted to his post-play plans. What he would teach at Rutgers. Maybe he would ask for a sabbatical to another country for research. *I could write a book*, Shantanu thought to himself. *But this hand pain I have been feeling. Probably carpal tunnel. I could get a ghostwriter.*

"I have to tell you something," Catherine said.

"This is never the start of a good conversation," Shantanu said.

"Do you remember my friend Renee?"

"Remind me."

"She works at the Getty in L.A.," Catherine said. Her hands gripped the steering wheel tightly.

"Right," Shantanu said. "I've never been."

His hands clutched the cooler with the same intensity that Catherine's were holding the steering wheel.

"She told me that the museum is looking for an associate director of programs," Catherine said. "I've always wanted to work at a place with that kind of prestige."

Shantanu slowly nodded.

"So are you going to apply?" Shantanu said.

"I did already," Catherine said. "A couple months ago. I got the job. I found out last week."

"You're just telling me this now?"

"You've been busy with the play," Catherine said. "I didn't want to distract you."

Shantanu's face was becoming progressively hotter. He had difficulty disguising his irritation.

"Didn't want to distract me?" Shantanu said. "Come on."

Shantanu looked away from Catherine and back at the passenger side of the highway. This time, he was not counting trees.

"'Congratulations' is the word you are looking for, by the way," Catherine said.

"You tell me this as I take you to spend a holiday with my family," Shantanu said.

"I didn't ask for this," Catherine said brusquely. "You did."

"Of course," Shantanu said sharply. "Once again, I'm *such* a burden."

The drive continued in an icy silence as both of them stewed. Shantanu turned the radio off, while Catherine rolled her window down slightly.

"I want you to come with me," Catherine said. "To Los Angeles. I think you'd like it there. After the play."

"You want me to move all the way across the country? On a whim? What about my job? And Mitali is here."

"You can find a new job," Catherine said. "You're off from work now anyways. And Mitali is a grown woman. She doesn't need you to babysit her. And you don't even have a place to get rid of."

"And my mother?" Shantanu said.

"You know that she would come too. All you have to do is ask her."

"I can't just pick up and move. And neither can Ma."

"You *can*, Shantanu. I'm telling you. You *can* just pick up and move. And start something fresh. And you can do it with me."

"You make it sound so easy."

"It *is* that easy."

"What if I say no? Would you stay for me? I've built a life here."

"You know the answer to that question. I'm going to L.A. Either you're coming or you're not."

"This is just like when we went to that dinner with Jerry to ask him to direct," Shantanu said. "You weren't up front about it."

"Notice how that worked out."

◇

After picking up Kalpana, none of the three said a word for the rest of the ride until they arrived at Jahar and Chaitali's. When Shantanu helped Kalpana out of the car, Kalpana whispered, *"Babu,* are you okay?"

"I'm fine, Ma," Shantanu said, looking over his shoulder at Catherine. "This is just an odd day," he clarified.

Kalpana pursed her lips and looked at the front door where Jahar and Chaitali were waiting to greet them.

"What a strange world," Kalpana said. "It always gets stranger."

Jahar offered Kalpana a *pranam* and took a cooler filled with curries from her frail hands.

"Shorshe maach? Torkaris? Lamb? *Luchi?"* Jahar said, looking inside the cooler. *"Didi,* this won't go well with our turkey."

"Eesh, you haven't even tried it yet," Kalpana said. "And besides, my *luchi* is a holiday tradition."

Jahar turned to Shantanu and extended his hand.

"Thank you for coming, Shantanu," Jahar said, speaking with an air of formality he typically used for conducting deal negotiations.

"Thank you for having us," Shantanu said, echoing Jahar's formality. He even gave a slight bow, for a reason beyond his understanding.

Chaitali offered to take Catherine's coat. Catherine stiffly obliged.

"Your home is very nice," Catherine said, also taking off a wool scarf. "It's very . . . contemporary."

"Well, we try," Chaitali said. "Are you into architecture?"

"Only in incredibly awkward moments," Catherine said.

Despite herself, Chaitali let out a laugh. She reached for Kalpana's coat and offered a *pranam,* just as Jahar did.

"Your sari is lovely," Chaitali said hesitantly.

"I wear it for special occasions," Kalpana said. "*This* is a special occasion."

The group shuffled in silence for several moments before they heard a knock on the door. Catherine moved to open it. It was Mitali, who had just arrived in an Uber. She greeted Catherine with a hug, as well as her mother. There was a *pranam* for her *shomadidi* and an apologetic glance at Shantanu.

"I'm sorry I'm late," Mitali said. "The bus was on time, but I put in the wrong address for the Uber driver. Neesh will be here soon. He hasn't answered my texts, so I'm assuming he's just asleep on the bus."

"His name is Neesh?" Jahar, his eyebrows raised, whispered to Chaitali, who nodded.

"Don't worry about it," Shantanu said. "You're right on time."

"Shantanu, why don't you keep your coat on?" Jahar said. "Would you like to join me on the back porch for a cigar?"

"I don't smoke. And I don't drink either."

"Would you join me as I have one? And we have ginger ale. Chaitali told me your family has an historic affinity for ginger ale. I can pour you a glass."

Shantanu could feel the eyes of the room on him.

"Lead the way," Shantanu said with forced cheerfulness. He followed Jahar, while Chaitali shepherded Catherine, Mitali, and Kalpana into the family room. She went to the kitchen to make tea for everyone.

Shantanu shivered on the back porch, but quickly hid his chills as he watched Jahar take puffs of his cigar. He sipped his ginger ale.

"I miss Thanksgivings with Supriya," Jahar remarked.

"How long has it been?" Shantanu said.

"More than twenty years," Jahar answered ruefully. "The last year with her was difficult. So many visits to the doctors. But we did get to have Thanksgiving together. With my son, too, for that matter. Everything fell apart after that."

"I know the feeling," Shantanu said, looking through the porch windows at Chaitali in the kitchen.

"You don't like me very much," Jahar said.

"I didn't say that," Shantanu said.

"You did not have to. I do not blame you. I hope you will believe me that this is something I never intended on happening."

"Well, as they say, that horse left the barn," Shantanu said.

"Indeed," Jahar said.

Jahar tapped his cigar in an ashtray sitting on a table nearby.

"It's just—" Shantanu stopped.

"It's okay, go ahead," Jahar urged. "You have waited a long time to say this."

"The girls viewed you as an uncle this whole time. A family friend."

"A *kaku*," Jahar said.

"A *kaku*," Shantanu sighed. "We used to see you at pujas. And then you end up offering Chaitali a lifeline. An escape from me. Us. A chance to start over. It felt unfair. It *was* unfair."

Jahar nodded.

"I never realized how much she needed that," Shantanu said. "I could never see through the anger I had at myself. I lost her. And I almost lost Mitali too."

"Looks like you have found yourself a lifeline as well," Jahar said, glancing at Catherine in the kitchen, who was sipping a cup of tea. "I would cling to her like—what are those things that cling?"

"Barnacles."

"Yes, right. Barnacles," Jahar said. "Look, Shantanu. I am not going to apologize for Chaitali and I finding each other. And I surely don't expect your forgiveness. But I would like to have a relationship with you and Mitali. And Catherine, of course. It's unconventional, I admit, but it's either that or we stay splintered. I know the effect that has on Chaitali, particularly her distance with Mitali. I'm not asking to be close friends. But there needs to be something."

Shantanu looked at the kitchen again, where Catherine and Kalpana were now huddled in deep conversation at the table. Mitali was helping her mother take trays out of the oven. Even though the gathering was unthinkable a year before, there was something about those interactions that felt filling for Shantanu.

"You're right."

Shantanu took another sip of his ginger ale.

"So who is this boyfriend of Mitali's?" Jahar asked. "Neesh?"

"He's a bit high-strung," Shantanu answered.

"What do you know about him?"

"Not much. He's been very helpful with the play. And he means well. He's a drummer. You'd like him."

"A drummer."

Shantanu turned and looked back inside the house.

"Yes. That must be him now," Shantanu said.

◇

Neesh's suit was rumpled and his face was pale. The bags under his eyes were more prevalent than usual. He hesitated for a second before pressing the doorbell.

"That must be Neesh! I'll get it!" Neesh could hear Mitali yell from the inside.

When the door swung open, Mitali's smile immediately disappeared.

"What's wrong?" she asked.

"Nothing."

"Okay, well, I hope you like stuffed mushrooms. They're hot off the stove. This suit looks good on you," Mitali said. "Where did you get it?"

"Consignment shop."

The bus ride to Howell was excruciating for Neesh, who suddenly had to confront the notion that his dwindling bank account would not be replenished by another paycheck and that his prospects for employment were slim. The bus was empty, since many commuters were already home for Thanksgiving or were off work. The space on the bus allowed Neesh to move between various rows to get some of his nervous energy out. He put his clip-on tie in his mouth and then took it out. His legs had become more restless as Jahar and Chaitali's house got closer. He dreaded telling Mitali about getting fired. Neesh would have to explain why. *Maybe I could tell her without giving her the real reason.* So far, Neesh had been able to hide his situation from Mitali. *No*, Neesh decided. He would tell her everything. Neesh wanted to be the one to tell his secret to Mitali.

"We have to talk about something after Thanksgiving," Neesh said.

Mitali's face scrunched.

"You're not going to break up with me on a holiday, are you?" she said.

"No, of course not. I would never." Neesh grabbed Mitali's hand. "I *will* never."

Mitali smiled and led him to the kitchen, where the rest of the family was.

"Ma, this is Neesh," Mitali said. Chaitali walked over and enveloped Neesh in a hug, something he did not expect.

"So this is the handsome drummer boy I've heard so much about," Chaitali said.

"He's our Goopy!" Kalpana gave a toothy smile from the opposite side of the kitchen.

"Hey, Catherine," Neesh said softly.

"Hey, buddy," Catherine said. "You learn the drum part to 'Hot for Teacher' yet?"

"Yeah," Neesh said. "It didn't take long."

Shantanu and Jahar walked in from the porch.

"Hi, Neesh," Shantanu said. "I like your suit. I don't own one, but if I did, it would look like that."

"Very funny, Baba," Mitali said.

No one seemed to notice the look on Jahar's face, which quickly morphed to confusion and rage as he took in the sight of Neesh. It wasn't until Neesh walked over and shook Jahar's hand to introduce himself that Neesh realized something was off.

"May I speak to you for a second?" Jahar walked Neesh to another corner of the kitchen.

"Thanks for having me," Neesh said. "I'm Neesh Desai."

"How *dare* you?" Jahar hissed. "It *is* you."

Neesh yelped as Jahar pushed him backwards, pinning him against the wall. His clip-on tie fell to the ground.

"What's going on?" Mitali said, noticing the sudden commotion.

"What the fuck?" Neesh said.

"Baba!" Mitali yelled. "Do something!"

"Jahar, what are you doing?" Chaitali gasped.

Shantanu grabbed Jahar by the collar and forcefully pulled him off Neesh. Jahar was breathing hard as he continued to glare. He held up a finger and jabbed it towards Neesh.

"This *man*," Jahar said. "This *kuttar baccha*."

"Do I know you?" Neesh said, brushing his hands over his suit. He bent down to pick up his tie.

Jahar scoffed.

"I know *you*," he said. "Do you still rob people? Have you already robbed her?"

Neesh's face suddenly turned to one of begging, just as it did when Mitali met Hector at his apartment. How could Jahar know? Neesh shook his head, as Mitali and Shantanu exchanged looks.

"Jahar," Chaitali said soothingly. She walked over and put her hand on his shoulder. This caused Shantanu to involuntarily wince.

"Neesh Desai used to be quite a con man in his day. Scalping fake tickets. Check scams," Jahar snarled.

"What?" Mitali said. "You must be mistaken."

"I'm not," Jahar said. "Ask him."

All eyes in the room turned towards Neesh. Neesh looked at the ground and said nothing. He briefly considered running out the door.

"And then there was his biggest accomplishment," Jahar said. "He once tried to steal antiques at a convention center. He was carried out by the police."

"This can't be true," Mitali said. "How would you know all this?"

"He didn't do all this by himself," Jahar said. He took a seat at the table and put his hand on his head.

Jahar then pointed at a picture frame on the far side of the kitchen. In it, there was a much younger-looking Jahar with his arms around a teenager. The pudgy teenager had one side of his lips curled upwards, holding an oar. Both of them were shirtless in front of a lake with a row-boat in the foreground. It was the kind of boat Neesh had dreamt of renting in his lowest moments. The resemblance between the two in the photo was uncanny. And Neesh recognized the boy immediately.

"Is that—" Neesh hesitated.

"Sandeep is my son," Jahar said.

"Neesh knows Sandeep?" Chaitali said.

"Knows him?" Jahar laughed. "They used to do all this together. When this bloody idiot was caught at the convention center, Sandeep came to me to help get them off. He told me how they were pressured and manipulated into being petty criminals. I had my colleague take Neesh's case pro bono. He got off with a misdemeanor, thanks to me. He could have been charged with a felony! But I never believed a word of what Sandeep said. Ever. There was never any manipulation. You were just avoiding jail time."

Neesh's palms were sweaty. He bent over and put his hands on his knees.

"Is this true, Neesh?" Mitali pleaded.

Neesh could see in her eyes that she was hoping against hope that it wasn't. That there had been some mistake. Some mix-up. Some way to put this spill back in the bottle. His throat was dry and he closed his eyes.

"Sandeep was never the same after Supriya," Jahar continued mournfully. "I begged him not to get involved with the wrong crowd. To finish college. To focus on his bass guitar. I told him to stay away from people like you."

"I did," Neesh said, looking into Jahar's eyes. "I swear. I never went near him after what happened. And I never made him do anything. He did it all on his own."

"I will not hear it," Jahar said, putting his hand up. "You are a liar. So is my son."

"I'm not a liar," Neesh said. "Not anymore."

"Sandeep begged me for help when it came to your arrest," Jahar said. "And I gave it to him. Because that's what fathers do."

"You can't blame yourself," Chaitali said soothingly. "Sandeep is an adult. He made his choices."

"I blame people like *him*," Jahar said. "Sandeep is a good boy with a good heart. He fell in with the wrong people. This man is one of them. I bet you still see each other. Have you seen my son?"

"He found me at a bar once a while back," Neesh said.

"Exactly!" Jahar said. "You could not stay away."

"Did you take any money from the play?" Shantanu asked in a measured tone. He seemed to be assessing the situation as he might a research paper. "The money for the set, for example?"

"No, never," Neesh said.

He closed his eyes and saw the young boy Chittesh, the merchant's son at the convention center. He would have been in high school by now. Neesh wondered if Chittesh was thinking about college and whether Madhar Gandhi, his father, was still as warm as he was in their encounter. Then he thought of the gun held to his head by the man at Desai Antiques in Chicago. And he remembered his father's words, the other ones.

Clean up the mess you made.

Chaitali was next to Jahar, her hand on his shoulder. He seemed out of breath but calming down. Mitali was standing at the built-in wooden nook, not able to make eye contact with Neesh. Catherine was standing up. Neesh did not think it was possible for her to look as concerned as she did, given her typically unflappable nature. Kalpana and Shantanu, however, wore the same facial expressions. They were looking at him with pity. Neesh could not bear the sadness with which they looked at him.

Neesh put his clip-on tie back on and straightened his suit.

"Happy Thanksgiving," Neesh said. "Thank you for inviting me."

He walked towards the front door. As soon as he stepped out, his walk turned into a jog, and then the fastest sprint of his life.

◇

Mitali and Neesh sat on opposite ends of her bed. It had been two days since Thanksgiving, but Neesh was still wearing the same suit.

"It wasn't supposed to be like this," Neesh said to an expressionless Mitali.

"What wasn't?"

Neesh grimaced.

"Any of it."

"You left," Mitali said. "On Thanksgiving. You just ran out."

"I know."

"And you didn't answer my texts or calls for hours. I was worried about you."

"I know."

"Was all that true? What Jahar said?"

Neesh looked down at the wool rug upon which the bed was placed. It was only visible on the edges of the bed, as if it was intruding on the bed's space.

"Yes," Neesh said softly.

Mitali leaned against the bed's headboard and brought her knees to her chest. She wanted more from Neesh. She wanted him to say that there was some explanation. Some reason it wasn't what it sounded like. But it didn't come.

"You lied to me," Mitali said, taking off her glasses. She pushed back her bangs.

"I didn't lie. I just didn't tell you about that part of my life."

"I feel lied to."

"I should have told you," Neesh said. "I wasn't proud. If I did tell you, would you have ever trusted me?"

"I don't know."

"Exactly."

"I didn't come across it when I first tried to look you up," Mitali said. "Lots of people with similar names to you, it turns out. I was mostly looking for your Facebook. How did I miss this? I work in digital marketing."

"I've never had a Facebook," Neesh said.

"Did you steal from a lot of people?"

Neesh slowly nodded.

"Why?"

"I had a cocaine problem and it got me fired from *Rock of Ages*. I needed money. And then I just got good at it."

"That's what you meant by it not working out."

"Yes."

"Did you ever steal from me? The play? Have you done anything like this in the last couple years?"

"No."

"I don't recognize you."

"Mitali."

"You look the same. You *seem* the same. But I don't *recognize* you."

"I'm the person you've known all this time."

"You can't say that. Nothing about you is the same."

"You're angry."

"Don't tell me what I am."

But Mitali admitted to herself that she was angry. That she felt betrayed. *Is this rational? I don't think he's lying anymore.*

"Please," Neesh pleaded. "Believe me."

But yet, when Mitali looked at Neesh, she couldn't help but picture Neesh at a convention center, skulking around thinking about who to steal from. The thought of how many victims there were of the schemes Neesh took part in was at the forefront of her mind.

"I think you should go."

Neesh tossed his head back and looked up at the ceiling and his right arm grabbed his tie. His left leg began to bounce. He turned to look at Mitali, and in an instant, he went perfectly still.

"Mitali. You're all I have."

The desperation Neesh was wearing clung to him more than the rumpled suit. But Mitali wouldn't meet his eyes.

She repeated again, this time with more of a cold, robotic monotone: "I think you should go."

SIXTEEN

Chaitali walked into the bedroom and found Jahar sitting straight up on the edge of the bed, holding a picture frame in his hand. It was the one of him and Sandeep that had been hanging in the kitchen. Jahar's face was expressionless, but his eyes were fixed.

"Jahar?" Chaitali whispered delicately.

The sun had disappeared outside, and Jahar had not turned on any of the lights. The flowery wallpaper and the surrounding picture frames usually brightened the room. The house was typically full of life.

"Are you all right?" Chaitali said, this time a bit louder. "Jahar."

Chaitali had seen this kind of blank look before, in the waning months of her marriage to Shantanu. Her stomach jumped. *Am I about to lose Jahar, too?* The mostly empty glass of whiskey sitting on the nightstand did not ease her fear.

"He looks so *strong* here," Jahar answered, not looking up from the picture. "Did I ever tell you this was taken at Lake Erie?"

Chaitali shook her head no. It was the only picture of Sandeep in the house, but she had never asked for details.

"It was the only trip we ever took together," Jahar said. "We went camping. Fishing too. It was for his birthday. I was proud of him. He kept the oar and we brought it home with us. We told the company the oar got lost in the water."

Chaitali thought of the oar Mitali stored underneath her own bed.

"As the years went by, I forgot his birthday," Jahar said, his voice filled with sorrow. "I got busier and busier with the firm. One day, before he moved out for good, I found the oar in the trash."

"Oh no."

"That night he called me to help with that Neesh boy. I told Sandeep I was worried about him. I tried to talk to him. I asked him not to hang up."

"Did he?"

Chaitali went to sit on the bed next to Jahar.

"He said, 'We don't have to pretend to be something we're not.'"

Throughout most of their relationship, Chaitali and Jahar had an unspoken rule: Chaitali would not ask about Sandeep, and Jahar would not ask about Keya. It was an extra bond they shared, aside from grief. They both had significant regrets as parents, and they found comfort in their shared failures. Sitting on the bed, Chaitali wished she could more comfortably break their vow of silence. They had broken so many norms by remarrying, to begin with. Why keep to this one? But Sandeep was a topic Jahar was always keen to avoid. This was a subject that she knew put him in a dark place.

In the rare moments that Jahar did mention his son, he had offhandedly said that he was always frustrated with Supriya's coddling. This, in turn, made Supriya even more protective, from Jahar's telling, especially when she became sick. Chaitali only briefly met Supriya at pujas and family functions, and barely remembered what she was like. When Supriya died of breast cancer, Jahar was left with a teenage son he knew very little about. Jahar recounted to Chaitali over dinner early in their relationship that he did not hesitate to tell Sandeep he was disappointed in him, from what little he knew, and that his mother likely was as well. That he had said this soon after Supriya's passing set a permanent fissure in their relationship.

"'When is my birthday, Baba?'" Jahar murmured in a higher voice, mimicking Sandeep on the bed. "I said it was April nineteenth. It was April thirteenth. *April thirteenth*. I will never forget it now."

"That's okay." Chaitali tried to console Jahar. "Your parents never celebrated your birthday. This isn't the reason you and Sandeep grew apart."

"No, it's not," Jahar said. "I used to think he was throwing away his life by dropping out of Rutgers. Even more when I found out about the kind of work he had fallen into. But the truth is that he was fine with that life.

It gave him more direction than I ever did. What does that say about me as a father?"

Jahar reached for his glass of whiskey and downed the rest.

"I should have listened to Supriya," Jahar said, his voice rising. "I used to avoid bringing Sandeep to pujas because I didn't want to tell those idiot *mashis* and *kakus* that my son was a D student. Little did I know: he *did* reach his potential. Just not in ways that we ever saw for him."

"Stop that, Jahar," Chaitali said, her tone sterner than she meant it to be. Jahar tilted his head up towards the picture frames on the bedroom wall. All of the ones that belonged to Jahar featured either Chaitali, Supriya, or his other extended family back in Kolkata.

"Do you wish I was Supriya?" Chaitali blurted out.

Chaitali could tell the question caught Jahar by surprise. She even surprised herself.

"Excuse me?"

"Do you wish I was Supriya?" Chaitali repeated more firmly.

She had never asked him this before. Chaitali was too afraid of the answer. Chaitali always worried that the answer was yes, that she was meant to fill an abyss in Jahar's life and was failing.

After all, Chaitali had left Shantanu behind, but Supriya was taken from Jahar. It made all the difference to Chaitali. She was a divorcée married to a widower. While she could give all of herself to Jahar, Jahar would never be entirely hers. They were in different worlds, no matter how much affection they had for each other.

Jahar jerked his head towards Chaitali and stared intently into her eyes.

"You are not Supriya," Jahar said.

Chaitali slid away from him slightly, feeling the familiar pit in her stomach. Jahar extended his hand to take Chaitali's. He squeezed.

"*You* are Chaitali," Jahar continued. "That is all any of us can be. Ourselves. And that is why—"

A pause.

"And that is why I—"

Chaitali squeezed back. Jahar didn't have to say anything else. The last time Jahar used the word he was having some difficulty saying was when they signed their marriage license. *There is no shame in love.* But in Jahar's generation, saying *I love you* was rarely said out loud. It was shown, not told. Still, Chaitali could tell it was what Jahar wanted to say. She felt a sheepish appreciation, for this seemingly small expression from Jahar was a giant show of affection.

"Have you spoken to Mitali?" Jahar asked.

"She's upset," Chaitali said.

"I tried to keep Neesh and the others from corrupting Sandeep way back when," Jahar said. He lay down on the bed and curled up into a fetal position. "I don't think either of them were honest about what happened at that convention center."

Chaitali felt a rush of pity for Jahar.

"You once told me that it wasn't too late for me to fix my relationship with Mitali," Chaitali said. "You were right. Now it's my turn. It's not too late for you to do the same with Sandeep. It's *never* too late. If there's one thing I've learned recently, it's *never* too late. Turning the page doesn't mean ripping it out entirely."

"My dear," Jahar said, now staring at the ceiling. "The truth is, you cannot reach someone who does not want to be reached."

◇

"I can't believe you cooked for the whole cast, Ma," Shantanu said, spooning a helping of butter chicken onto his plate in the George Street Playhouse hallway.

"This is an important day," Kalpana said, dressed in a white-and-purple sari. "Here, take a *paratha*."

Shantanu eagerly accepted pieces of the fried bread and stacked them on his plastic plate next to a small pile of basmati rice. He carried the plate into the auditorium and sat in the front row, near where Chaitali and Jahar were sitting with their own plates. Mitali, looking forlorn, was down the row, picking at her plate, while Pamela sat in the row behind her, nervously looking through a printout of her play. The six members of the cast were onstage with their food, as was the stage manager, a woman in her midthirties whom Jerry had hired.

Shantanu's attention was focused on Mitali.

"Has she been like that all day?" he asked Chaitali.

"Days. Weeks. I feel terrible." She glanced at Jahar and lowered her voice to a whisper. "Ever since Neesh."

"Is there anything we can do?" Shantanu said. "I'm not very good at these things."

"Not unless you can move time forward," Chaitali said.

"You don't have to whisper," Jahar interrupted. "I'm right here."

"We were just saying Mitali has looked quite sad since Thanksgiving," Chaitali said.

Jahar put a *paratha* down on his plate and looked at Mitali.

"Perhaps I was too hard on him," Jahar said softly. He opened his mouth to say something else, but then closed it. His gaze drifted straight ahead, as he became lost in his own thoughts. Shantanu and Chaitali exchanged looks. He beckoned towards Mitali, and Chaitali nodded.

"We're going to be right back," Chaitali told Jahar, as she and Shantanu stood up. Jahar didn't seem to hear.

Shantanu and Chaitali walked over with their plates and sat next to Mitali, who had not made much progress on her food.

"You have to eat, *sona*," Chaitali said.

"The next couple days are going to be a blur," Shantanu said. "You need to rest and eat and whatever else."

Mitali weakly smiled and put a piece of chicken in her mouth. Chaitali picked up the water bottle off the ground and handed it to Mitali, who took a swig.

"Mitali, look." Shantanu pointed to the back corner of the auditorium. Chaitali and Mitali turned to look. Jerry was in the doorway, gesturing wildly towards the stage. He was in an animated conversation with a man Mitali did not recognize.

"What's he doing?" Mitali said.

"Enjoying his perch," Shantanu said.

"What do you mean?" Chaitali said.

"That's a *New York Times* theater reporter," Shantanu said. "Hannah was able to get him to come interview him for a story. I believe he's over there talking about his reinvention as a director."

"Everyone has a part to play," Chaitali said, as Kalpana shuffled into the auditorium with her cane and looked around.

"*Shomadidi*, come sit here." Mitali waved her arms, but Kalpana did not notice. "*Shomadidi!*"

Shantanu and Chaitali joined in. Suddenly, all three were yelling "*Shomadidi!*" This time Kalpana heard them and limped down the aisle towards them.

"*Eesh!* My hearing in my old age is getting worse!" Kalpana said as she sat next to Chaitali and Mitali.

The Dases continued to eat, mostly in silence.

"I cannot believe this is the last dress rehearsal," Shantanu said with his mouth full.

"Me either," Mitali said. "I'm surprised at how smooth the run-throughs have been, all things considered."

"That man might need hospitalization, though," Kalpana said, pointing at Jerry. "He yells too much. It is unhealthy."

Shantanu and Chaitali laughed. Mitali couldn't help but do the same.

"Can you believe we are all here? Did any of you think we would all be sitting here together?" Shantanu said.

Chaitali shook her head.

"I wonder what Keya would think of all this," she said.

"She would be back there with Pamela trying to make the play perfect," Mitali said. "And then she would repaint the elm tree so that it would be her favorite kind of blue."

"That she would," Shantanu said.

"You spilled on yourself, Shanti," Chaitali said, reaching for a napkin in her purse.

Shantanu wiped the stain on his shirt with his hands, making the stain worse.

"Luckily, I have twelve other plaid shirts like this one," Shantanu said. "Mitali, are you really okay with me and *Shomadidi* moving to California?"

"I worry about you," Kalpana added.

Shantanu's relationship with Catherine was always *complicated*, given that he had never expected to meet anyone after the divorce. He had seen himself as a failure—a failed husband, a failed father. Why try and fail again?

But it was her exhortation in the car—*You can, Shantanu. I'm telling you. You can just pick up and move*—that made him realize things in his life were simple: Catherine had changed his life for the better and he had affection for her. She believed in him. So he would move because she asked him to. Sometimes, things really were black and white. *Complicated* was such a cop-out, Shantanu came to realize. In his case, it was a stand-in for *scared*. Shantanu had been *scared* of forgiveness. He had been *scared* of moving on from the past, unlike Chaitali. He was *scared* of admitting that he was in love.

"I think when you meet someone like Catherine, you should follow her wherever she leads," Mitali said. "I'll miss you guys, but I'll come visit. I'll have Ma here and Jahar Kaku. And Ne—"

A brief pause.

"I'll be fine."

"Catherine reminds me of my favorite Tagore quote," Kalpana said. "Have I ever told you what it is, Shantanu?"

"No, Ma."

"'You can't cross the sea merely by standing and staring at the water.' That woman never stares. She just crosses. She's good for you."

Shantanu looked at Chaitali.

"Yes, she is," Chaitali said.

"The couch up there reminds me of the one Keya picked out for me and Amitava," Kalpana said. "I wish he was here to see this."

Suddenly, Mitali's head jerked up. She stared at the makeshift elm tree on the stage, as well as the couch that caught Kalpana's attention.

"I am not so sure that I would want Baba to be here," Shantanu said.

Mitali stood up.

"I have to go," she said.

"Where are you going?" Chaitali said.

"To the city." Mitali began quickly packing up her belongings. She handed Shantanu her plate of food.

"You're not staying for the rest of rehearsal?" Shantanu said.

"There is something I have to do," Mitali said.

◊

Neesh was repeatedly scrolling his phone's contact list until it got to two names: Jared and Sandeep. And then he'd keep scrolling. There weren't many names in his phone. There was the studio, Mitali, Shantanu, Griselda, Hector, Gary Whyte, and assorted college friends he had lost touch with over the years. One entry was titled "Home." But he hadn't dialed that number in years. Neesh had been repeating this scroll for hours, considering whether to go through with calling his old partners. When he'd come close, he would walk around the apartment or go play his electric drum kit. He didn't have much else to do, having already gone for a run that morning. Now it was dark outside and eerily silent, save for the occasional siren.

Neesh's scrolling was interrupted by Hector, who gently hit him in the head from behind the couch with an envelope and handed it to him.

Neesh opened it. There were hundred-dollar bills in there. He didn't know how many.

"What's this?" Neesh said.

"Should be about a thousand dollars," Hector said. "Should get you through rent this month."

Neesh took a deep breath.

"Thanks," Neesh said.

"Consider us even for you letting me crash here after I got evicted," Hector said.

"Okay."

"You've got no job. No girl. You're going through it," Hector said, before turning back and heading into his room.

Even with Hector's help, Neesh needed money. He didn't know how long it would take for him to get a new job, and even if he could get one right away, what would pay him enough to live? *Maybe Sandeep is the answer.* Neesh literally slapped himself after thinking that. *Jared and Sandeep are the reason you're in this mess, dumbass.* Neesh lay down on his couch and stared up at the ceiling. *But they're good at creating income streams. And they cared about me. Who else can I say that about right now? What's the harm of one phone call?*

The buzzer in the apartment went off. Whomever was outside was holding the button, meaning the high-pitched buzz continued ringing throughout the living room.

"Hector, are you expecting somebody?" Neesh tried to yell over the noise. He didn't get an answer, so he ran to his speaker. "Hello?"

"Can you let me up?"

The sound of Mitali's voice caused Neesh's body to convulse. Then he froze. *Is this really her? Maybe it's someone else and the person hit the wrong apartment. That's right. It has to be a mistake.*

"Neesh?"

"Yes. Hi. Yes. Yes. Hello," Neesh said. "Do you know what time it is?"

"Are you letting me in?"

"Right," Neesh said. "Of course."

He pressed all the buttons on the speaker. Neesh knew he had a couple minutes to get the apartment in order, given the six floors of stairs Mitali had to climb. He grabbed the broom and frantically swept the living room area. He was a whirlwind as he picked up clothes and takeout containers off the ground. Neesh threw them in a pile in a closet as he heard footsteps echo in the hallway. When he turned around, he saw Mitali in the doorway.

"Hello," Neesh said.

"Hello," Mitali repeated back to him. She stood there, waiting for Neesh to invite her in. But he just stood there, frozen.

"Can I . . . ?" Mitali motioned towards the torn couch.

Neesh snapped out of his daze and nodded vigorously, leaping onto the couch, while Mitali gingerly sat down.

"I have something for you," Mitali said stoically.

"Okay?"

Mitali reached into her purse and took out a playbill with THE ELM TREE written across the cover. She opened to the page marked by a pink Post-it and pointed to where it read PRODUCER/SET DESIGNER: NEESH DESAI.

"I'd like you to come to the show," Mitali said.

Neesh took the playbill and held it as if it was a rare antique, the kind that would stock his father's shelves.

"I can't do that," Neesh said, while flipping through the playbill.

"Why not?"

"All I am is an ex-con to your family. And to you. There is no coming back from that."

Mitali brushed some dust off the couch.

"The dress rehearsal was really nice tonight," Mitali said. "My mom was there. Jahar. My dad. My grandmother. We were all together in the room. Being with each other. I never thought we'd get to that place ever again."

"That sounds nice," Neesh said, thinking about what his own parents were doing. *Probably at the shop.*

"And then my grandmother brought up the couch onstage," Mitali said. "The blue one you picked out. She said it reminded her of the one that Keya bought for her. And it hit me. You're the reason this all happened. You thought of doing the play. And you worked so hard on the set. And the tree. This play is as much an accomplishment of yours as it is ours. I can't take that away from you."

Neesh looked away.

"Remember that line about cosmic forces? *You* were the cosmic force. You are the planets and the stars aligning in the way my family needed them to," Mitali said. "So, I would like you to come to opening night."

"I'm broke. I don't have a job. And you're my ex-girlfriend. If I went, it would just be a reminder of everything I've lost."

"The play is a reminder of everything *we've* lost," Mitali said. "But you made the play happen. I want you to share that with us."

"I don't know."

"I want you there. And Keya would want you there."

"If Jahar sees me, he'll throw me through a window. He's old, but he's strong."

"I have an idea for that too, actually."

SEVENTEEN

Pamela thought that she would be nervous. But standing backstage on opening night, as she watched Swati and Seema run lines in a corner, she felt at ease. The play was ready. There were no more scenes to write or tweak. No more rehearsals. No more of this weight on her shoulders. She was wearing a dark blue skater dress with a cardigan, which matched the blue streak in her hair. Pamela couldn't remember the last time she wore the dress, but she wanted to look the part of a distinguished playwright. Most of her tattoos were hidden. She drew the line at heels, though, opting for black leather loafers instead. Her lip and nose rings remained prominent. She wondered how hard Keya would laugh at her "distinguished" look.

Weeks before, Jerry had walked up to her and said, "This ending. Don't change a word. It's locked. Now, let me make it look good."

That was the moment when Pamela felt at peace.

Pamela walked to the lobby, where *The Elm Tree* posters were all over the wall and audience members were beginning to file in. She considered going to the bar and ordering a glass of wine for herself but thought better of it. Pamela ran into Catherine, who was scolding a teenage boy for knocking one of the posters off the wall. Their eyes met and Catherine winked.

The show had sold out two of the three nights, which gave Jerry hope that the show might be able to continue on in some way after the run. Jerry now stood near stairs that led to an upper mezzanine level, balling and unballing his fists, while muttering to himself.

"Are you okay?" Pamela asked.

"Pre-show routine," Jerry said. "Leave me alone."

Pamela began to walk away.

"No, come back," Jerry said. "Don't mind me. I'm cranky. Come with me."

Jerry led Pamela into the auditorium and pointed near the front of the stage.

"Do you see who is sitting there?" Jerry said.

Pamela followed Jerry's outstretched finger to a completely bald man in a gray suit.

"That's Nicholas Simmons," Jerry said. "The idiot *Times* critic. He's here to review our show."

"Is that bad?" Pamela said.

"I'll decide later."

"This is a big night for you," Pamela said.

"For us."

Pamela scanned the crowd and looked for more familiar faces. She could see Deidre in the front row. There were some other high school classmates she recognized, who were probably drawn to the play because of Deidre's Facebook posts. That morning, Pamela smiled at Jerry's mention of her in the *New York Times* interview, the only other person Jerry mentioned in a piece examining his comeback. There was one seat in the front row which was taped off. Pamela had suggested after the last dress rehearsal that one seat have a sign on it that read RESERVED FOR KEYA. The proposition caused both Chaitali and Shantanu to tear up.

"There you are."

Pamela and Jerry turned around. Janine and Roger were standing with tickets and playbills in hand.

"There *you* are," Jerry said. "I'm guessing that you must be Pamela's parents. I'm Jerry Santucci."

"You're the director," Janine said. "It's a pleasure to meet you. What am I in for tonight?"

Janine shook his hand.

"A whole lot of truth," Jerry said. "If you'll excuse me. I must go backstage."

Jerry walked to the lobby and began navigating through the crowd.

"Do you want me to help you find your seats?" Pamela said.

"No, you go on," Janine said. "We'll find our way."

"Break an arm," Roger said.

"A leg," Pamela said. "You mean 'Break a leg.'"

"Break something. I don't know," Roger mumbled.

As Janine and Roger began to walk down the aisle, Pamela tapped Janine.

"There's something—" Pamela paused. Janine looked at her, waiting for her to finish. "Never mind. I'll see you after the show."

Pamela turned around and headed backstage. When she arrived, she saw Kalpana standing near Shantanu, Mitali, and Neesh. Pamela was surprised to see Neesh, after what she had heard happened. He looked sharp, though, in an all-black suit.

"Nice threads," Pamela said. Neesh sheepishly smiled.

"Ma, let's get you to your seat," Shantanu said.

"Hold on," Kalpana said.

Kalpana placed her hands on Shantanu's head.

"*Durga, Durga.*"

She did the same for Mitali.

"*Durga, Durga.*"

And then for Neesh.

"*Durga, Durga.*"

Kalpana noticed Pamela nearby.

"You too," Kalpana said.

Pamela walked over and dutifully lowered her head.

"*Durga, Durga.*"

Shantanu began to lead Kalpana away, but she stopped and turned back to Pamela.

"Do you recognize the sari I am wearing?"

It was a turquoise color. Pamela thought that it brought the best out in Kalpana, who seemed radiant, and not at all sorrowful.

"I wore it the night of *42nd Street*," Kalpana said. "You have given us a great gift."

She continued to slowly walk with Shantanu. Neesh and Mitali peeked out the side of the stage to look at the crowd. Mitali motioned for Pamela to do the same.

"There's so many people," Mitali said. "Look over there."

She was pointing to Jahar's seat. He was sitting next to Chaitali in the front row. But he was deep in conversation with another man next to him.

"Do you see that?" Mitali said to Neesh.

Neesh peered into the front row.

"So he came," Neesh said. "I didn't think he would."

"How did you convince Sandeep to agree to come?"

"It took a while. And then some."

Mitali gave him a worried look. But she took his hand anyway.

◇

Shantanu helped Kalpana to an aisle seat and took his own next to her. Catherine had not returned to her seat yet, which was next to his. He craned his neck to see who was in the crowd. There were several acquaintances and distant friends he had seen at pujas over the years. Many, like Pallavi, the elder *mashi*, were dressed in traditional Indian clothing. Some former students and fellow professors. Carl, his improv teacher. But there was a face exactly six rows behind, which interested him the most.

"I'll be right back, Ma." Shantanu got up and walked up the row. As he made the trek, he heard some shouts of his name, and occasionally, a familiar face would tap him, shake his hand, and wish him good luck.

Six rows back, Shantanu extended his own hand.

"You made it," Shantanu said, crouching down next to the seat, wincing as he did so.

"I'm not here," Dr. Lynch said in a red seersucker suit that was drawing looks from others sitting in his row. "Or rather, I didn't see you, and we didn't have this conversation."

"Okay."

"There's usually supposed to be a separation of church and state for this kind of thing. Ethically and all." Dr. Lynch looked around as if he was afraid of being seen, which was difficult given his outfit. "But I would never miss a billable hour. And trust me, I'm billing you for this."

"I didn't think you would come," Shantanu said.

"I never thought you'd do this." Dr. Lynch winked, clasping both hands around Shantanu's.

Dr. Lynch surveyed the auditorium.

"Quite a turnout," he said.

"Indeed."

"So, California," Dr. Lynch said. "You're really doing it."

"I am."

"Good for you. But again, I must remind you that you didn't see me here."

"Thank you, Doctor."

"Moving all the way across the country. Was it something I said?"

"It was," Shantanu said, smiling. He straightened up and headed back to his seat.

◇

Pamela took her seat in the back row of the house, on the aisle. She had purposely requested it so she could not see the audience's reactions. She overheard the elderly couple sitting next to her as they flipped through the playbill.

"I haven't heard of most of these names," the man said. "Except Jerry Santucci."

"Apparently, this was written by teenagers," the woman said.

"Imagine that," the man answered.

"We should've brought the grandkids," the woman said. "While they're at home playing video games, their classmates are doing *this*."

Pamela reached into her pocket and pulled out a piece of paper. It was folded. It had a hand-drawn heart with the words "Writing Scenes" on it. She unfolded it.

Hi!

I'm just sitting here bored at lunch so I thought I would write. I was just thinking about what my favorite parts of the play are so far. I like the stuff about being an individual. And about feeling significant to someone. How do we get more of that into this? I feel "significant" to you. And I feel like an "individual" around you. That's what we're trying to say here, right? That's what we all want. That's the theme, which is what Mr. Romino always says a play needs. A theme. I'm rambling. I'm sorry. I've just been thinking about this all day. There's a lot left to write but I'm so glad we are doing it together. Do you think it would be too arrogant to cast ourselves in it when we make it into a real thing? Gah. Okay. I need to stop. Let's finish it first. Okay, lunch is going to end soon. Talk to you later.

—*K*

Pamela grinned. The houselights came down. The curtains rose. *The Elm Tree* began.

Acknowledgments

Very little of what we do in life is a single, solitary achievement, and this book has reminded me how much that is true. This book is less my doing and more me jumping on a cresting wave and riding it as far as it would take me.

But I did not create the wave. I am just its beneficiary. The wave began with the Bengali community I grew up around in New Jersey. Most of the characters are composites of many people I knew in my childhood who in real life (like Keya Mashi and Chaitali Mashi) provided me comfort and guidance growing up.

Behind the scenes, the biggest reason this book exists is Zachary Knoll, who championed the book from the very beginning and elevated the prose at every turn. He has my eternal gratitude and friendship. As does Emily Graff and the rest of the wonderful team at Simon & Schuster, including Brittany Adames, who tirelessly advocated for the book. They have made me feel like a real author instead of an impostor.

There is also Dave Larabell and the rest of the CAA team. Dave is the reason I have any sort of a literary career and helped me find something I love.

Thank you to Anna Kambhampaty for giving the book an initial edit.

There were so many early readers who helped me shape the plot as the book went on, including Trisha Chakraborty, Ali-Asghar Abedi, Adi Joseph, Mayeesha Cho, Susan Rigetti, and Sam Vadas. As I said, riding a wave. The story doesn't happen without their suggestions.

My thanks to Sanjena Sathian and Diksha Basu for their early support of the book.

Of course, the biggest part of the wave is Wesley Dietrich, my muse in all things.

About the Author

SOPAN DEB is a writer for the *New York Times*, where his topics have included sports and culture. He is also the author of the memoir *Missed Translations: Meeting the Immigrant Parents Who Raised Me.*

Before joining the *Times*, Deb was one of a handful of reporters who covered Donald Trump's 2016 presidential campaign from start to finish as a campaign embed for CBS News. He was named a "breakout media star" of the election by Politico.

At the *New York Times*, Deb has interviewed high-profile subjects such as Denzel Washington, Stephen Colbert, the cast of *Arrested Development*, Kyrie Irving, and Bill Murray.

He lives in Washington, DC, with his wife and dogs.